SMELLING OF ROSES

Also by Eric Sykes

UFOs Are Coming Wednesday
The Great Crime of Grapplewick

SMELLING
OF
ROSES

Eric Sykes

This edition published in 1998 by
Virgin Books
Thames Wharf Studios
Rainville Road
London W6 9HT

Reprinted 1998

First published in Great Britain in 1997

A catalogue record for this book is available from the
British Library.

ISBN 0 7535 0280 1

Typeset by TW Typesetting, Plymouth, Devon
Printed by Mackays of Chatham PLC, Lordswood,
Chatham, Kent

CHAPTER

ONE

Sergeant Beaconsfield had had a bellyful of the North African desert and, judging by the way it hung over the waistband of his khaki shorts, this was quite something. He took a drag at his cigarette butt and dropped it, scuffing sand over it with his boot. He wasn't a particularly careful man – it was just something to do. He looked around at his gun crew preparing the twenty-five-pounder for action.

'Supercharge?' asked the loader. It was a joke.

'Bloody 'ell, no,' replied the Sergeant. 'Same as last week. It's only five thousand yards, we're not shooting at Berlin.'

He wandered over and checked the angle of sight. He nodded and the crew relaxed.

They were young, tanned, the colour of walnut. He envied them their vigour and enthusiasm as they eagerly exchanged bets on the result of the fall of shot. They'd seen action in the last few months, albeit a retreat. The firing of a few hurried rounds, hitch up and race back a few miles, unlimber, fire a few more rounds over open sights, then back again. They were good lads, he reflected, so it was a relief to be finally posted to this comparative calm. But now, after three weeks, boredom had set in – that is except for Wednesday. This was the shooting match.

'Ten on us, Sergeant?' asked one of the lads.

'You're on,' agreed Beaconsfield without interest.

The ten referred to cigarettes – big deal. But then it was something to relieve the monotony. He scratched the knotted khaki handkerchief on his head, disturbing the flies that were trying to get through to the Brylcream, and gazed towards the distant horizon dancing in the heat haze of the North African desert.

Some three miles ahead on a rocky escarpment the young gunner in the forward observation post shook his head to clear the sweat from his eyes. A droplet splashed the rock in front of him and a lizard skittered over his hand, scaring the living daylights out of both of them. God, what a bloody desolate place to end up in! He would have liked to step back into the shade of an overhang in the rock face but he'd heard too many old sweats' tales of scorpions lurking in the dark places. Once disturbed, they'd be up the leg of his voluminous shorts, and this was one gunner who intended to go home with his dowry intact.

Suddenly he stiffened as he caught a flash from the escarpment some distance away across the flat desert. And then he relaxed. It was his opposite number, the German spotting for his eighty-eights. They sometimes waved to each other. From the corner of his eye, he noticed a movement below and lifted his binoculars. Here we go again, he thought, as an Arab leading his camel came into view. Lowering his glasses, the young gunner turned around and cranked the field telephone. The tinny voice of Sergeant Beaconsfield answered, 'Yes?'

'Arab and camel now approaching target area, Sarge.' He replaced the handset.

At the other end Sergeant Beaconsfield smiled with satisfaction, turned to his gun crew and put up his thumb. The loader rammed home a shell in the breech of the gun and the crew looked around to the Sergeant expectantly. The Sergeant signalled with a curt nod, turned away with eyes closed and fingers in his ears . . . bang! The old artillery piece leapt back startled, bouncing the overhanging camouflage netting, and a crowd of flies rose from a dixie of yesterday's McConochies stew on the trestle table.

In the forward observation post the young gunner was dry-mouthed, apprehensive and fearful of what was to come. A sudden gout of flame and black smoke erupted in the desert well to the left of the target, followed by the dull crack of the twenty-five-pounder.

The camel shied violently, almost lifting the Arab off his feet. With a stream of invective the camel driver jerked savagely at the halter until the beast steadied. He spat, then eased his grip on the camel's rope, and the ludicrous plod continued. He was fatalistic. Soon after, there would be another thundering in the air followed by yet another great bang. Each time he made the journey across this stretch from the oasis to Matruh, he was a target. So be it – he was in the hands of Allah. If it was written, he'd be hurled from this dung heap of a world, so let the accursed infidel do their worst, Allah be praised. He closed his ears to the second rushing in the air coming from the opposite direction. This was followed by another great explosion, closer this time. The sand spattered them and steel fragments shrieked through the air, compliments of Krupps Munition Works, Essen. The camel, unlike his master, having no religious faith, plunged and bellowed swinging his master about like a bundle of rags. Docilely, the camel driver allowed himself to be thrown up and down – a doll in the hands of a demented puppeteer. Eventually the beast wearied of the sport and stood unconcerned awaiting the beating. However, its driver's hands had no feeling and his wrists were too badly chafed, so the pleasure would have to wait. Steadily he settled on his course once more, never deviating by one degree from the track forged by his father, and his father before him back to the days of the Pharaohs, a track now pockmarked by explosions from previous contests.

3

Each Wednesday the Arab and his camel passed over a certain strip of desert under observation by both British and German gunners. The object of the game was to see which artillery team could bracket the target without actually demolishing it. This was a stand-off period following the short decisive battles of Tobruk and Mersa Matruh, and the first battle of El Alamein, a time when Rommel and his staff were frantically trying to build up their supplies for the final push. The British remained close to their own supplies but did not have enough ordnance to help them regain the initiative.

The field telephone rang again and Sergeant Beaconsfield lifted it from its cradle. 'Yes,' he said, as he flicked the wheel of an enormous lighter and held his head to one side in order to light a fag without scorching his nose, but the cigarette remained unlit. 'Say that again,' he said into the mouthpiece, all attention now. The lads watched him warily. 'OK, if you say so.' Then he replaced the telephone and walked over to check the elevation of the gun.

'Who won that one, then?'

The Sergeant didn't look round. 'Nearly blew the arse off it. Too close for comfort.'

Excitedly, the gun crew was all smiles and a wave of clenched fists but the smiles quickly disappeared when the Sergeant added, 'They were, not us.'

The loader sniffed. 'What chance have we got with this clapped-out drainpipe against their eighty-eights?'

'Hey,' said one of the lads, delighted. 'You owe me ten, Sarge.'

The Sergeant ignored this.

'Up five hundred yards,' he said and watched as the adjustments were made.

The Sergeant was unmoved. It was only cigarettes after all and he was already owed over forty and ten bottles of Stella beer. Some of the lads maintained he

4

dropped the spotter a nice backhander to phone in false reports, and they were not far off the mark.

'Right, lads,' said the Sergeant. 'Eyes down for Round Two.' But the lads, half rising, were gazing over his shoulder to where a fifteen-hundredweight truck was approaching at speed. Beaconsfield turned and shielded his face as the truck screeched to a halt in a swirl of hot white dust.

The young driver sat to attention at the wheel looking sheepish. The thin, slightly built Second Lieutenant adjusted his goggles on to the peak of his cap as he stood up, holding on to the top of the windscreen.

One of the lads nudged his mate. 'It's Rommel, in'it?' he whispered.

The Sergeant eyed him with distaste. 'If that's Rommel, we'll all be back home in a week.'

The young officer stepped down and looked curiously about him before making his way forward. The Sergeant, hands on hips, watched him warily as he approached, noticing the angry redness of his knees. His thin pointed nose was more vivid still and already peeling, and with the large white circles round his eyes where the goggles had been, he looked like an owl that had had a go at the jam pot.

'Who's in charge here?' he piped.

'Captain Brown, sir, but he's in Alexandria.'

Lieutenant Jampton sniffed and sauntered over to where the crew were now pretending to be busy with the twenty-five-pounder. He walked round it and looked down the barrel. The breech was open and the gunner's face at the other end said, 'Hello, sailor.'

Lieutenant Jampton jerked his head back, embarrassed, collected himself and wandered over to the Sergeant. 'Artillery, eh?' he said.

'There's not a lot gets past 'im,' muttered one of the lads, and the others sniggered.

Lieutenant Jampton whirled round with his nose glowing like an inhaled cigarette but before he could convene a court martial Sergeant Beaconsfield spoke. 'Yes, sir, D Battery, 86th Field Artillery.'

'D Battery, eh?' muttered Jampton and marched over to a trestle table where he pushed aside a filthy mess tin and spread out his map. Beaconsfield looked over to the driver, still seated at the wheel of the steaming fifteen-hundredweight, sweat streaming from under the rim of his tin hat. The Sergeant shrugged and strolled over to the table where the Lieutenant was staring earnestly at his map. He was nodding to it, then he consulted a compass strapped to his wrist.

'Ah ha,' he murmured and looked ahead, then back at the map, then he looked behind, and eventually he turned a full circle. 'Right,' he snapped and started to fold the map.

The Sergeant noted idly that it had been upside down.

'Carry on,' said the young officer sternly and, adjusting his goggles, he climbed back into the fifteen-hundredweight.

His driver, anticipating, was already revving the engine awaiting the orders to advance. Jampton pointed ahead and they began to move. Sergeant Beaconsfield was galvanised into action and waved his arms. 'Whoa,' he shouted to the driver, who slammed his foot down on to the brake so hard that his CO almost did a somersault over the windshield on to the bonnet.

Beaconsfield said, 'Sorry, sir,' as the young officer regained his composure, 'but whatever you're looking for it isn't that way.'

He pointed in the direction in which they were facing.

'Ah,' replied Jampton brushing himself down. 'I'm looking for the Special Ordnance Group.'

The Sergeant looked up at him innocently. 'Ours or theirs?'

'Sergeant –' he began, but Beaconsfield cut him short. 'Well the only thing ahead of us here is the Jerries.'

'The enemy?' He stood, raised his binoculars and looked ahead, apprehensive lest he should see the whole of the Afrika Korps bearing down on him. He turned and looked back. 'That way, eh?' he murmured.

'Yes, sir. You'll see plenty of Division signs about six or seven miles back on the coast road.'

'The coast road?'

'Yes, sir, parallel to the sea. You can't miss it – it's full of ships.'

The young Lieutenant leant towards him. 'What's your name?'

'Sergeant Beaconsfield, sir.'

The Lieutenant nodded. 'Well, Sergeant Beaconsfield, I can do without your sarcasm, thank you.'

'Yes, sir.'

The Lieutenant made a rotating sign with his hand and the driver accelerated and screeched round in a full circle, disappearing completely in his own hot dust.

The Sergeant stepped back, expecting to see the vehicle emerge and speed on its way, but it didn't. As the dust settled, the Lieutenant beckoned and he walked forward.

'Sergeant,' he said, 'just before I arrived, you were firing. What was your target?'

The Sergeant looked down at his boots, then over to the gun. He was bored now with this new jumped-up officer, and he didn't like being beckoned. He sprang to attention, sweat flying off him in all directions, looked straight ahead and roared, 'Nothing . . . *sah*!'

The Lieutenant glanced sideways at his driver, triumphant.

'Nothing?' he asked, head to one side.

'No, *sah*, nothing. Time-honoured custom, *sah* . . . that was the noonday gun, *sah*.'

Enlightenment dawned – the noonday gun; he'd

7

heard about that. Of course, he should have known. He pulled himself together. 'Very well. Carry on, Sergeant, and the next time we meet I hope you're properly dressed.'

Fortunately for him the roar of the engine drowned the laughter and as the fifteen-hundredweight shot forward he was jerked back into his seat but he was happy; he was well pleased with his handling of the situation. As the fifteen-hundredweight raced away, he looked back, but anything behind was obscured by the dust of his own passing. He leant across and shouted to his driver, 'Noonday gun . . . it's these traditions that make the British Army the finest in the world.'

Gratwick didn't quite hear what he said and yelled back, 'Thursday, sir.'

Luckily, Jampton didn't hear the reply either. The heat was beginning to bother him. He opened his knees wide to ease the heat rash in his crotch. He desperately wanted to scratch it but not in front of the men.

He made a mental note to write home to his Aunt Dorothy about the noonday gun – she would be thrilled. It wasn't until they had travelled a few miles that it suddenly occurred to him that it wasn't yet eleven o'clock. Could the Sergeant's watch be wrong? He was shaken out of his reverie when Gratwick pulled up by the side of a nest of divisional signs – 1st Armoured, 4th Indian, 151st (Durham) and, almost indecipherable, the Special Ordnance Group, and in brackets (Ladies Welcome). This caused a cluck of disapproval from Jampton and he ordered his driver to follow the arrow. Unfortunately the arrow had pointed towards the desert, and, as every old sweat knew, the desert was a big, unforgiving stretch of nothing – a waste land known as the blue where only the stars or a good compass can guide, and at eleven o'clock in the morning Lieutenant Jampton had neither.

Inevitably, after a couple of hours, they were totally

and completely lost. Jampton called a halt and dismounted. He walked around the front of the truck and spread his map on the shimmering bonnet of the fifteen-hundredweight, then yelped and sprang back as his elbows came into contact with the hot metal. Fortuitously for him, Gratwick was gurgling away at his water bottle and hadn't noticed, so he was able to maintain his officer's dignity. He consulted his inadequate compass, then he made his way to the top of a rocky escarpment and surveyed the surrounding desert through his binoculars.

Gratwick watched him dispassionately. He wished he could take his tin hat off in this stifling heat but he had done that once and received a stern rebuke from his CO to be properly dressed at all times. The sun was directly overhead and he'd never known it so hot or so still. He was frightened now and had visions of driving about this desert long after the war was over, missing in action. He saw his father opening the telegram and felt a lump in his throat, then the officer was back.

Jampton eased himself into the seat and pointed vaguely to the left. Gratwick started up and they were bouncing and shuddering over the escarpment and down into the shallow depression.

'Ah,' said Lieutenant Jampton and pointed.

There, over to the left on the shimmering floor, were the burnt-out wrecks of a bygone battle: blackened hulls of tanks, and a couple of burnt-out Bren-carriers.

'Somebody copped it here,' muttered Jampton, with slitted eyes.

Gratwick's heart sank. They had passed this battlefield three hours ago but he wasn't going to let on. He knew then that they had been going round in circles. Several miles later Jampton suddenly looked back, then he glanced sideways at Gratwick.

'We passed that battlefield this morning.'

'Yes, sir,' said Gratwick, trying desperately to miss the potholes.

9

Jampton spread the map across his knees but the jolting of the wagon made it impossible to read. He shaded his eyes to glance up at the sun.

'Well at least we're travelling east,' he said, and pointed forward. 'The sun sets in the west.'

'Yes, sir,' said Gratwick miserably. Everybody knew that.

They bucketed on for another few miles, when suddenly Gratwick braked hard as they almost ran into a troop of four Crusader tanks. Jampton, although holding on to the windshield, was actually looking the other way at the time and caught his back a tremendous wallop as he was thrown against it.

'Bloody 'ell,' said the tank gunner, a mug of hot tea halfway to his lips. 'I know our camouflage is good but it don't make us invisible.'

Suspicious eyes watched as the Lieutenant dismounted stiffly and walked towards the tanks as easily as he could. By now the chafing of his shorts against his sunburnt knees was agony. His gait was not lost on the deeply tanned men of the Tank Corps. The Lieutenant was either new to Africa or he'd just had an attack of dysentery.

'Who's in charge here?'

Lieutenant Jampton hadn't meant to croak but his water bottle was long since dry. He hadn't expected the desert to be quite so vast or that he would be away from human contact for so long. The tank men looked at one another and shrugged. Jampton's stomach gave a lurch and he took a pace backward. These men were stripped to the waist, showing no insignia or badges of rank; they could be Germans. His eyes flickered uneasily to the camouflaged Crusaders but he was too new to know the difference between a Tiger tank and a water bowser.

Luckily one of the men spoke. 'What d'you want, then?'

The Lieutenant let out a sigh of relief. It could easily have been '*was wollen Sie?*' He smiled – or he tried as much as his lips would allow. 'Oh, er, I'm looking for the Special Ordnance Group.'

The men seated round the brew-up relaxed. For one awful moment they thought he was going to belong to them. The Lieutenant gestured with his map and looked all around him.

'They're in this vicinity somewhere.'

One of the men rose to his feet and sauntered towards him.

'That's where they're supposed to be,' said Jampton, and prodded the map hesitantly. The man studied the map for a few moments, then shook his head.

'That's where we are now.' He pointed. 'You're about ten miles adrift as the crow flies.'

One of the other men had come across and was craning over Jampton's shoulder. 'Yeah, and then some. It all depends how old the crow is.'

The first tank man laughed. 'Take no notice of Lofty, sir. He's bomb happy.' But Jampton wasn't listening.

'Ten miles, eh?' he said almost to himself.

'Well, ten miles or thereabouts. Just keep on a south-southeast bearing.'

'South-southeast?' asked Jampton.

'That's about it,' said the tank man. 'Carry on, south-southeast.'

Jampton looked at his compass, then he gazed in the direction of the Special Ordnance Group, over the limitless stretch of desert. Foreshortening his gaze, he looked at the fifteen-hundredweight and saw that his driver was fast asleep over the wheel. It had been a long day for Gratwick too. Jampton's shoulders slumped. He'd had enough. He was hot and dusty and dried out. Irritation fluttered within him; after all, it was the driver's job to find the location. Why did he have to make all the decisions just because he was an officer?

11

Pettishly, he stamped his foot; he was ready to take his bat and ball and go home.

'Cheer up, sir,' said the tank gunner, and handed him a mug of hot, sweet tea. 'Get that down you,' he said.

Jampton looked blankly at the tall, tanned man and took the proffered mug. 'Thank you,' he muttered, although he would have given his right arm for an ice-cream cornet.

'It'll be sundown in an hour,' said the man. 'No sense in chasing across there in the dark unless there's a flap on.'

'No, there's no rush,' said Jampton, sweating more now because of the hot tea.

In addition, his nostrils had picked up the aroma of frying. He couldn't identify the smell but whatever it was it smelt delicious. Had he had enough juice in him, his mouth would have watered. Jampton was about to ask if he could join them when he realised with a start that he'd already been invited.

'Oh, thanks, thanks, I could do with, er, whatever's going.'

One of the other tank men walked over and shook Gratwick, whose neck was getting the full benefit of the dying sun.

Gratwick's head shot up.

'Yes, sir,' he yelped. 'Coming, sir.'

The tank man patted his shoulder. 'OK, son, relax, you're staying with us tonight. But there's a bit of daylight left so you'd better get some camouflage over your vehicle.'

Gratwick was still disorientated and looked around for a tree or a bush. He realised where he was and his heart sank. The tank man took pity on him.

'Been out long?'

Gratwick stared at this father figure. Here was a real fighting man, and old, too: he must have been about thirty-odd.

'No,' he said. 'Disembarked yesterday and had my

12

orders to be Lieutenant Jampton's driver. We came over on the same boat.'

The old man looked over to Jampton and sighed. They'd be taking them out of the cradle next.

'OK.' He glanced at the fifteen-hundredweight. 'I see you haven't any netting then.'

Gratwick looked back over his shoulder. 'No, they didn't issue us with any. It was a rush job, you see.'

Again the man sighed – it was going to be a long war.

'Right, drive over to that dune and park.' He pointed to a spot some fifty yards distant. 'Shovel some sand over the truck and make it look like a derelict.' He looked over the back. 'They've given you a shovel, I see.'

'Yes, sir.' Gratwick was glad he wouldn't have to drive any more that day.

The man was about to join his comrades when he stopped. 'Oh, by the way, you don't have to call me sir. Corporal Dunnett. I'm just a tank driver.' And with that he strode to the shade.

Gratwick smiled after him; there was a man he could admire. He turned back to the truck and frowned as he humped Jampton's bedroll off the back. He wasn't to know then but that was the first and last time he would have this chore; fate was to take a hand and before he was much older he would never again see Lieutenant Jampton or the Special Ordnance Group. His war would be over.

Some time later Jampton slid gingerly into his sleeping bag and tried to settle down, but it was no use. His knees and arms were burning like the clappers, while the rest of him shivered. The night was black and cold – good grief, was it ever! From the heat of the day to the sheer freezing chill of the night, it was almost impossible for anything to survive. No wonder the desert was arid and desolate. He lay in his blankets in the foetal position with his hands between his thighs for warmth. By jingo, it was cold. The blanket covered his head in the hopes that his breath might add some heat, but it was useless. He snatched the blanket off and the raw night air froze his face.

There were the usual flashes on the horizon but they didn't bother him now. He'd seen all that on the previous night and for a moment he felt good; he felt he could handle the war. A slight snap jerked him up into a sitting position and he held his breath, eyes desperately trying to pierce the blackness. He waited a moment, then slowly he lay back again and drew his blankets close. It could have been one of his knee joints. Then another quiet crack. He was sitting up again. Then an almost inaudible pop. His head swivelled almost three hundred and sixty degrees but there was nothing to see. Panic began to take over. Flashes on the horizon were one thing but these were sounds – and close. Should he waken one of the tank men? Luckily, he dismissed the idea. They wouldn't be too happy being roused to listen to the natural phenomenon of the desert, the creaks and cracks as the earth's crust cooled after the scorching heat of the day. The sounds were benign but Jampton was too fresh and too callow to understand. To him every slight noise was the hobnailed boots of an enemy patrol.

Sleep was impossible now but the cold was forgotten, all his antennae straining for the first signs of disaster. Suddenly in the distance he heard a thin ethereal wailing. He was on his feet now, clutching his blanket. The howl came again. It was inhuman, he thought; and he was right: it happened to be a jackal. It howled again, and why shouldn't it? This was its own back yard; humans were the interlopers. Somewhere closer came the answering call and for the first time in his life Jampton's bowels began to know fear. It was physical and it could have been disastrous had he not been constipated. It might have been the manly thing to wrap

14

himself in his blankets to sleep rough in the open while Gratwick dozed in the cab of the fifteen-hundredweight. But, damn it, after all, he was the superior and this was one of the times when discretion was better than valour. He eased himself in the seat next to his driver and closed the door as softly as he could. This wasn't out of deference for the sleepers round him. In fact they should all be awake after that howling. No, the reason he closed the door with care was purely self-preservation. He wasn't going to give away his position.

He glanced over at the dark shape of Gratwick slumped over the wheel. He was no consolation. Jampton wrapped his sleeping bag around himself and fell into an uneasy shallow doze. Suddenly he was jerked awake by the high-pitched whine of the electric starting motor, then another, then four tank engines roared into life. A few minutes later in the darkness of the pre-dawn he watched with stirring panic as the Crusaders disappeared in line astern. Gratwick, also awake now, watched open-mouthed as the great armoured leviathans rumbled into the darkness. In a few minutes all was silent again. It was as if they had never been – but long after departure the blue diesel fumes that hung in the still night air reminded them that it wasn't a dream. Jampton had never felt so alone in his miserable young life.

After a few moments Gratwick excused himself to answer the call of nature and stumbled out into the black, cold night. And now, to judge from the grunts and gasps coming from the darkness, he hadn't gone far enough. Damn the lower classes: they couldn't even defecate decently. He ground his little teeth in frustration. What was he doing here anyway? Shouldn't he be in Alexandria discussing the state of the war with Uncle Charles?

Somebody somewhere had dropped a monumental clanger.

15

TWO

But there had been no mistake. His movement had been carefully orchestrated . . . no one could have foreseen the dire consequences which were to follow.

Whilst Lieutenant Jampton was struggling up the gangplank of the troopship moored in Southampton water prior to his passage to North Africa, a letter by diplomatic pouch was delivered to a large brownstone house in Mina Street, Roushdi, in Alexandria. A brass plaque to the side of the tall doors proclaimed it to be the Ministry of Agriculture and Fisheries – it fooled no one. This was the headquarters of British Military Intelligence.

In a room on the fourth floor, Colonel Charles Brunswick signed for the letter and passed the clipboard back to the courier. Ordinary people posted their letters into a pillar box, but then his wife was Lady Dorothy Belvedere-FitzNorman, her family being one of the oldest and most powerful in England – certainly superior to the Royals and only slightly lower than God. Unfortunately Lieutenant Jampton was also their adopted nephew, loved and worshipped by Lady Dorothy almost as much as he loathed the little prat.

The Colonel sighed. He'd come a long way from his humble origins. Born 1900 in a squalid house in Solihull, Charles Brunswick and his sister Emily grew apathetically through childhood, measles, whooping cough and mumps, avoiding, by the grace of God, rickets. Their mother, a shadowy figure, said little except 'time for bed', or 'eat it up, it's good for you'. Their father was even more obscure. He owned a small carpet shop in the better part of town, which wasn't saying much. And to his credit he was away from home sometimes for a week or so. In fact his visits home became more infrequent as the children grew.

Charles's fourteenth birthday was momentous: World War One was declared – and as if that wasn't enough his mother died. By the time their father had arrived back from wherever he'd been to this time and had heard the news, he'd proclaimed that changes would have to be made. Charles's sister Emily had made up her own mind, however, and was already training to be a nurse. If the war didn't end by Christmas, she'd be somewhere in France and bugger Solihull. Charles was immediately installed in his father's shop in order to learn the wefts and warps of carpet making.

By 1916 his sister was looking after the boys at a field dressing station somewhere in France. And thankfully, two years later, he received his call-up papers. He and the newly formed battalion 'The Midland Pals' no sooner set foot in France than peace was declared.

In 1920, serving in Cologne in the Army of Occupation, Charles received news of his father's death and was granted compassionate leave to attend the funeral. It was a happy affair being reunited with his sister Emily. In all fairness, their father had been away so often they'd never got to know him. And whenever he was at home he wasn't a person you looked at. He rarely spoke and when he did you listened whilst staring at the floor. On the occasions of birthdays and Christmas, you accepted the new penny and thanked his waistcoat buttons. In fact they would have had difficulty in picking him out of an identity parade. Up to this moment, for young Charles and Emily, their

17

lives had been about as colourful as trudging slowly across a rain-sodden slag heap.

But this was all about to change. The summons to a solicitor's office should have alerted them. People of their class didn't make wills. They just died and the relatives came out of obscurity and swept through the rooms like marauding Goths opening drawers and cupboards, looking under cushions and beds as though it were a bargain sale in a second-hand shop, even as the dead lay quietly on a table in the cold front room.

The sunshine bombshell that exploded when the Last Will and Testament was read hit them like a warm wind in winter. It also explained their father's long and mysterious absences ... He had bequeathed to them a large carpet shop in Bond Street, London, two carpet shops in the expensive part of Birmingham, others in Edinburgh and Glasgow, all these assets exceeding Fifteen Million Pounds ... It was unbelievable! Incredible! Whichever way you said it Fifteen Million was a foreign language. What kind of a man had their father been? A man with that kind of money in the bank and yet one who would walk a mile rather than pay for a penny tram ride. Emily, white-faced as a piece of foolscap, stared across at her brother. She was afraid to faint in case she came to to find that it had all been a dream ...

Poor Emily, thought Charles. Only six weeks before, she'd married one of the men she'd nursed in France, a Lance Corporal Jampton, and, apart from having lost a leg on the Somme, he was in fairly good nick. If only she could have waited another month: with her newfound wealth she could have done better – at least have someone with both legs intact.

On the other hand, the born-again Charles Brunswick was footloose and fancy free. He travelled the world first-class, shedding bits of Solihull along the way, but after his third Grand Tour he discovered that

England wasn't such a bad place after all. He continued his carousel with the smart sets in Mayfair and when that palled he bought himself a commission in a fashionable cavalry regiment, a change of direction that steered him towards hunt balls, regattas, mentions in the gossip columns of *The Times*, *Punch* and *Tatler*, and he was considered to be the second-most eligible bachelor in England – the Prince of Wales came first.

To be fair, only a small percentage of this popularity was due to Charles Brunswick himself. The great attraction was his large bank account at Coutts and wheels were already beginning to churn. At a mess ball Charles was casually introduced to Lady Dorothy Belvedere-FitzNorman, a debutante of no great beauty and not many offers of matrimony even though she came from one of the oldest, most distinguished families in the land, so powerful they were able to maintain a twenty-bedroom mansion set in thousands of acres of Shropshire countryside, with no money. This lack of funds is not uncommon among the high-bred aristocracy. However, one thing they all have in common, although money is never mentioned, is a nose for it.

So the meeting between the dashing, rich, young subaltern and Lady Dorothy was certainly not by chance. From this came an invitation to a hunt ball – and by chance Lady Dorothy was present – followed by a weekend at a country house, and again by chance another of the guests was Lady Dorothy. His leaves from the regiment became more frequent and in many cases extended. His Commanding Officer began addressing him as 'Charles, old boy'. He was already in the machine and no match for the establishment and inevitably in August 1923, hardly knowing what day it was, Charles found himself walking under the archway of sabres held up by his fellow officers, Lady Dorothy on his arm. And, like it or not, he was now married and

19

the regimental band was playing 'Here Comes The Bride' to prove it.

The only bright spot at the wedding for Charles was again meeting his sister Emily, who was now heavily pregnant. Her husband, ex-Lance Corporal Jampton, seemed jollier than on their last meeting. And so he should. He'd certainly fallen on his feet, or to be more precise his foot. Emily had laughingly pointed to her husband's artificial leg. 'If that bullet had been eight inches higher I wouldn't be having this,' she whispered, patting her extended stomach.

Years later Charles Brunswick was to curse the aim of that unknown German sniper who missed the target by eight inches. It would have saved a lot of heartache.

Colonel Brunswick, white with shock now, read his wife's letter again. 'Dear Brunswick,' it began. She never used the name herself but always addressed him as Brunswick as if he was the boot boy.

Dear Brunswick,
    Wilfred will be arriving, all being well, on or about . . .

She'd told him who the Captain was, the name of the Vice Admiral in overall charge of the convoy – all highly classified information privy only to an exalted few in the Admiralty.

Brunswick slammed the letter on to his desk. Bollocks to all that, he thought. He wasn't going to be saddled with the obnoxious little twat of a nephew. He had enough on his plate being Director of Military Intelligence. The war was going badly enough without the added hassle of having young Jampton under his feet. Brunswick groaned. He, God help him, would be expected to . . . He couldn't think of what he was expected to do but certainly he wouldn't be standing at the foot of the gangplank with a bunch of flowers in his hand and a welcome speech on his lips.

He picked up the letter again. His wife had engineered the posting of Jampton to Alexandria. Why, for God's sake? And a horrible thought struck him. Could his wife and her family be Nazi sympathisers? He shuddered and gulped down his third large whisky of the morning. Then suddenly he was hit by inspiration. No way was he going to be lumbered with the festering presence of his nephew. He smiled as he lifted the telephone and asked to be connected to the Regimental Transport Officer at the docks. Then he poured himself another choda peg. There's more than one way to skin a cat, he thought.

Lieutenant Jampton, the object of this love-and-hate saga, crouched disconsolately in his fifteen-hundred-weight. Had it really been only twenty-four hours since he had landed in North Africa? He tried to reconstruct the events as they happened; Aunt Dorothy would want to know every little detail and they were bizarre to say the least.

At two o'clock in the morning the great troop ship had nudged against its berth and even before it was secured he had been tannoyed to report immediately to his disembarkation point on B deck. Jampton remembered the curious stares of other officers as he pushed his way through, feeling a little apprehensive, wondering why he had been picked out to disembark before anybody else, and when he finally came to the top of the gangplank he was reluctant to go any further. He might have been paralysed . . .

He stopped at this point in his recollection.

The bit about being tannoyed would certainly intrigue his Aunt Dorothy. And also his being first off the ship – this would certainly raise her eyebrows. Rapidly in his mind he began to compose his letter. Why not embellish it a little? Why not say that the ship's captain saluted him and the Royal Marine Band played him on to the dock? But as quickly as the thought came, it was cancelled. The Royal Marine Band would not be playing at two o'clock in the morning on the dockside. They were more likely to be playing dance music at a senior officers' club ... He could imagine his Aunt Dorothy passing his letter around the dinner table with pride and a tearful eye. He went on with his composition. It was all harmless of course, and it was codswallop. In truth, the facts of the matter were slightly different. Indeed there was a vast gulf between the ramblings of Jampton's adolescent mind and what actually happened.

Thousands of eyes watched the young Lieutenant as he stood at the top of the gangplank gazing down at the unknown, blacked-out dockside of Alexandria. Shaded blue torches bobbed and weaved between pools of bright moonlight like heavily sedated fireflies. He might have stood there until the end of the war, when someone remarked, 'What's he waiting for, the National Anthem?'

This caused a roar of laughter and Lieutenant Jampton, relieved that in the darkness they couldn't see his face, struggled down the gangplank dragging his weighty blue suitcase. It was only when he got to the bottom that he realised the rest of his kit was still on board. He turned to make his way back up again, but his path was blocked by a beared sailor who had followed him down.

'It's all right, sir, I've got the rest of your kit here,' he said. Over one shoulder he carried Jampton's bedroll and haversack and under his other arm was the portable, collapsible canvas bath (Officers, For The Use Of), and without stopping he strode purposefully along the dock.

The young officer picked up his suitcase with an almighty effort and scurried to catch up, trying to block his ears to the whistles, jeers and catcalls that came from the massed troops leaning over the rails of the lower decks. The seaman stopped behind a fifteen-hundredweight parked in front of the Regimental Transport Office and dumped his load in the back. Unfortunately, this area was lit by the moon as if from a spotlight in the theatre, and when Jampton staggered out of the blackness with his suitcase the sailor turned towards him and saluted. Jampton put down his suitcase in order to return the salute. A great cheer went up from the ship at this soldierly tableau. The sailor escaped into the obscurity of the dock. Lieutenant Jampton grunted as he picked up his suitcase again and was about to heave it in the back of the wagon when a very young soldier in a too big battledress poured out of the cab.

'Private Gratwick, sir, your driver.' He stamped to attention and snapped up a salute.

Jampton put down his suitcase again and returned the compliment. When the door of the office burst open a red-faced Major wearing an armband identifying him as the Regimental Transport Officer stared unbelievingly at these two idiots facing each other at the salute.

'Never mind all that crap,' he snarled. 'If it's Lieutenant Jampton, get yourself in here pronto.'

Jampton followed him into the little office.

'Right,' said the RTO without preamble. 'Here's your movement orders. Special Ordnance Group, about 200 miles in the blue.'

Jampton looked baffled. 'Blue, sir?' he asked.

'Desert to you, laddie,' replied the Major not unkindly. He handed over the movement orders.

A phone rang and the Major lifted the receiver, and whilst he talked into it Jampton read his orders. 'You are to proceed immediately to Special Ordnance Group at the following map reference. Report to Sergeant Major Puller on arrival.' Jampton reread the orders. He was to report to a Sergeant Major whoever he was? It was a mistake surely; an officer shouldn't report to an NCO. He looked over to the Major, who was just putting down the receiver. He turned to Jampton.

'Still here?' he asked.

Jampton proffered him the Movement Orders. 'There must be some mistake, sir. It says here that I'm to report to a Sergeant Major.'

'Well, what's wrong with that?' asked the RTO.

'I'm sorry, sir, but I was under the impression that when an officer joined a new unit, it is customary to report to the CO.'

The RTO snatched the papers and put on his spectacles. Angrily he scanned the papers, then he slapped them triumphantly. Patiently he held the orders out so that Jampton could see them.

'If you read on a litle bit more,' he said as if each utterance gave him pain, 'you'll see that this Sergeant Major Puller will then acquaint you with all the information you require as you take command.'

He thrust the papers back into Jampton's hand. 'And that means you, m'lad. You're it.'

Lieutenant Jampton was dumbstruck. Commanding Officer. He stared unseeing at the paper in his hand. 'Commanding Officer,' he whispered. It took his breath away. First posting, first command.

'It's only an Ordnance mob,' said the Major. 'It's not a post in the Cabinet. Now bugger off, I've got work to do.'

Jampton turned to leave as if in a trance.

'Good luck, lad,' said the RTO. 'You'll find a map amongst those papers.'

'A map?' repeated Jampton, still dazed.

'Yes, but don't worry about that now. I've tacked you on to the back of a convoy of six three-tonners that will take you more than halfway.'

'And what happens then?' asked Jampton fearfully.

The RTO looked at his watch, exasperated. 'Look,

sonny,' he said, 'I would love to come with you and show you the way but I've got a bloody big troop ship to unload – preferably,' he added, 'before Rommel gets here.' With this he gave Jampton a push and slammed the door.

Still in another world, Jampton took his seat beside his driver. In front of them was the back end of the last vehicle in the convoy. A Captain walked down the line of trucks and tapped on the window of the fifteen-hundredweight. Gratwick hurriedly wound it down.

'All set?' asked the Captain.

'Yes, sir,' mumbled Gratwick.

'Good. Just keep your distance, but whatever you do don't lose sight of the tail lights of that truck in front. Otherwise you might end up in the Transvaal.'

'Right, sir,' squeaked Gratwick sitting to attention, looking directly ahead.

The Captain nodded and without another word strode up the line of vehicles and climbed into the leading one, and the convoy moved off smoothly; that is, all except for the little fifteen-hundredweight at the rear, which leapt forward in a series of frantic spasmodic jerks as if eager to get at Rommel's jugular. It finally stalled.

Jampton picked his hat up from the floor of the cab and murmured, 'Been in Africa long?'

'No, sir,' mumbled Gratwick, desperately trying to start the motor. 'I came over on the same ship as you.'

Jampton was a little peeved. He hadn't been the first to disembark after all. The motor roared into life and with a better takeoff they found the convoy waiting patiently for them at the dock gates.

A bright flash that lit up the inside of the cab followed by a loud bang suddenly jerked Jampton out of his dockside reverie. It came from the direction the tanks had taken. Had they fired at something? Had they run into a minefield? He wheeled round to the empty driver's seat. Where the dickens was Gratwick? He desperately needed reassurance. He shivered and pulled his sleeping bag tighter around his thin shoulders. What he wouldn't have given for a steaming hot bath. Did it ever get light in this part of the world? he wondered.

Then he remembered that Gratwick was still out there somewhere. Surely he must have finished by now. He thought about his driver for a moment and wasn't terribly encouraged. If the rest of the British Army was like him, it was going to be a long uphill struggle.

A sudden panic gripped him. Had the fool finished his toilet and then walked away in an entirely different direction? His thoughts immediately turned to the gallant Captain Oates in the Scott Expedition. 'I'm going out now, I may be some time,' and with these historic words Oates had left the tent to be lost for ever in the Antarctic wastes.

Had his driver emulated Captain Oates? No, it was unthinkable. In any case 'I'm just whipping out for a crap, sir' wasn't exactly heroic. But then another horrific thought crossed his mind. Could it be that Gratwick had crouched and relieved himself on to an antipersonnel mine? Another flash followed by a bang. Thank God Gratwick was out there somewhere alive and well. After more worrying minutes he decided to parp the horn. But even as he reached out for the wheel second thoughts stopped him. What if the Germans had listening devices in the desert? He had visions of a Panzer Corps homing in on him, and suddenly his bowels weren't exactly secure. Firing a Very pistol was also out of the question. If a battle was being prepared, it might easily start off the attack prematurely.

But how to contact Gratwick? A brilliant idea struck him, and taking a shaded torch from under the dashboard, he climbed out and gave three quick flashes

26

to the north, similarly to the west and south, and shivering he waited and listened. But all he could hear was the thumping of his heart and the chattering of his teeth. Good grief, he'd never been so cold in his life.

Warmth now took precedence over the missing Gratwick. And in a sudden flash of inspiration he thought of his suitcase in the back of the fifteen-hundredweight. Of course, what a fool he'd been, what a ninny. Why hadn't he thought of it before? In the suitcase there were two Fair Isle jumpers, his long trousers and his greatcoat. Oh blessed suitcase! He shuffled round to the back of the truck and clambered in. His groping hands encountered the canvas of his pack, his portable bed. Then he touched what felt like a blanket. He was puzzled. Was it slightly warm? He slid his hand over it and Gratwick sat up with a jerk, startling Jampton, who let out a frightened yelp.

From the darkness came Gratwick's voice, outraged. 'Let's have less of that – I'm not one of them.'

Jampton tried to gain the initiative. 'One of what?' he asked bewildered.

'A brown hatter,' blurted out Gratwick.

The Lieutenant hadn't the foggiest idea what Gratwick was on about, but he most certainly objected to being addressed in this surly manner.

'May I remind you, Gratwick, you are speaking to your superior officer.'

The driver, now fully awake and regretting his outburst, replied, 'I'm sorry, sir, but I thought –'

'Never mind what you thought,' squeaked Jampton. 'You're not paid to think.'

It was a ludicrous exchange, two voices in the middle of nowhere.

'Next time,' went on Jampton, 'when you leave your post to relieve yourself, you will report back to me immediately on completing and not go sneaking into the back of the truck without my permission.'

In the blackness Gratwick listened with tongue out and thumbs against his head while he waggled his fingers.

'Is that clear?' said Jampton.

'Yes, sir.'

'Good.'

Jampton climbed out over the tailgate. 'Now,' he said, 'if you will hand me my suitcase, then return to your post, which is at the wheel . . .'

There was a silence from inside the truck.

'Did you hear what I said?' piped Jampton. 'My suitcase.'

Again there was a pause, then, 'What suitcase, sir?'

'My blue suitcase,' replied Jampton impatiently, 'I left it outside the RTO's office on the dockside.'

'Yes, sir, I remember it,' said Gratwick.

'Well?' asked Jampton, a sickening feeling beginning to stir inside him. He knew how this conversation was going to end.

'Didn't you put it on the back?' he prompted.

'No, sir,' replied Gratwick, 'nobody mentioned it.'

Mercifully, his Commanding Officer's face was indiscernible in the dark. It's not a pretty sight to see a man weep but Jampton was on the verge. His nerves were shredded; he wanted to fling himself down screaming and kick his heels against the hard surface of the desert. But before he could begin his tantrum, a lighter thought saved him. After all, the suitcase had his name and rank stencilled all over it. Surely the RTO would send it on. Of course – that's what would happen. Who knew? It may even be waiting for him at the Special Ordnance Group even before he arrived. With this optimism, he walked round the truck and swung himself into the cab. Gratwick followed and they sat together in surly silence for about ten minutes.

Jampton couldn't rid his mind of 'brown hatter'. What the dickens had Gratwick meant? The only solution he could come up with was that, before his call-up, Gratwick had sat high up on the Twinings tea van whipping up a team of matching horses. Yes, that must be it. They all wore brown bowlers. After satisfying himself with this observation he turned to look out of the side window and noticed that the stars were beginning to lose their glitter and the darkness on the ground seemed to be lightening. The dim shape of the rocks ahead was now faintly recognisable. It was the false dawn but Jampton wasn't to know this. He decided to follow the example of the tanks and move off. He settled in his seat and consulted his wrist compass, shook his arm, peered at it again and ordered the advance. His driver switched on the engine and they moved off in the direction of his CO's pointing finger.

Gratwick was desperate to keep the steering wheel firm so that he might continue in a straight line on a south-southeast bearing. He wasn't unduly worried: his job was to drive. Where they ended up wasn't his pigeon – that was the officer's responsibility.

On the other hand, Lieutenant Jampton was dead worried. It didn't seem to be getting any lighter and he had little faith in his driver, but as the miles went by he was less enthusiastic with the south-southeast direction. It was highly probable they would miss their objective by miles. Further doubts crept into his thoughts. He remembered vividly the tank man saying south-southeast but then had he *meant* south-southeast or did he have a stutter? At least, he thought, trying to cheer himself up, it's getting light.

CHAPTER

THREE

At the beginning of the desert campaign in North Africa, the 41st Light Infantry were at the sharp end under the command of General Wavell, and were known as the Cyrenaica Force. They almost succeeded in driving the Italians out of Africa but these heady victories ended when the Afrika Korps under the command of Kesselring and a little-known General called Rommel entered the lists, and this was an entirely different kettle of fish. The British were now forced back, conceding all the ground gained from the Italians. The 41st Light Infanty were fighting a rearguard action, backtracking all the way to Tobruk . . . It was their last battle.

When the Stukas peeled out of the dawn skies to begin the attack, it heralded the last rites of the sadly depleted 41st Infantry. The screams and crash of the bombs was augmented by a bombardment from the eighty-eights of the German artillery. Flames and smoke, the bangs of exploding shells, the rattle of small-arms fire, the screams and curses, it was a Dante's *Inferno* and in the midst of this madness the panzer tanks bucked and rocked over the rubble and smoking masonry followed by the infantry divisions of the Afrika Korps.

By the afternoon, Sergeant Major Puller, on the point of exhaustion, found himself in charge of what was left of the 41st, the command post having suffered a direct hit and all of the officers killed or wounded. He made up his mind quickly. Enough was enough – the regiment was finished. He hadn't enough men left to form a decent glee club and he passed the word round they would be pulling out under cover of darkness. But there was an hour of daylight left and as they retreated street by street the Sergeant Major began to wonder how many would be left by the time it got dark.

Mercifully, when night fell, Sergeant Major Puller, commandeering all the serviceable transport he could find, assembled his convoy and travelled as fast as the rubble-strewn streets and the slowest of the vehicles would allow. Fortune was with them. On the outskirts they found gaps in the perimeter wire and, luckiest of all, some white tape had been put down leading them through a heavy minefield, and thence into the blue, where they stopped. Sergeant Major Puller, after a quick check that the convoy was in order, swung himself into the lead truck and followed his compass on an easterly course. His intention was to put as much distance as he could between his pathetic convoy and the blood-red sky, the flashes and the explosions that were once Tobruk.

Some hours later when the sun rose, unconcerned, to light up the desert, Sergeant Major Puller finally called a halt. They'd lost one vehicle when the back axle broke. Now they were six three-tonners, a half-track and a fifteen-hundredweight. The Sergeant Major was the only one to alight; the rest slumped and slept, too weary and dispirited to move. He walked over to the second three-tonner and checked over his supplies, jerry cans of water, thank God, and food packs. But still the situation was critical. He reckoned this sustenance would last three or four days at the most. If they didn't stock up soon, they may as well have stayed in Tobruk. He decided to go at once to Alexandria and seek help. He would take two vehicles and, siphoning the petrol

31

from the other wagons into five-gallon drums, he set out for Alexandria.

Private Dusty Miller was driving the lead truck accompanied by the Sergeant Major, while the second three-tonner was driven by Private Sparks, and his passenger was a girl wrapped in a blanket, white-faced and shell-shocked. There didn't appear to be any superficial damage but God knew what state her innards were in. And besides, she was the only woman and you couldn't leave a woman in the desert. So the Sergeant Major decreed she should go with them and they'd deliver her to the military hospital. Poor little sod, thought Sparks. It was he who had rescued her from the pile of rubble that used to be the Hotel Imperial and it had been a close-run thing.

His mind went back a day. He remembered the heat and the dust and noise as he'd been spread-eagled on a pile of debris, Bren gun levelled at a corner of the street some three hundred yards away awaiting the enemy infantry or, worse, a panzer tank to poke its nose round the corner. Shells had been crashing round him too close for comfort and he had been about to scamper to a better place of concealment when suddenly he froze as something brushed gently against his ankle. He had snatched his leg away with revulsion (he smiled wryly now at the recollection). He'd thought it was a bloody rat, but as he looked round he saw that it was a hand – white, small and human. With a quick glance to the street corner, he'd left his Bren gun and scrabbled away at the rubble. From a doorway opposite, Dusty Miller saw what was happening and dashed over and gave him a hand to free whoever it was. It turned out to be a girl. By the time they'd dug her out, the German infantry were edging round the corner of the street. While Sparks stumbled back carrying the girl, it was Miller who'd covered their retreat.

Sparks paused in his recollections and gave the girl a sidelong glance and offered her his water bottle, but she ignored it, gazing straight ahead with unblinking eyes, and for one frightening moment he thought she was dead. But then she took the bottle from him and he breathed a sigh of relief. Eventually, when they arrived in Alexandria, the Sergeant Major alighted from the truck and brushed some of the sand and dust from his uniform. He made his way to the truck behind and said to Sparks, 'See her to the hospital first and I'll meet you here at eight o'clock sharp tomorrow morning. I'll have something sorted out by then. I've told Miller.' He slapped his hand against the door and Sparks pulled into the traffic while Miller, in the second truck, followed.

The girl riding in the cab with Sparks had still not uttered a word but at least she looked more alive as she pointed out the directions – presumably, Sparks thought, to the hospital. But he began to have doubts when she directed him up a narrow street. This couldn't be the way, surely. Had her experience in Tobruk unhinged her mind? Was he driving around haphazardly with a nutcase? He was almost convinced when after about a hundred yards she made a sign that he stop. He did, and looked out of his side window to see a large shop front and over the top a sign: ABDUL BEN HUSSEIN, IMPORT AND EXPORT. In the window itself was a load of tourist rubbish: brass urns, cheap costume jewellery, ivory and some tatty-looking rugs.

Miller came round to his door and looked up at Sparks. 'Buying her a present, are you?'

But the girl leant across Sparks and pressed the horn several times.

Sparks looked down at Miller's face and raised his eyebrows. 'She's lost her marbles,' he explained, but Miller wasn't listening. He was looking over Sparks's shoulder at something else.

'Bloody hell,' he breathed.

The whole shop front was swinging slowly inward and when it finally stopped the girl motioned for Sparks to drive in. He did so and Miller hauled himself into his own truck and followed. It was a bloody big garage; it was more than that, there was room for a small tank regiment. They were suddenly plunged into darkness as the shop front swung back into place. A light came on – it couldn't have been more than a forty-watt and didn't do much to relieve the gloom. Sparks jumped to the ground and came round the opposite side to lift the girl down. He was intrigued with his surroundings; after all it could be the hospital's back entrance. More light spilled in as a door opened and a fat Egyptian in fez and European suit minced down two steps to greet them. His face lit up when he saw the girl and they embraced each other.

'Yasmin, my little desert flower. I thought you had forgotten your poor old uncle.'

It was then the girl spoke for the first time. 'These are my friends. I think his name is Miller.'

The fat man bowed. This must be Abdul, Sparks thought.

'And this one –' her voice softened '– is Sparks.'

Sparks shuffled his feet and nodded, embarrassed when she added, 'He saved my life.'

Abdul's face brightened. 'Ah then, you will be my honoured guests tonight. My house is your house.' He bowed. 'Come, Yasmin,' he said, 'we have much to talk about.'

Sparks and Miller looked at each other, horrified. They didn't want to spend the night here. They knew a couple of better places in town where they could whoop it up and they wouldn't have to sit cross-legged on a cushion drinking tea.

'Yes, well, er, thanks for the invitation but . . .' He tailed off. The fat man, arm round the girl's shoulder, was going up two steps and through the inner door. Miller shrugged.

'Ten minutes, that's all,' he hissed to his mate, and they followed.

Sergeant Major Puller didn't seem to be having too much luck either. Alexandria was a madhouse; nobody wanted to be bothered with his problems, they had enough of their own, and he was shuttled from one authority to another. They were all too busy burning code books, depositions, unit strengths, movement orders – in fact, almost everything except letters from home ended up in the back of the furnace. The Sergeant Major was now desperate. He had about eighty men way out in the desert with not much food and very little water.

He thought of his options. In the middle of all this disorganisation and muddle, it would have been easy for him to walk into any motor pool and load up at the divisional Quartermaster Stores, but he knew this wouldn't be enough, merely a sticking plaster on an amputation. Then he suddenly remembered his old mate, an RSM of the Royal Army Service Corps. He might not even be in Alex – he might even be dead – but it was a chance the Sergeant Major had to take. It was as he was about to leap into a taxi that he heard his name being called.

'Sergeant Major Puller?' the voice enquired.

He turned curiously and then snapped rigidly to attention and saluted. Colonel Brunswick didn't return the salute, but stuck out his hand.

'Sergeant Major Puller.' He beamed. 'I heard you were in Alex ruffling a few feathers.'

The Sergeant Major shook his hand warmly. 'Good to see you again, sir. Long time.'

'Indeed it is,' replied the Colonel. 'Hyderabad in '38 if I'm not mistaken.'

'Yes, sir, happy days.'

The taxi was still waiting but Colonel Brunswick dismissed it with a peremptory wave. The driver shouted a stream of obscenities in Arabic and sped off.

'And the same to you,' shouted the Colonel after him. Turning back to the Sergeant Major he said, 'Right then, come with me and we'll see if we can't solve some of your problems.'

Reminiscences of old times, large whiskies – then the Sergeant Major poured out his troubles. Colonel Brunswick listened without interruption and then buzzed for his Adjutant and while they waited the Colonel poured a third glass for him. Ten minutes later Sergeant Major Puller had to repeat his problems to the Adjutant, who took notes and finally rose.

'Right, sir, I'll see what I can do.'

Colonel Brunswick looked at him steadily.

'Don't see what you can do, Jimmy, do it. Tomorrow,' he went on, 'Sergeant Major Puller must be on his way across the desert with mission accomplished.'

'Yes, sir,' replied the Adjutant, and left.

Sparks and Miller were still guests of Abdul ben Hussein but they were in a better frame of mind. They were seated at a table smiling at a bottle of Johnny Walker Black Label but this was only the beginning of the joy to come. They had already consumed a magnificent four-course meal and were about to make their excuses and exploit the night life of Alexandria when a small black man in a tuxedo came in and began to pick out a gentle tune on the piano. Abdul followed with a bevy of girls, introducing them all one by one. Beaming, he said, 'Take your pick, you are my guests tonight.' The girls were an international blend of beauty and elegance; these were Abdul's words and he wasn't far out.

The two soldiers couldn't believe their luck. They sat there stunned, then Miller relaxed and his face broke into a broad grin. Immediately all the girls, who had been looking a little apprehensive, smiled back and the ice began to break. They subsequently learned that Abdul not only owned the nightclub they were in but on the floors above were several well-furnished bedrooms. In fact, Abdul also ran the best brothel in North Africa and he wasn't backward in exercising a little trade in hashish ... It was a memorable night.

They didn't see the girl, Yasmin, again until the following morning, and it seemed that a good night's sleep had done the trick – she wasn't half bad. After bidding her uncle farewell she'd climbed up in the cab with Sparks and, strangely enough, it seemed perfectly natural.

'You'll have to show me where the hospital is,' he said.

She looked at him with wide eyes. 'Why do you want the hospital?' she asked. 'Are you not well?'

'There's nothing wrong with me,' said Sparks. 'It's you.'

She smiled. 'I'm fully recovered, thank you.' And she settled back.

'Where to?' he asked.

She shrugged. 'With you,' she said.

Sparks laughed. He hadn't quite sobered up and it didn't seem like such a bad idea.

At five minutes to eight o'clock Sergeant Major Puller waited for his two three-tonners. His hangover hadn't quite caught up with him and he was in a good frame of mind with a pocketful of orders stamped and signed giving him permission to draw this and to draw that from the stores. In fact, he had permission for almost anything that could be put on the truck. Two lorries approached and pulled up in front of him. He noticed the girl in the cab and he strolled over.

'Feeling better?' he asked.

'Yes, thanks,' she replied.

The Sergeant Major looked at her and nodded. There didn't seem to be anything else to say. He clambered up beside Miller and they set off for the Supply Depot.

Two hundred miles away in the desert, somewhere around midnight, Puller's nomads – hungry, thirsty, and still reliving the horrors of Tobruk – huddled over fires or tried desperately to sleep in the back of their three-tonners. It wasn't the best policy to light fires after dark but on this occasion it turned out to be a godsend. Those pinpoints of light were a homing beacon for Sergeant Major Puller's convoy of vital life-support supplies: tents, uniforms, blankets, and so forth, and, even more importantly, food and, best of all, two water bowsers. It was going to be like Christmas. In addition to the necessary supplies, there were plenty of cigarettes, boiled sweets and, for recreation, cricket bats, cricket balls, footballs and pingpong balls. He could have had a full-sized billiards table but transport was the problem. (In any case, the balls for this had been lost in a slight fracas with some American GIs.) And to cater for the less energetic and less erudite minority there were snakes and ladders and ludo. In order to facilitate further supplies, they were given the official title Special Ordnance Group, under the temporary command of Sergeant Major Puller.

And three weeks later they were pretty well organised. For what, it would be anybody's guess – but at least they were fed and watered and receiving regular supplies. A fair description would be that it was the only rest home in the western desert.

But their days were numbered. Even now an officer was on his way to take overall command, albeit a Second Lieutenant. Even had they been privy to this

38

information they would have greeted the news with a wave of indifference. Little did they know they would have made a grave mistake in being too complacent. This was no ordinary Second Lieutenant: this was Wilfred Ronaldsway Jampton.

The day broke sunnily, as it had done for thousands of years, and the SOG awoke cursing and scratching as Reveille broke the silence. The bandsman blew his bugle from a horizontal position, staying awake just long enough to complete the piece. It was his first duty on awakening, whenever that was. Sometimes he didn't get up until well after midday. In five minutes it was full daylight after the blackness of the African night, but it would be another hour before the sun rose over the horizon to warm the land. Coughing with the cold and 'V' cigarettes, those with appetites shuffled like zombies to the cook's marquee. When the sun rose it would be hot, too hot for comfort, and the flies weren't up yet. In fact, breakfast time would have been the best part of the day if it wasn't for the breakfast. By the time the sun was appearing over the horizon, those who had been filing past the cooks for powdered egg and something else were now forming up outside the latrines.

But all the attention was focused on the marquee that housed the MO and served as a hospital. Nine o'clock was sick parade but it was a joke. If there was anything that bothered anybody, they visited the MO at any time of the day or night, and if he was sober he usually prescribed aspirins, or grazes and desert sores were painted with gentian violet, a blue dye, and as desert sores were commonplace most of the unit looked like an ancient tribe of Iceni with not enough woad to go round.

However, on this momentous morning there was a mob craning and bobbing to see round the man in front into the dim interior of the tent. Only the desperate ones stayed in line for the latrines. Even the Sergeant

Major, freshly shaven, strolled across to see what the commotion was about.

'It's Miller, sir,' said one of the spectators helpfully.

The Sergeant Major nodded; he'd had a suspicion it might be. Rifleman Miller had been a good infantryman with the old 41st. He had joined the Army without any feeling of patriotism, King and country. His had been a straight choice. The magistrate had had enough, either he enlisted or it was prison again. Miller hadn't taken long to make up his mind. Escape from prison was almost impossible but there were no bars round an Army Camp. Now he was up to his old tricks and there weren't many he didn't know.

'Get out,' came the MO's voice from inside the marquee, and the crowd pulled back as Miller was hustled blinking into the harsh sunlight.

The lads nudged one another in delighted anticipation. Most of them, unlike the Sergeant Major, had known Dusty Miller only since Tobruk, but he had established himself as camp comedian. The MO ducked out after him, the effort of being in the bright new sun bringing out pimples of the morning's gin on to his forehead. He belched softly; then, bending again, he scooped up a handful of sand.

'This is sand, see, sand.' A little of it trickled through his fingers.

Miller stared at him uncomprehendingly and looked at the crowd in puzzlement.

A wag at the back shouted, 'Who got you ready then?' and a laugh went up.

Dusty Miller was in full uniform, greatcoat buttoned up to the neck with a blanket round his shoulders and a balaclava underneath his tin helmet. He held his gloved hands to the crowd as if to say 'What's the matter with the MO this morning?'.

The MO struggled to maintain his composure. 'If this was snow I'd be able to make a snowman, wouldn't I?'

The crowd latched on, and there were a few giggles.

'Do you understand, Miller? We are not in the frozen north. This is not snow; this is desert sand, limestone dust and camel droppings.'

This brought a better response from the lads; this gave them the complete picture. Miller was realising that what had once seemed a good idea was dribbling away like the sand in the MO's cupped fists. He cleared his throat and prepared to cut his losses.

'I didn't say it *was* snow, sir. I said it *felt* like snow.' He beamed at the Sergeant Major. 'Oh yes, I can see it's sand now. It's warm. But when I got up I was cold and shivering and the next thing I remember I'm standing at your table.'

The MO wasn't letting him off lightly. 'Yes,' he replied silkily. 'You staggered in and said if they don't find us today we'll have to eat one of the dogs.'

This brought a howl from the crowd. After all, they'd been starved of entertainment and this was better than Flanagan and Allen.

Miller eyed the MO with a puzzled expression. 'I don't remember saying that, sir.'

'Well you did,' yelled the MO, losing his cool. 'And although your memory has been on the blink lately, you always seem to remember where my damn tent is.'

He held on to the guy rope for support; this last effort had brought the sweat pouring down his face. He decided to end the matter, have a large gin and go back to bed.

'Sar'nt Major,' he croaked.

'Sah.' The Sergeant Major sprang to attention.

'This man is malingering. Put him on extra guard duty.'

With that he staggered back into the marquee to leave the rest of the sick to the medical orderly. The Sergeant Major relaxed and stared at Dusty Miller thoughtfully. The crowd, now sensing that the morning's entertainment was over, began to disperse.

The Sergeant Major shook his head in despair. 'Well, my little desert flower, you've done it again, haven't you?'

Miller shuffled his feet and stared off into the far distance; he shrugged and looked back at the Sergeant Major. They had been togther since '36 when the Sergeant Major was a corporal so they had the measure of each other.

The Sergeant Major shook his head again and sighed deeply. 'OK, get your bedding off and relieve Taylor in the Bren pit!'

Miller rallied. 'But, Sar'nt Major, I'm supposed to be off duty.'

The Sergeant Major took a step forward until his nose was within an inch of Miller's. 'Listen, lad, there's no off-duty till the war's over, and with blokes like you around I can't see any possibility of that.'

Miller sulkily took the blanket from his shoulders and was about to unfasten the buttons of his greatcoat. The Sergeant Major was quicker.

'Leave those buttons alone,' he rasped. 'I want you on guard duty properly wrapped up and properly dressed.'

Miller's mouth fell open. 'But, Sar'nt Major, it's hot now and it'll get hotter.'

The Sergeant Major smiled grimly. 'Yes, it will, won't it? But we don't want you catching cold again, do we?'

Miller was about to reply but the Sergeant Major cut him short. 'Ten-*shun* . . . right turn at the double to the Bren pit, eff right, eff right . . .' and Miller doubled off to the jeers of his mates in the sick queue outside the MO's tent.

One wag shouted after him, 'At least you won't get frostbite.' The outpatients laughed good-humouredly and the Sergeant Major whirled angrily towards them.

'If you feel good enough to laugh you don't belong in

42

a sick parade. Do something useful for a change.' And sheepishly they turned away and dispersed.

In the Bren pit Private Sparks eyed his mate Dusty Miller as he joined him and wondered idly why he was well wrapped up. Were they expecting bad weather?

Miller took a swig from his water bottle. What was visible of his face glistened with sweat. He estimated he had already lost half a stone in weight.

Sparks shook his head sadly. 'Do you know,' he said, 'if I was MO I would let you out on the grounds of sheer stupidity.'

'Yes, but this one's never sober,' growled Miller. 'Four days I've been going around in this lot and he didn't take a blind bit of notice.'

'I've watched you,' replied Sparks, 'staggering about, flapping your arms, blowing on your hands: pathetic.'

Miller shrugged and muttered bitterly. 'He used to be a good MO too. I fell at his feet yesterday and he just stepped over me.'

Sparks snorted; even he was beginning to sweat now. Just looking at his mate was enough. Then he laughed. 'You've been in this lot long enough to learn there's no way you can get out on a mental kick. They can see through it a mile off. You'd be better off acting normal – you'd stand a better chance then.'

There was a pause, then Miller spoke defensively. 'It has been done though.'

Sparks's eyebrow went up. 'Oh yes,' he replied, 'but as far as I can recall only once and that was in my old regiment at Catterick, but there wasn't a war then.' He lifted the Bren gun from the sandbags and took out an oily rag.

Miller looked at him quickly. This was Sparks all over. He would start something and then leave it dangling in the air while he went off to do something else. But he wasn't going to get away with it this time. 'What happened?' said Miller.

Sparks looked up. 'Eh?'

Miller looked away in exasperation. 'What happened to the bloke at Catterick?' he said as if talking to a child.

'Oh him,' said Sparks. 'He was really off his rocker, he was. He thought the Adjutant was his mother.'

'Get away,' replied Miller disbelieving.

'He really starved once. He wouldn't eat till the Adjutant fed him with a spoon, and if he had meat the Adjutant had to cut it up for him.'

Miller's heart sank. They didn't have an Adjutant for starters and meat only came out of bully beef tins so what might have been a good idea was a non-starter. He eyed Sparks speculatively. 'Was he really round the twist?'

'Oh yes,' replied Sparks. 'He used to cry every night and wet his bed.'

Miller snorted. Sparks looked directly at him. 'I ought to know,' he said, 'I was in the bunk underneath.'

Miller was intrigued, visualising the scene. Then he pulled himself together. 'Yes, but in the end, this bloke, did he work his ticket?'

Sparks examined the breech of the gun. 'Like I told you,' he said, 'the last I saw of him he was in the back of a three-tonner with the Adjutant reading him *Jack and the Beanstalk*, and they took him to the nuthouse.'

'Was he in there long?' asked Miller after a pause.

'Nah, not long,' said Sparks. 'He was out in a couple of months.' He took a long swig from his water bottle and, slapping back the cork, said, 'They kept the Adjutant though.'

Miller by this time was almost bubbling with heat. Even putting a cigarette to his lips brought another rash of perspiration but his mind was on the Adjutant.

'How long ago was this?' he asked.

But Sparks wasn't listening. He was looking far beyond the opposite end of the camp.

* * *

The Sergeant Major, standing outside the mess tent holding a mug full of cold tea, was also watching the approach of the vehicle. The MO emerged from his tent and followed the Sergeant Major's gaze.

'One of ours?' asked the MO dispassionately.

The Sergeant Major nodded. 'Looks like it, sir.' He shaded his eyes.

When it was about two hundred yards away, the vehicle suddenly changed direction and shot behind a rocky escarpment. The MO, swishing his gin and tonic round his glass, looked quizzically at the Sergeant Major who shrugged back at him. They waited a few moments, then a flash from the top of the small rise told them they were being observed through binoculars.

The MO took a deep swig and murmured, 'Whoever it is, he's very interested in us.'

'Yes,' said the Sergeant Major laconically. The MO glanced down at his glass and found it was empty. 'Let me know what transpires,' he said and ducked back into his tent for a refill.

After what seemed an age, the small truck re-emerged and trundled its way warily forward. The Sergeant Major, identifying it as a fifteen-hundredweight, watched as it groaned up the slight incline towards the camp. Men strolled from the mess tent with bulging mouths to view the arrival; more faces poked around tent flaps and a row of heads appeared above the canvas wall of a latrine looking for all the world like a coconut shy at a vicar's tea party. All silently observed the arrival of the labouring vehicle. Apart from the sound of its approach, the camp was gripped in an unnatural stillness.

The silence was suddenly broken by a shattering, racking early-morning cough as a tall thin figure in a tin hat, khaki vest and boots staggered from his tent in order to shake the detritus of the night from his blanket – sand, dust, cigarette ash. From the Sergeant Major's point of view it looked as if he were flagging the vehicle down. In any event it slowed, whereupon the barely dressed swaddie stepped forward holding the blanket in front of the bonnet of the fifteen-hundredweight and then, in the style of a matador at a bullfight, he whirled the blanket round him executing a passable veronica. '*Olé*!' – the cry went up from a dozen of the lads followed by a laugh. The blanket man turned to them and bowed low to acknowledge the *Olés*. Then he turned back to the vehicle. As the occupant said something, the matador took a small stub of a cigarette from his lips, bending forward while he had his second rattling cough of the day, and, straightening, returned the stub to his lips and pointed in the direction of the SM.

Jampton looked over to the Sergeant Major and back to the wheezing matador. He wanted to say something else but he couldn't think what. He was outraged! When the pseudo-matador had bowed towards the crowd to acknowledge his applause his vest had ridden up and Jampton had found himself staring at a big, bare, hairy backside. Good grief, the Officers' Training Corps hadn't prepared him for anything like this. Bereft of words, he peremptorily signalled Gratwick to drive on and, in the short stretch to the Sergeant Major, Lieutenant Jampton regained some of his composure.

Sergeant Major Puller watched the fifteen-hundred-weight approach with dismay. The driver looked exhausted and certainly scarcely old enough to hold a driver's licence. The officer, standing upright and holding on to the windscreen, was covered in white dust. Even his goggles were coated, so how he managed to see anything was a miracle. The Sergeant Major had a sinking feeling in the pit of his stomach. He knew that this was going to be a memorable day and he'd had enough memorable days in the past not to find them pleasurable.

The first thing Lieutenant Jampton noticed was the leather strap on his left wrist bearing a crown. So this was the legendary Sergeant Major Puller. Secretly he complimented himself on his powers of observation.

'Sar'nt Major,' he croaked.

'Sir?' replied the Sergeant Major.

Jampton was irritated. The man had not come to attention, nor had he saluted. Indeed he was standing easy in a very casual manner, hardly befitting a noncommissioned officer in the presence of his superior, and, what was worse, in full view of the men. Jampton thought for a second whether to take issue but decided there would be time for that later.

'This is the Special Ordnance Group, I take it.'

Puller's heart sank. His worst fears were confirmed: this was the man to be in charge. He shook his head sadly and surveyed this dust-covered apparition from a Dickens novel and knew for a certainty the war was lost.

'Well, sir,' he replied, 'we used to be the 41st Light Infantry. There are only a handful of us left now.' He sighed unhappily and continued. 'What we have now is anybody's guess. It's just a hotchpotch of cooks, drivers, Indians, Foreign Legionnaires; in fact all the last people to get out of Tobruk. So yes, you are right, we are now on record as being the Special Ordnance Group.' He grimaced as he said it.

'Ah ha,' said the dust-covered Lieutenant. 'I thought as much.'

He gazed imperiously round at the camp. His sight was impaired by the dust on his goggles but he wasn't going to let on.

He turned to address the Sergeant Major, who, much to his annoyance, was bending down to pet a flea-bitten mongrel. 'Have you had your breakfast yet?' said the Sergeant Major.

Jampton had a sudden vision of a steaming plate of

47

bacon and eggs with mushrooms. He was about to reply when he realised that the Sergeant Major was talking to the dog.

'Sergeant Major,' Jampton commanded tapping the windshield with impatience.

The Sergeant Major shooed the dog towards the mess tent and shouted after it, 'And don't give it any bacon, he's too fat as it is.' Then, brushing his hands together, he turned to the fifteen-hundredweight. 'Yes, sir?'

'Thank you for your time, Sergeant Major,' said Jampton sarcastically. He would put this man in his place, medal ribbons or no medal ribbons. 'Sergeant Major,' he repeated, 'I am Lieutenant Jampton, your new Commanding Officer.'

He paused to let this sink in. The effect, however, was completely ruined as the dog shot out of the mess tent with a large lump of something in its mouth followed by two pans and an irate cook in a dirty white apron. 'Bloody thief,' he yelled. 'If I catch you in here again it'll be dog pie for supper.' He looked over to the Sergeant Major. 'That bloody dog of yours is a menace.' He stooped to pick up the pans and disappeared back into the shade of his domain. The Lieutenant was aghast. If cooks could yell at the senior NCO, where was the discipline?

The Lieutenant glanced down at Gratwick, who was dozing over the wheel. No moral support there. He addressed the Sergeant Major again.

'I repeat, I am Lieutenant Jampton, your new Commanding Officer.'

The Sergeant Major looked coolly up at him as if to say 'so what?' Jampton ignored this dumb insolence. He went on, 'Why was I not challenged?'

'Challenged, sir?'

'Yes, challenged.'

He decided to remove his goggles to give the Sergeant Major the full benefit of the steely glint in his eyes.

48

Unfortunately as he was lifting the strap he caught the visor of his cap and it fell to the floor. As he bent down to retrieve it, he caught his head a fearsome smack on the corner of the windshield. The Sergeant Major winced and looked away. That was all they were short of, an accident-prone CO. The crowd now had all the information they needed and moved away in order to discuss it.

Lieutenant Jampton, trying desperately not to rub his forehead, eyed the Sergeant Major and the surrounding camp. Now that he could see clearly his worst fears were confirmed – it was like a run-down gypsy encampment. He was about to speak when a voice behind him caused more consternation.

'Care for a drink, old boy?'

Jampton whirled round but before he could disgrace himself further the man spoke. 'Allow me to introduce myself. Captain Witherspoon. I'm the Medical Officer.'

Lieutenant Jampton gazed blankly for a moment and pulled himself together. Another man of breeding; at least he would be someone to talk to in the officers' mess.

'Lieutenant Jampton, your new CO.' He stood to attention and saluted.

'Good ho,' said Captain Witherspoon. 'Follow me and I'll crack open another bottle.' He walked unsteadily towards his tent and disappeared.

Jampton stared blankly after him. Was it his birthday? he wondered. If it was he had a birthday every week.

Captain Witherspoon hadn't been one of the original 41st Light Infantry. He'd been MO to the garrison in Tobruk and after his surgery had gone up in smoke and flames he was the last person to join Sergeant Major Puller's retreat. He was hauled over the tailgate of the last three-tonner and all he had with him was his doctor's Gladstone bag containing not, as expected, medical supplies, but four bottles of Gordon's Gin and two of Scotch.

Standing in the Bren pit, Miller and Sparks watched the young Second Lieutenant. The red, burnt legs, white at the back, did not go unnoticed. Miller winked at his mate and said thoughtfully, 'You know, he'd make a good mother.'

Sparks frowned and they carried on with their game, flipping stones at a passing beetle.

Jampton ordered the Sergeant Major to take him on a tour of inspection around the camp. The Sergeant Major hesitated for a moment. What was there to inspect? The Lieutenant was already four paces ahead tapping the guy ropes of the mess tent with his swagger stick.

'Very sloppy, Sergeant Major. See to it.'

'Yes, sir,' replied the Sergeant Major and immediately forgot about it.

Jampton stopped and gazed around him. 'These are all just tents, Sergeant Major,' he said, waving his arm.

'Yes, sir,' replied the Sergeant Major, baffled. What were they supposed to be, for God's sake? Terraced houses?

Jampton eyed him sternly, slapping his stick into the palm of his hand.

'Well, Sergeant Major?' He waited for a moment and then, exasperated, he followed on. 'Where is the guard tent? Where is the mess tent? The orderly room? My tent? The officers' mess? If you have these locations, why are they not signposted?'

The Sergeant Major was an old soldier, too well trained and too much in command of himself to let his anger show – well, some of it. His mouth set in a grim line and his nostrils went white. These were the only visible signs that Jampton had just avoided hospitalisation.

'With respect, sir,' he started, 'there are no signs

because over half this lot don't speak English.' He spread the fingers of his left hand and tapped each point off. This conveyed the impression that he knew what he was talking about and it gave his hands something to do so they didn't stray around the scrawn that joined Jampton's head to his shoulders.

He went on.

'The situation here is that we are only temporary, and any day now –'

'Excuses, excuses,' broke in Jampton snappishly, and suddenly he stopped.

One tent, set apart from the others, intrigued him. He minced across to it and poked in his head. It was crammed full of unused cricket balls, bats, footballs in pristine condition – in fact all the sporting paraphernalia the Sergeant Major had so joyfully brought into camp three weeks ago.

'What's all this?' snapped Jampton, withdrawing his head.

'Give 'em time, sir. They'll come round to it.'

The little Lieutenant was appalled. 'This is supposed to be a military camp on active service,' he yelped, 'not a sports centre. What about a swimming pool?' he asked sarcastically.

'Water's the problem, sir,' replied the SM helpfully.

But the bossy young prat wasn't listening. He turned to carry on the camp inspection only to find his path was blocked by a line of washing strung between tents. A large blanket was being pegged to the line. But it wasn't the laundry that had stopped him dead in his tracks. It was the hands doing the pegging: they were delicate and well shaped. His gaze travelled down the blanket – and the bare legs behind it were not the hairy, thick-type legs that had marched across Africa. These limbs would be more at home in the Folies Bergère.

The young Lieutenant looked enquiringly at the Sergeant Major, who sighed and nodded. Jampton went forward and ducked under the washing line and his suspicions were confirmed. It was not only a girl, it was a beautiful girl with long black hair. That's all he took in – he wasn't old enough to look at the rest of her. Instinctively he made as if to take his cap off, then noticed she was wearing an outsize khaki shirt with two stripes sewn on the arms.

The girl turned and moved towards him and stared into his face. Jampton, disconcerted, realised he was in her way and hurriedly stepped back a pace. This was a mistake: he fell over a bucket. The girl watched him without expression but in that short observation she had taken in the small beak nose, the mouth that looked like the slit in a piggy bank and, more important, the one pip on his shoulder. '*Merci*,' she said tonelessly and jabbed the peg on to the blanket.

Jampton struggled to his feet and in order to regain his composure said 'Carry on, ma'am' and went to tap the peak of his cap with his stick in salute. Unfortunately he was in such a tizzy he missed the peak of his cap altogether and nearly knocked his eye out. The Sergeant Major walked away as if he hadn't seen anything. What a pillock, he thought. With the lump on his forehead getting larger by the minute and a streaming red eye, Jampton was a walking wounded – and nobody had laid a finger on him yet.

Jampton ran after the receding figure and planted himself in front of him so he had to stop. 'Well?' he snapped.

'We call her Corporal Smith, sir. Don't know her real name.'

'A foreigner?' asked Jampton.

'Half Arab, half French, I think,' replied the Sergeant Major.

'But what does she do – come in once a week to do the laundry?' queried Jampton.

The Sergeant Major replied, discomfited, 'Well, no,

sir. She's also the camp barber and sometimes helps in the sickbay.'

Jampton digested this and raised his head to look over the Sergeant Major's shoulder to the washing, but the girl had already gone. He cleared his throat and looked the Sergeant Major in the eye.

'I want a straight answer,' he said.

'Of course, sir.'

'Am I to take it that – er – Corporal Smith is on our ration strength?'

'Yes, sir,' replied the Sergeant Major defiantly.

Jampton was astounded. He still couldn't take it all in. He carried on relentlessly. 'And what recruiting office paid her the King's shilling?' he asked sarcastically.

'There are extenuating circumstances, sir,' the Sergeant Major explained patiently. 'Private Sparks found her under a pile of rubble when we were pulling out of Tobruk, and we were moving all the time – never seemed to get a chance to dump her. In any case she wouldn't have gone unless Sparks went too, but we had enough problems on our hands with the Afrika Korps.' He shrugged. 'Eventually we wound up here.'

'And who does she – I mean where does she sleep?' asked Jampton.

'In the back of one of the trucks, sir,' answered the Sergeant Major.

'This is the British Army, Sergeant Major, not a . . .' Jampton struggled to find a suitable comparison. 'Not a Trade Union Congress.'

The Sergeant Major blinked. He couldn't quite make the connection, but then neither could Jampton, who wished he hadn't said it.

'Just look around you, Sergeant Major.' He paused. 'I arrive –'

He suddenly stopped. From the distance came a low growl rapidly reaching a crescendo as, with an ear-splitting roar, a fighter plane buzzed the camp at about thirty feet. Jampton ducked involuntarily and yelped, 'What was that?'

'A sand fly,' murmured a passing soldier. 'Plenty more by the latrines.'

Jampton looked quizzically at the Sergeant Major. The remark was obviously a joke but strangely enough nobody seemed concerned or even curious. Again a scream and a roar and the plane zoomed over, lower this time so that it disturbed a long trail of desert dust.

Suddenly Jampton knew what had niggled him on the first pass. He whirled round to the Sergeant Major. 'That's a German plane,' he gasped.

The Sergeant Major nodded. 'Messerschmitt 109, sir. The lads call him the Red Baron.'

Jampton stared at him perplexed. 'Then why didn't we fire?'

'Well, sir, he comes over every day,' replied the Sergeant Major.

'Every day?' squeaked Jampton, and whirling round he shouted towards the sandbagged Bren-gun pit. 'What's the matter with the Bren? Why don't you shoot?'

Sparks and Miller this time were flipping stones at a passing column of ants. They looked at each other puzzled, and glanced up at the plane, now banking for another run in.

'Shoot, dammit!' screamed Jampton. 'Why don't you shoot?'

Miller shrugged, turned to the gun resting on the sand bags and let off a short burst. He turned towards Jampton and put up his thumb.

Sparks was not best pleased. 'Now what did you want to go and do that for?' he hissed. 'I've just cleaned the bloody thing.'

'Well you heard him,' said Miller.

'Doesn't mean you have to listen to the stupid git,

54

does it?' retorted Sparks, and angrily he whirled on the gun and fired off a long burst.

The Messerschmitt jinked round the upcoming tracer and made height, moving in a graceful arc to set himself up for another approach. By this time there was no lack of interest from the lads in the camp. As soon as the staccato fire burst from the Bren gun, every eye watched fearfully. As the plane approached, the roar of the engine increased and suddenly lights speckled along the leading edge of the wing, spraying bullets and shells. Astonished, everyone flung themselves to the ground. Again the pilot made height in a graceful climbing turn to set himself up for the *coup de grâce*. The lads in the camp watched dry-mouthed, fearful of what was coming next. Some of them rose to their feet and ran madly in every direction.

Sparks and Miller flattened themselves on the floor of the Bren pit. It was three feet deep and comparatively safe. Even so, they would have preferred the Grand Canyon. They listened to the plane for a moment, then Miller muttered, 'Oh Gawd, he's coming round again.'

Jampton, the Sergeant Major and the driver Gratwick lay prone behind the fifteen-hundredweight. The Sergeant Major muttered, 'Gawd, we've upset him now.'

'Upset him?' repeated Jampton.

The Sergeant Major replied, 'He doesn't usually bother us.'

He ducked as the plane, guns blazing, zoomed towards them.

Dusty Miller, in a panic, reached up and without looking fired a short burst from the Bren. It was a token gesture and no one was more astonished than Rifleman Miller when the roar of the departing Messerschmitt suddenly cut out, then it spluttered and coughed. Heads were raised cautiously as the plane struggled to gain height. Black smoke was pouring from it and, as it shrank to a speck in the sky, the faint noise of the engine cut out abruptly. There was a small pinprick of light as if the sun had caught the perspex of the canopy, followed thirty seconds later by a slight crack. Then the plane began the spiralling descent, out of control, black smoke corkscrewing behind it. When it finally crashed into the desert about five hundred yards from the camp, it was almost an anticlimax. There was little left of the plane anyway, just a large smoking black patch.

Dusty Miller couldn't believe his eyes. Sure, he'd fired the Bren many times before with intent when the sky was full of enemy planes, and to his knowledge he'd never hit one yet. But this, this was beyond belief. He'd actually shot one down!

Fifty yards away Lieutenant Jampton stared at the blackened smoking patch of sand. The Sergeant Major eyed the young CO curiously. He was a strange sight, half crouched, holding his shorts away from his crimson, shiny knees, hopping from one foot to the other. God, thought the Sergeant Major, he looks as if he's about to join in a hoedown, poor little bugger.

'Don't let it bother you, sir. There's plenty more where that came from.'

Jampton, encouraged by the SM's support, said eagerly, 'It was either us or him.'

The Sergeant Major shook his head. 'Oh I doubt that, sir. If he'd been serious you'd be writing condolences to a lot of mothers tonight.' He pointed to the vehicle park. 'That's all he took out: the supply wagon. He was teaching us a lesson.'

Jampton looked across at the blazing three-tonner and was galvanised into action.

'Gather the men together, Sergeant Major, and form a bucket chain.'

He took a khaki handkerchief out of his pocket and tied it over his mouth and nostrils before running to the blazing vehicle, but after a few paces he realised he was alone. He turned, but the men and the Sergeant Major hadn't moved. They were standing about watching him curiously.

Jampton tugged the handkerchief down to give his mouth freedom and yelled, 'Didn't you hear me, Sergeant Major. Form a bucket chain.'

But still nobody moved.

Then one of the lads shouted, 'There's ammunition on that truck, sir.'

Jampton turned quickly back to the blazing wreck, then panic-stricken he ran behind his fifteen-hundred-weight yelling, 'Stand well back, everybody, there's ammunition on that truck!' And, crouching, he watched wide-eyed as the flames lessened and with a tired lurch the bed of the burning truck collapsed. Then from the dying embers a bright ball shot lazily into the air about fifteen feet, like a very cheap Roman candle, and with a soft bang slowly fell to earth. It was all over.

'Ammunition?' asked Jampton sarcastically.

'I could have sworn we had more than that,' sighed the Sergeant Major, trying hard not to laugh.

The CO rose to his feet, got into the cab and ordered his driver to take him over to the Bren pit.

Dusty Miller was in full flow. 'Ah,' he said modestly, 'it was nothing. He was gettin' on my wick flying over every day showing off.'

'He won't be coming again,' shouted one of the crowd.

Sparks, still in the Bren pit, snorted. Over the last few months he'd seen his mate in action against the Italians and then the Afrika Korps, but what had happened in the last few minutes was straight out of *Comic Cuts*.

The crowd jumped out of the way as the fifteen-hundredweight screeched to a stop. Lieutenant Jampton rose to his feet and rapped on the windshield with his stick to gain attention. He decided this was as good a time as any to introduce himself. It never crossed his mind that the shooting down of the enemy plane was a million-to-one chance, a miracle in his romantic adolescent imagination. He thought that soldiers, especially infantrymen, shot down enemy aeroplanes every day of the week.

'Men,' he began. But he might have been invisible. They were still excited, laughing and chattering with Miller the focus of their admiration.

Jampton clapped his hands and tried again.

'Men,' he screeched.

But Miller had the floor and it was he who shushed the crowd and looked across at the scarecrow of his surrogate mother beating the metal of the windshield in frustration.

Miller raised both arms. 'All right, lads, that's enough,' he bellowed; and the noise of the chattering crowd subsided. He bowed towards Jampton. 'Sorry, sir,' he said humbly. 'Carry on.'

Sergeant Major Puller, arms folded, shook his head sadly at the sheer farcical effrontery of it all. Jampton looked at him enquiringly. 'Private Miller, sir,' muttered the SM.

'Thank you, Sergeant Major,' said the Lieutenant and cleared his throat. 'Men,' he began again, 'now is as good a time as any to introduce myself. I am Lieutenant Jampton, your new Commanding Officer.'

He paused for effect and somebody at the back shouted, 'Speak up!'

'That's enough,' barked the SM, asserting himself, and, turning to his CO, said, 'Carry on, sir.'

'Men,' continued Jampton, this time louder. 'On the first day of my command we have destroyed an enemy plane.'

A match rasped and somebody lit up a fag. Jampton glared at the tall bearded smoker and was about to order the Sergeant Major to take that man's name when a voice bellowed, 'Get on with it, it'll soon be dark.'

Jampton was puzzled. What was the man on about, it wasn't yet midday.

'Right,' he continued uncertainly, 'that plane was shot down by whom?'

They all turned their heads to where Miller was standing trying to look modest.

'Yes,' went on Jampton, his voice rising, 'the only man in the camp apart from the Sergeant Major who is properly dressed.

This was greeted with ironic cheers, whistles and 'Good on you, Dusty.'

The young Lieutenant was gratified he'd made his point. When the noise subsided he began to drive his point home.

'The Special Ordnance Group from this day is about to be reborn.'

He wasn't looking at them now. Carried away with his own oratory, he had a vision of his Aunt Dorothy standing, hands clasped in front of her, head tilted slightly to one side. There was a half-smile on her face as she gazed in open admiration at his mastery over this ill-dressed slovenly mob.

His vision faded. Somewhere along the line he'd lost his hold over his new command. They were all looking curiously beyond him where some were pointing. He jerked his head round to see what was the cause of the distraction and saw a figure striding purposefully towards them carrying what appeared to be a bundle of washing; it subsequently turned out to be a parachute.

It was the pilot of the Messerschmitt and from the way he strode purposefully into the camp it was evident that he was not a happy man. He stopped and took in the scene. Then, slinging down his parachute, he made a beeline for Lieutenant Jampton, who was still standing upright in his fifteen-hundredweight.

The pilot spoke through gritted teeth. 'Who is in charge of this –' he gestured disdainfully to the men '– band of gypsies?'

His English was excellent, so much so that Jampton was unsure of himself. He stepped down from his vehicle.

'I am Lieutenant Jampton, the Commanding Officer,' he said shakily. He didn't know whether to salute or offer to shake hands. This man obviously had breeding.

The pilot looked him up and down, then turned to the crowd. 'Which man was responsible for shooting down my plane?'

'You're only required to give your name, rank and number,' squeaked Jampton behind him, trying desperately to regain the initiative.

'I'm waiting,' the pilot said icily.

Some of them turned towards Miller, and the pilot, following their gaze, strode towards the Bren pit as the crowd parted for him to pass.

As he reached Miller he shouted, '*Dumbkof, puta*, cretin, arsehole.' Obviously he was well travelled. To emphasise each word he slapped Miller's face.

Sparks leapt out of the Bren pit, an entrenching tool in his hand and murder in his eyes.

'That's enough, Sparks,' rasped Sergeant Major Puller quickly.

Sparks stopped dead. It was as if he'd walked into a closed door. He didn't look at the SM, his eyes still on the German pilot, who returned his gaze coolly. It was anybody's guess what would happen next; then somebody sneezed and that broke the spell. Sparks' shoulders slumped and he turned away. 'Bollocks to the lot of 'em,' he muttered.

There was a light touch on his arm and he turned to look down into the beautiful dark eyes of Corporal Smith. For a moment it was as if he didn't recognise her. Snatching his arm from her hand he said, 'And bollocks to you, too,' and pushed his way through the crowd.

Lieutenant Jampton watched it all open-mouthed and

felt it was time to take charge of the situation. He clapped his hands together like a gym teacher about to call for another game of netball.

'Right,' he squeaked, not quite in control of his voice.

'Why?' barked the pilot.

Jampton stepped back a pace.

'Why,' repeated the pilot, 'did you allow this oaf to open fire?'

The Sergeant Major cleared his throat; he'd heard enough – it was time to end the pantomime.

'All right,' he barked, 'you and you.' He pointed to two of the spellbound audience.

He was about to order them to take charge of the German pilot when Jampton intervened. 'Thank you, Sergeant Major,' he piped. 'I'm in command; I can manage if you don't mind,' he added waspishly.

'*Got in Himmel*,' muttered the pilot. 'When you have quite decided who is in command, I must warn you that you haven't heard the last of this.' He glared at Jampton. 'You, little man,' he said, 'are responsible for a wanton act of destruction contravening the Geneva Convention of War.'

Unsure of the validity of this statement, Jampton replied, 'You are an enemy and it was our duty to shoot you down.'

Ignoring this last fatuous remark, the pilot carried on. 'As you will have no doubt observed, I am too old to fly as a fighter pilot in battle. I am merely a test pilot, a noncombatant.'

Lieutenant Jampton shook his head vigorously, leaving his cap askew.

'Hear me out,' barked the German.

Sergeant Major Puller turned away in disgust. Why didn't the little prat just detail two men to take him prisoner?

The pilot continued, 'For the past days I have entertained this pathetic outpost – aerobatics of daring

61

and brilliance, far in advance of your Spitfires. I was under the impression that you enjoyed these displays of superiority and,' he added modestly, 'appreciated my undoubted skill as a pilot.'

'That's all very well –' broke in Jampton.

'I'm talking,' said the pilot icily, 'and may I remind you my rank is higher than yours.'

'Not in the British Army,' piped Jampton.

Trying desperately to decipher the logic of this last remark, the pilot took in the slight, thin apparition before him. *Mein Got*, if this was the best England could offer, what was taking General Rommel so long? Then he glanced quickly at his wristwatch and, like a businessman dismissing an interviewee, declared, 'Well, it's getting late and I'm hungry for my lunch.' And, whilst everyone was spellbound by this sheer effrontery, he marched over to the fifteen-hundredweight and climbed in beside Gratwick.

'Drive on,' he commanded.

Gratwick looked round to his CO with frightened eyes.

Jampton was flustered. 'What do you think you're doing?' he bleated.

'Isn't it obvious?' replied the German coolly. 'You have destroyed my plane and as I am already overdue I certainly don't intend to walk back.'

Jampton whirled to the Sergeant Major for support but the great man shook his head slightly and nodded towards the fifteen-hundredweight. The German pilot was now holding his service pistol at Gratwick's head.

'Do we go,' he asked calmly, 'or do I blow his head off?'

Jampton remained rooted to the spot.

'Drive on,' said the pilot, and Gratwick, on the verge of filling his pants, put the truck into gear and hurled it into the desert.

Coming to his senses, Jampton sprang into action.

'You there,' Jampton shrieked, pointing at Miller, 'the Bren gun, quick!'

Miller, open-mouthed, looked at the Sergeant Major for confirmation.

'It's no good, sir, you're too late,' said the SM.

But Jampton didn't hear. He was struggling to get his own pistol from its holster. Whilst he hurried forward the fifteen-hundredweight was already five hundred yards away and getting smaller but that didn't deter him.

'Halt or I fire,' he screamed and pulled the trigger.

There was a click. He tried again, and again there was a click. He shook the gun angrily.

Sergeant Major Puller began to turn away wearily. Had nobody told the useless little pillock about the safety catch? As he turned he heard the loud report of the revolver. At last, he thought, he's found out what the safety catch is for. Then he noticed the look of disbelief and incredulity on the lads' faces. Was it possible the young Lieutenant had hit the fleeing truck at what must be half a mile away by now? But as he turned to Jampton he realised what had transpired. The damn fool had inadvertently slipped the safety catch off while returning the pistol to its holster and the bullet was buried deep in the sand, an inch from his foot. Dear God, thought the Sergeant Major, considering seriously a transfer back to an Infantry regiment, Paratroops or Commandos. Any one of these postings would be safer than this.

'Sergeant Major,' yelped the almost hysterical Second Lieutenant, 'he's escaped!'

The Sergeant Major eyed him warily. He didn't like the way Jampton had yelped, 'He's escaped,' as if he, the Sergeant Major, was responsible. He'd been in the Army long enough to step from under this particular can.

'Yes, sir,' he replied, and ever so gently he shifted the

ball back into his CO's court with, 'You did what you could, sir.'

Jampton was beside himself. 'Yes, but dammit, man,' he shrieked, 'that truck. All my equipment was on that, my bedding and ... and ...' He struggled for words trying to remember what exactly was on the back of the fifteen-hundredweight and what was in his suitcase left on Alexandria docks.

'And,' replied the Sergeant Major smoothly, 'the driver, don't forget the driver, sir. He's in the bag before he's had a chance to get his knees brown.'

Oh God, thought Jampton, of course, Gratwick. He'd have to mention that in his report.

Some of the lads, feeling the excitement was over, drifted back to their tents, some to see if there was any tea going, and quite a few straggled across to the blackened patch of desert looking for souvenirs from what was left of the Messerschmitt. Too much had happened in the last hour – a day that would crop up in conversation when most of the SOG were drawing old-age pensions.

Half an hour later, hunched over the MO's table in the medical tent, Lieutenant Jampton composed his report. It was a slow, laborious, difficult task. After all, to whom did he send the report, it being the Special Ordnance Group? He'd naturally assumed that the Royal Army Ordnance Corps would be the recipient but Sergeant Major Puller had been adamant that this might put the cat amongst the pigeons. He doubted very much that the RAOC had any record of the Special Ordnance Group and the last thing the Sergeant Major wanted was to kick the sleeping dog while it lay. The fewer people who knew about the SOG the better as far as he was concerned. So, on his advice, Jampton was addressing his report direct to Colonel Brunswick of Military Intelligence. This cheered him up a little.

Colonel Brunswick was also known to him as Uncle Charles, his legal guardian. He sighed and began to write, and two hours later a dispatch rider would be on his way to add to the confusion in Alexandria.

Lieutenant Jampton sat back wondering what he should do next. A frown crossed his face. What was it Sergeant Major Puller had said to him? Suddenly he remembered – a letter of condolence to Gratwick's parents. Of course, that shouldn't take long and, after all, it was his duty as Commanding Officer. The grieving parents would shortly be receiving a telegram from the War Office informing them that Gratwick was now a prisoner of war. He reached for the flimsy letter form and unscrewed the cap from his fountain pen. He began writing.

'Dear Mr and Mrs Gratwick,' he started, and then a thought struck him. Supposing one of them was dead? It was a tactless beginning. He screwed the paper up and took another letter form. This time he'd think it out before committing it to paper. 'Dear Sir or Madam.' No. No 'Dear'. Best to ignore that. 'I regret to inform you that your son . . .' Again he stopped. Good grief, he didn't even know Gratwick's first name.

Private Albert Gratwick, 6120345, of the Base Army Service Corps, six months ago had been delivering meat on a butcher's bike in Oldham. Unfortunately it wasn't a reserved occupation and in any case the size of the meat ration didn't warrant a delivery boy and so, along with thousands of other eighteen-year-olds, Gratwick received his call-up papers and reported to the Army Camp at Catterick. Here he was inoculated, uniformed, numbered, fed, and on top of all this they gave him a few bob to spend on himself. Then after a few days the Army taught him to march, drill, stand still, salute – all under the banner of discipline. He was given a rifle and taught how to oil the barrel, the use of a pull-through, how to smack home the magazine containing five bullets; naturally there weren't any bullets – there weren't enough to go round. He was posted to Swaffham in Norfolk, where he drove, reversed, learnt to drive at night with slitted headlamps, and how to move in convoy. But once again, just as he was on the verge of settling in, making friends and finding a girl, he was back in Oldham on embarkation leave. It wasn't a particularly happy homecoming. His parents had let his room and he had to sleep next door at Mrs Taylor's and, what's more, she charged three pounds ten for room and board. All his old mates were either in the Forces or down the coal mines, so it was a great relief to report to Southampton and from there to North Africa, Lieutenant Jampton and the desert.

Gratwick reviewed his first day on the ration strength of the Special Ordnance Group ... and that was a laugh: he hadn't even had time for a corned-beef sandwich before he was whipped away into the blue, chauffeuring an enemy pilot to God knew where. How would he ever be able to answer 'What did you do in the war, Daddy?'. He resolved never to get married.

For the first hour after leaving the camp, the German pilot and Driver Gratwick hadn't exchanged a word. The pilot, after consulting his wrist compass, silently pointed out directions from time to time. Suddenly he jerked up, alert, and squinted ahead. Approaching was a cloud of dust and Gratwick changed down the gears.

'No, no,' said the pilot. 'Keep going.'

Gratwick did as he was told and, as the oncoming vehicles approached, his spirits jumped – three half-tracks, and, more important, they were British.

'Don't stop,' yelled the pilot over the noise of the engines.

Gratwick was undecided – but only for a moment, until he felt the pressure of the service revolver against his side. When they drew level, the German smiled cheerfully and waved to them and – Bugger me, thought Gratwick incredulously – they waved back. It was hardly surprising, though, as Gratwick was driving a British fifteen-hundredweight.

One hour later, Gratwick – having been stopped twice by enemy patrols, and, after brief exchanges between them and the pilot in rapid German, having been waved on with much merriment – was now a guest of a crack enemy artillery battery.

The first thing he noticed when they entered the German camp was an eighty-eight-millimetre artillery piece. It was awesome. Surely the British hadn't anything to match one of these. But then Gratwick was hardly in a position to pass judgment. The only British gun he'd seen in his short military career had been the twenty-five-pounder yesterday, and that piece reminded him of the cannon on display in Werneth Park, Oldham, which was supposed to have been captured at Sebastopol. He looked again at the haughty, malevolent barrel of the German artillery piece and wondered if the Special Ordnance Group was within its range. He shuddered. Good grief, it looked so lethal it probably could flatten Cairo.

The pilot ordered Gratwick to stop and eased himself stiffly to the ground and bade Gratwick do the same. He beckoned two of the Wermacht over and spoke swiftly in German, to which one of them clicked his heels and said, '*Jawohl, Herr Hauptman.*'

The pilot turned to Gratwick. 'I'm going over to the officers' mess. These two will take care of you till I get back.'

He spoke again to the two bronzed giants and they pointed him to a small marquee. He nodded. '*Danke,*' he said, and left.

Gratwick looked round furtively. The stares of the soldiers embarrassed him. He felt like a pile of dog droppings in Kew Gardens. He'd never come across a bunch of lads like this. These were real soldiers. If the rest of the Afrika Korps was the same, it was no contest. They had to be the master race.

'Come,' said the fair-haired one and led Gratwick to a trestle table in the shade of a canvas awning. One of them leant across the table. 'I in London . . .' He corrected himself and held up three fingers. 'Tree years past, in town of Canning.'

Gratwick smiled, shaking his head and not understanding. A few yards away a group of the young supermen burst into laughter. Gratwick had a feeling they were laughing at him. It was the last straw. With all that had happened to him it was too much. He laid his head on his folded arms and sobbed himself to sleep. It was the dreamless sleep of the dead; and when a hand shook him awake he blinked and it was several moments before he realised where he was. Somebody slapped down a plate of some kind of processed meat and a tin cup of water.

Good grief, he thought, why for heaven's sake couldn't they let me sleep?

It was only then he noticed that the shadows were long and soon it would be nightfall. He must have slept through the afternoon. Gratefully he gulped the water but ignored the food – if that's what it was. He looked around and saw the German pilot approaching. He was a changed man, a beatific smile on his face. He slapped one of the men on the back as he passed and threw a gabble of German over his shoulder. Several of them laughed; their morale was high with the prospect of victory.

The pilot looked over to Gratwick. 'Come on, lad. Let's be on our way.' He swung into the fifteen-hundredweight and lit a cigarette. The hospitality in the officers' mess had been more than lavish.

Gratwick stiffly clambered behind the wheel and, to much handclapping and waving, the barbed wire was pulled aside and they trundled off into the blue, heading straight for the setting sun. After a few miles, the yellow sun was now orange and touching the rim of the horizon.

'Stop here,' commanded the pilot. They sat together for a few moments. 'Did you ever see a sunset like that, eh?'

Gratwick didn't reply. 'No' seemed inadequate and he couldn't think of anything else. He was tired and for the first time in his life he was homesick. They sat in silence, then the pilot said, 'By the way, my name is Rudolph and I'd like you to call me Rudy. Everybody does.'

Gratwick, sitting morosely with his hands in his lap, nodded.

'What do they call you then?' asked the pilot. Gratwick muttered his name softly. Rudolph leant towards him. 'Sorry, I didn't catch that.'

Gratwick cleared his throat. 'Gratwick, sir, Albert Gratwick.'

'Albert,' mused the pilot. 'Then I shall call you Albie and less of the "sir", young fella, I'm Rudy. And how are you enjoying the desert, Albie?'

Gratwick looked away, then in a low voice he said, 'I don't know, this is my first day.' After a pause he went on. 'I thought it was going to be all sand.'

He suddenly wanted to cry. 'And now I'm a prisoner of war.' A tear trickled down his cheek, but luckily the light was going and it went unnoticed.

Or perhaps it didn't, because Rudolph spoke softly.

'Come on, Albie, cheer up. For you the war's over. You will be well treated. We're not all barbarians, you know. We have no quarrel with the British. As a matter of fact I once knew a very nice boy at Oxford.'

'I don't want to be a prisoner,' squeaked Gratwick stubbornly.

'Oh come now, Albie. It is only until the war is over

and it won't be too long now. Hey, just think of the letters you can write home to your sweetheart. "Hello my darling, I was captured fighting in the Western desert." Yes, she will think you are quite a fellow.' He paused then said, 'Do you have a sweetheart?'

Gratwick, unable to trust himself to speak, shook his head.

'What?' said the pilot laughing. 'A young man like you with no sweetheart.' He clucked his tongue. 'Well perhaps you'll find yourself a nice buxom *fräulein* when you get to Germany.'

Gratwick spoke through his sobs. 'I don't want to go to Germany.' His voice rose to a wail. 'And I don't want a buxom *fräulein*, either.' He sat staring at the last vestige of the sun, blinking back his tears.

The pilot studied him silently for a few moments, then he said quietly, 'You know, Albie, you have very long eyelashes for a boy.'

FOUR

In a cluttered office high in the building that housed British Military Intelligence, Captain Shelley pushed another coloured pin into a large wall map of the streets of Alexandria. For several months now the British Intelligence had been engaged in a joint Anglo-French operation to track down an enemy transmitter sending and receiving information to Rommel's headquarters. The normal transmission times were at 2100 hours. But at that time several rogue transmitters opened up, all in code. It was a system deliberately designed as a smokescreen for the real transmitter and for the intelligence services it was almost an impossible task, like looking for a particular flea in a Marseilles flophouse.

Another night and another fruitless raid on a small café in the native quarter of the city. Four French agents had teamed with six British and taken the place apart, but their only success had been an old Cossor wireless blaring Arabic love songs continuously as a jerky background cacophony. Captain Shelley had been on the raid purely as an observer and once again he had the niggling feeling that the French were just going through the motions as if they knew it was to be a wasted effort. He rubbed his eyes wearily. He was Adjutant to Colonel Brunswick and, having compiled his report on the abortive night's proceedings, he wondered whether or not to acquaint his boss with his foreboding as to French cooperation. But then he rejected the thought. It was only conjecture and he was too tired for a lengthy in-depth discussion. Better he stick to the facts.

The telephone jangled and he picked it up. 'Captain Shelley,' he said tersely. He listened for a time, then said, 'Be right down, sir,' and replaced the earpiece. He sighed. Something was biting his governor and it had little to do with enemy transmissions.

Colonel Brunswick had just received the dispatch from his nephew, Lieutenant Jampton.

'What kind of a bloody report is this?' he said incredulously after reading Jampton's communication for the third time. He gazed round his sparsely furnished office and then looked at the document again – it was incredible, unbelievable. Certainly the correct protocol for submitting reports was obviously of low priority in the present Officers' Training College. It was written more in the style of a chatty newsletter from boarding school. It began 'Dear Uncle'. Dear Uncle, for God's sake. If this report was dispatched in its present form, he'd find himself in charge of the latrines at Aldershot.

There was a knock on the door and his Adjutant entered. 'You sent for me, sir?'

'Yes, Jimmy,' replied the Colonel. He handed over Jampton's report. 'Read that,' he commanded tersely. Then he opened the filing cabinet and took out a bottle of Dimple Haig.

The Adjutant read quickly, then started again in order to give it a more thorough examination. Finally he put the flimsy down on the desk.

'Lieutenant Jampton,' he murmured neutrally.

'My nephew,' replied the Colonel, taking a large swig from his glass. 'I told you about him. He only disembarked two days ago.' He stared morosely into his whisky. 'My wife's family connections – a Brigadier

General, a Vice Admiral, a Bishop, two high-ranking members of Parliament, one of them a cabinet minister.' He paused and stared bleakly out of the window. 'With that kind of clout it wasn't difficult to have him posted here, the idea being that I should keep an eye on him.'

His Adjutant nodded understandingly.

The Colonel took another swig. 'I wasn't having him here under my feet – we have enough problems as it is.'

The Adjutant nodded again.

The Colonel went on. 'I arranged with the Regimental Transport Officer on the docks that as soon as he set foot on dry land he was to have him whisked into the blue.'

Enlightenment dawned. 'Ah, yes, sir, he was to report and take charge of the Special Ordnance Group.'

'Yes,' murmured the Colonel, 'a quiet enough billet I would have thought, and far enough to be out of my hair. And on the first day this . . .' He tapped the report angrily.

There was a silence between them, the Colonel back at his window gazing while the Adjutant stared longingly at the half-empty bottle. Finally he broke the silence.

'We can't ignore it, sir.'

'I'm aware of that,' snapped the Colonel testily, 'but if I submitted this to the powers that be, they'd have me certified.'

He snatched up the report again. 'Apart from shooting down a German plane, the rest of it is *Boys Own* paper.' He put on his glasses and read, ' "To my astonishment the German pilot marched into camp, slapped one of my men across the face, the man incidentally who had shot down the plane. NB, the name of the soldier and full particulars are attached to my report, with a strong recommendation for a decoration, also Private Sparks. Details following." '

The Colonel put down the report and took off his

73

glasses. Wearily he put his hand over his eyes. The Adjutant took out his handkerchief to stifle a chuckle. He could picture the scene.

'It's not funny,' barked the Colonel. 'He even goes on to describe in detail how the pilot climbed into the fifteen-hundredweight and, with a revolver pressed to the driver's head, ordered him to take him back to the German lines and with that was driven off.'

The Colonel stopped reading and lowered the paper. 'Ye Gods,' he muttered, 'this isn't a report: it's straight out of *Woman's Own*. All we're short of is "what's the weather like?" and "wish you were here".'

An idea began to form at the back of the Adjutant's mind. The Colonel looked at him shrewdly. 'Out with it, Jimmy,' he said. 'Have you got the solution?'

The Adjutant pondered for a moment, then nodded slowly. 'I think we can handle this, sir. The German being driven off has just given me an idea. May I, sir?' He held out his hand for the report and Colonel Brunswick passed it over. The Adjutant took it. 'Back as soon as possible, sir,' he said and left the room.

After half an hour or so he returned with his amended version of the report and the first thing he noted was that the bottle of Dimple Haig was empty. This was going a bit, even for the old man, but he gave him the benefit of the doubt: perhaps he had knocked it over.

Colonel Brunswick chuckled as he perused his Adjutant's work. It was a masterly example of double talk.

'That's great, Jimmy,' he said handing it back. 'You should have been a politician.'

'Thank you, sir,' replied the Adjutant. 'If it hadn't been for the war, I'd have been a politician.'

'Really?' said the Colonel. 'See that it's transmitted immediately. And by the way, Jimmy,' he added in a low voice, 'I never saw this.'

74

The Adjutant looked at him for a moment and left the office.

Colonel Brunswick stared at the door after he'd gone. Jimmy, lad, he thought, had you been a politician there might not have been a war. And he smiled happily. He rubbed his hands together with satisfaction but his euphoria was premature. If only he'd burnt the report and claimed he'd never received it. That was the best line of approach. If only . . . if only . . . if only people thought before stepping out into the road just as a bus was approaching, there'd be a lot more of us about. In Colonel Brunswick's case, the fuse was lit and the flame started to flicker towards the gunpowder.

There is very little to be read in medical journals regarding morale. But that doesn't mean to say that lack of it shouldn't be classified as an ailment. As one takes two aspirins for a common cold, for low morale a stiff dose of propaganda will do the trick, and sadly it was a time when a low-morale epidemic was sweeping the country and the medicine chest was bare.

Newspaper editors were grasping any straws: eating carrots gives night-fighter pilots better vision . . . Hitler calls in heart specialist . . . Liverpool welcomes GIs . . . pictures of the King and Queen shaking hands with bombed-out Londoners . . . Winston Churchill in blue boiler suit and tin hat shaking his cigar defiantly at the skies.

Fleet Street had rung the changes many times. What was so desperately needed was a victory somewhere, or better still the German High Command signing an unconditional surrender, with the Brandenburg Gate in the background – at least a little stronger medicine than the King and Queen shaking hands with bombed-out Londoners/Churchill/carrots.

It was at this low point that help was mercifully on its way in the form of Lieutenant Jampton's report, or,

75

to be more exact, Captain Shelley's jazzed-up version of it, circulated to the media by the Ministry of Propaganda. A victory at last! Small, yes, but then so is an aspirin. It was a little sunbeam floating through the gloom; that's what it seemed at the time, but it turned out to be more like a cloudburst in the Gobi Desert.

The newspapers couldn't wait to rush it into print, but unfortunately the news would not hit the streets until tomorrow morning. The British Broadcasting Corporation, however, were jubilant. All they had to do was to slip the dispatch in front of the newsreader and the radio would scoop the tabloids by at least twelve hours. The editors in Fleet Street were undismayed, however. Already the teleprinters were busy alerting journalists and photographers on the spot in Alexandria. The nine o'clock news broadcast would merely be the appetiser. The roast beef and two veg would be served up by the national newspapers – pictures, in-depth interviews, a rundown of the young Second Lieutenant perhaps.

The first domino, given a gentle nudge, was already wobbling.

Colonel Brunswick was standing at a corner of the bar in the officers' mess nursing a glass of whisky. He was tired. Until an hour ago he'd been closeted with his French counterparts in Intelligence, a meeting soured by acrimony, each side endeavouring to shift the blame for the abortive raid on the café. Pressure from both Intelligence Services was being brought to bear. The enemy transmitter had to be found but, more importantly, the codes broken. It was vital for the survival of North Africa. Captain Shelley broke into his thoughts by handing him another Scotch. The mess was half full, the usual collection of worried-looking base wallahs, all the life and jollity coming from a group of young tank officers, easily identified by their light cavalry-twill trousers, brown suede shoes and silk neckwear, enjoying a few hours' relaxation. But their noisy antics were enough to keep the Colonel's conversation private.

'I think you're right, Jimmy,' said the Colonel. 'I have a feeling the Frogs are holding something back.' He looked at his whisky. 'I feel it in my guts. There's something they're not telling us.'

He gulped down half his drink, then he gazed around the room.

'What's the latest from the cypher johnnies?'

The Adjutant shook his head. 'Nothing new I'm afraid, sir.' The Colonel nodded morosely. 'In fact they're now of the opinion that the transmitters that don't matter are sending out Mickey Mouse stuff . . .'

He left the sentence unfinished.

'Yes,' said the Colonel. 'Until we find the one transmitting the real information, we're up a gum tree.'

The Corporal behind the bar turned up the volume of the wireless on the shelf. It was time for the nine o'clock news. The noise in the club subsided as they gave it all their attention.

'. . . And this is Alvar Liddell reading it.' There was a faint rustle of paper, then the newsreader continued. 'In the Western desert a small unit of British soldiers under the command of a Second Lieutenant were attacked from the air. The unit, not yet up to operational strength, returned the fire, and one of the enemy aircraft, a Messerschmitt, was shot down in flames. The enemy broke through the perimeter, engaged in hand-to-hand fighting and after a short skirmish the enemy was driven off. Our casualties were light: one man was taken prisoner and two of our vehicles were destroyed.'

The second item announced by Alvar Liddell was drowned by the ironic cheers of the tank men. The Corporal behind the bar switched off the set. It would have been impossible to hear in any case. Colonel Brunswick stared at the now silent wireless. His mouth was open. Could he possibly have heard Alvar Liddell announcing Jampton's report? He turned incredulously to his Adjutant who, anticipating his question, nodded. He was equally amazed. Then the Colonel found his voice.

'How the bloody hell did the BBC get hold of it? It's classified information.'

The Adjutant shrugged and took a large gulp of whisky to avoid a reply. He didn't know the answer either.

The Adjutant leant towards him. 'Try to look happy, sir. You're attracting some very curious stares,' he said in a low voice. The Colonel screwed his face into a fatuous grin and beamed round the room.

'Don't worry, sir. It's just a one-off. By this time tomorrow it'll all be forgotten.'

Colonel Brunswick nodded gloomily. Oh yes, it would be forgotten all right, provided something bigger came along, like two divisions of German paratroops dropping on to Hyde Park; or perhaps the King and Ivor Novello could sing 'Hitler Has Only Got One Ball', at a charity concert. Another large whisky appeared before him and he began to cheer up. What the hell! Jimmy was right: it was a one-day wonder. It would all be forgotten by tomorrow. In a much lighter mood he drained his glass.

'Must be off, Jimmy. Sign the chit, will you?' And he made his way unsteadily towards the exit. His *joie de vivre*, however, was premature. He of all people should have known the folly of lowering one's guard.

Life may be a bowl of cherries but in every cherry there's a stone. In this case the long fuse which had been lit by Jampton's report was now dangerously close to the powder barrel.

* * *

The explosion came with the strident tones of the bedside telephone rousing Colonel Brunswick from his happy stupor. He groped for the handset and by the illuminated fingers on his watch he noted that it was only 2 a.m. Good grief, only a few hours ago he'd been in the mess getting rid of the stock of whisky so that it wouldn't fall into enemy hands.

'Colonel Brunswick,' he muttered into the telephone, then, 'Jimmy, do you know what time it is?'

He listened for a few moments, then he shot upright into a sitting position; he was wide awake now.

'Good God,' he murmured, 'sweet merciful saviour. Where the bloody hell did the press get their permits from?' he asked.

He listened again. 'But how did the Ministry of Information know? Only a few of us were privy to the exact location of the Special Ordnance Group.'

The Colonel groaned. Of course, the Regimental Transport Officer would have a record of the map reference.

'Listen Jimmy,' he barked, 'we've got to head off the press before they reach the camp. If they start to question Jampton, we're all up the creek without a canoe. Be round at the factory soonest. I'll see you there. And I trust,' he said coldly, 'that you come up with something better for this one.'

He slammed down the receiver and staggered over to his trousers, which were still warm.

The Adjutant put down his end more thoughtfully. He understood his Colonel. The wily old bastard was beginning his retreat, dumping the whole shoddy mess on to yours truly. He remembered the Colonel's last words when he had left the office to tart up Jampton's original dispatch: 'And by the way, Jimmy, I never saw this.' In his mind's eye he visualised the Colonel in full dress uniform, stiff as a ramrod facing the Courts Martial reporting in a clear military voice that up to the unfortunate incident appertaining to Second Lieutenant Jampton's report, Captain Shelley had carried out his duties as an Adjutant in an exemplary military fashion. Jimmy shrugged. After all, he wasn't a regular. It just meant his demob would come up that much sooner.

There was little to be done about the press, however. They were already well into the blue and by early morning reporters, war correspondents and photographers would be all over the Special Ordnance Group. He groaned inwardly. God help us when they besiege Lieutenant Jampton, he thought. Naively, the stupid little twit will stick to his original story of the farcical happenings.

His thoughts were scattered by the door bursting open.

'Transport, Jimmy.'

'Yes sir, but –'

'I know, I know, they've got a head start. Our mission will be damage-limitational if that bloody nephew of mine has blown the gaff. And to make no mistake, Jimmy, if he does you'll be better off driving straight on to surrender yourself to the nearest German outpost.'

The Adjutant accepted this and hurried out to organise things.

When he'd gone the Colonel paced up and down. Damn the war, damn his wife Dorothy for sending out the little prat. Suddenly a happy thought unexpectedly came to mind. When the German pilot made his own report, it wasn't without the bounds of possibility that there would follow a reprisal air raid. He visualised the Stukas screaming down to go into the attack and with any luck the first bomb would land plumb on top of Jampton. As quickly as these thoughts appeared he dismissed them, ashamed and a little frightened by how desperate he'd become.

* * *

At about 9 a.m. the first truckload bearing the press correspondents entered the camp of the Special Ordnance Group. Stiff and weary they jumped down with cameras, microphones, and other paraphernalia, and looked around, feeling slightly embarrassed at the curious vacant stares of the soldiers.

Sergeant Major Puller walked from the mess tent wiping his lips with the back of his hand. He looked at the new arrivals, noting their press arm bands, and slowly approached the group.

'What's all this about?' he enquired.

'Press,' said one of them, and some of them nodded, holding up identification.

After a pause the Sergeant Major asked, 'Are you lost or something?'

One of them laughed easily. 'Come off it, Sergeant Major, you know why we're here; that little to-do you had yesterday morning.'

The Sergeant Major was still puzzled. The to-do the man referred to was the Messerschmitt and loss of Gratwick. But that was nothing, certainly not enough to bring a posse of newshounds this far into the blue. They all looked round as another press vehicle arrived, a square of cardboard behind the windscreen identifying it as BBC.

The Sergeant Major made up his mind.

'Right then,' he said. 'You'll be tired and hungry so if you'll make your way into the mess tent –' he pointed '– get yourself a brew-up and a plate of powdered egg.'

As they made their way over, the Sergeant Major caught hold of one of them by the arm.

'Just a minute, lad,' he said when the others were safely out of earshot. 'What's all this about?' he asked quietly.

'You're the flavour of the month,' he said. 'Didn't you hear the nine o'clock news last night?'

The Sergeant Major was intrigued; he shook his head. 'No. Nine o'clock news?'

'Everybody else did,' said the reporter, and showed a page of his notebook to the Sergeant Major.

It was a transcript of the news bulletin read by Alvar Liddell. When he'd finished reading, Puller's eyebrows went up. He whistled softly to himself. That report must have been a masterpiece of overstatement. He gazed towards the CO's tent. Maybe I've misjudged the little fella after all, he thought.

He shoved the pressman towards the mess tent. 'Better get your breakfast while there's any left,' he said, and he made his way over to his CO's tent.

The little fellow in question hadn't heard the arrival of the press. He was looking over a manuscript of military tactics, which he was in the process of writing. He heard the rap on the tent pole.

'Sergeant Major Puller, sir.'

Jampton's head jerked up. 'What is it, Sergeant Major?'

'The press are here, sir.'

'Press?' Jampton was puzzled. He turned down a corner of the page he'd been writing headed 'Hannibal's First Mistake', put it to one side and unfastened the tent flap.

'Come in, Sergeant Major.' He stepped back. 'What's all this about the press?'

'A pack of 'em, sir.' He smiled. 'Something to do with that report you sent in yesterday. Apparently it was given first priority on the nine o'clock news last night.'

'Gosh,' said Jampton and immediately regretted it. He should have said something like 'Really?' but he couldn't contain his excitement. Aunt Dorothy was bound to have been listening. She never missed the nine o'clock news. Then with a slight frown he remembered the events of yesterday morning's sad affair. Apart from shooting down the Messerschmitt, there was nothing to be proud of. The German pilot being driven off, with Gratwick at the point of a gun. Surely that hadn't been broadcast on the nine o'clock news.

'Have you any idea what exactly was said?' asked Jampton fearfully.

'I've just been talking to one of 'em, sir, and I don't know what you put in your report but whatever it was it seems to have done the trick.'

Jampton looked at him blankly. 'What I put in my report to Colonel Brunswick,' he said tartly, 'was classified and confidential. I put down the events exactly as they happened. Yes, even to the German pilot holding a pistol to my driver's head and making his way into the desert in my fifteen-hundredweight.'

The Sergeant Major stared at him incredulously. Then it came to him in a flash. Of course, he could imagine his old Colonel reading the report and could well understand the reaction it would provoke. No way would that report in its original form be sent to London.

'Right,' snapped Jampton. 'I think the time has come to meet the press.' He began to button his shirt.

Sergeant Major Puller was aghast. He visualised the pompous little prat holding court telling them exactly what had happened. It didn't bear thinking about. That would certainly put the cat amongst the pigeons. He made a quick decision: whatever happened, Second Lieutenant Jampton must be kept away from the media. He was used to making quick decisions – they had saved his life on more than one occasion.

'With due respect, sir,' he began, 'the press are out in force and in my experience when interviewed on occasions like this, an officer or noncommissioned officer must be properly dressed.'

Lieutenant Jampton looked at him sternly, then decided that the Sergeant Major was only trying to be helpful.

'I agree with you, Sergeant Major, but war is a mitigating circumstance and in any case all I own at present is what I stand up in.'

He smirked in what he thought was a comradely 'Jack the Lad' attitude.

'Don't worry, Sergeant Major,' he went on. 'I'll explain it to the press people how all my kit was on the fifteen-hundredweight. They'll understand. It may even raise a laugh.'

'Yes,' replied the Sergeant Major desperately, 'but will the mandarins, the brass hats in Whitehall, take a lenient view when they see your picture all over the front page of the *Daily Mail*?'

Jampton gulped. He could see his Aunt Dorothy staring at his picture on the front page, and him hardly distinguishable from the men, especially if the Sergeant Major took it in his head to change into his ceremonial dress . . . It wasn't fair. All his possessions had been on the fifteen-hundredweight when Gratwick had driven the German officer away. In any case his dress uniform, complete with his sword, had been packed away in the suitcase that was still lying on the docks at Alexandria.

'I've got nothing else to wear apart from what I stand up in,' he bleated.

The Sergeant Major sighed sympathetically. 'Well it looks like you'll have to wear that then.'

'I've got no alternative, Sergeant Major,' snapped Jampton stamping his foot.

Then the Sergeant Major smiled suddenly, as if hit with a brilliant idea.

'Well, what is it?' squeaked Jampton.

'Give me your uniform, sir, and I'll nip smartly over to Corporal Smith and we'll have it back to you clean and crisp like it's just come out of Burton's window.'

The CO was undecided for a moment, then he quickly began to unbutton his shirt. The Sergeant Major watched him fascinated. That chest reminded him of the half-carved chicken at the Christmas dinner – not a pretty sight. He watched as the CO started to unfasten the top button on his shorts. This could be interesting, he thought. At least he'd know if Jampton had joined the right branch of the service.

Jampton stopped suddenly.

'Do you mind waiting outside, Sergeant Major?' he said coldly.

'Sorry, sir.' He ducked out through the tent flap.

He was over the first hurdle. A few moments later a thin white stick of an arm, red from the elbow down, poked through a gap in the tent flap and the Sergeant Major took the pathetic bundle of soiled khaki clothing over to Corporal Smith.

'Yes?' she asked.

The Sergeant Major handed over Jampton's uniform. His instructions were short and quiet and to the casual observer he might have been saying 'and not too much starch on the collar'. Whatever he did say, Corporal Smith nodded and carried the stuff away.

He watched her go, then shook his head. She was unflappable. Since knowing her he'd never ever seen a flicker of emotion cross her face, even when she looked at Sparks, and everyone in camp knew that she was his bint. Like an icicle on a drainpipe, that one. He shrugged. He had more important matters to attend to inside the mess tent.

The Press Corps had bolted down their powdered egg and were gathering their equipment together when the Sergeant Major strode in. He went to the head of the trestle table and rapped on it with his knuckles.

'Gentlemen, my name is Sergeant Major Puller and I'm in charge of this operation.'

Conversation died as they turned expectantly towards him.

'Gentlemen,' he repeated, 'in order to save time I'll take you over to the Bren-gun pit where most of the

85

action took place . . . and I'll arrange for Privates Miller and Sparks to be present and you can interview them there.'

'Who're Miller and Sparks?'

'Ah yes,' said the Sergeant Major. 'Private Miller is the one who actually brought down the Messerschmitt. Sparks was number two on the gun.'

A ripple of excitement went through the group. Some of them jotted down notes and one or two rose from their seats.

The Sergeant Major raised his hand.

'I must ask you all to remain here till I organise things. This will be the quickest way as I know you'll all be in a rush to get back with your interviews and stuff. For those with cameras, what's left of the plane is about five hundred yards away and you might like to get some shots of our burnt-out supply wagon.'

'Can we do that now?' asked one elderly gentleman picking up his camera.

'Why not?' replied the Sergeant Major. 'Get your stuff together and Hardesty here will take you.'

The photographers began to gather up their equipment while the Sergeant Major drew Hardesty to one side.

'They're not to speak to anybody, understand?' he hissed.

'Why me?' objected Hardesty. 'I'm the bloody cook.'

'Yes,' replied the Sergeant Major. 'Well for the next hour you're excused potato peeling. Just make sure they take pictures but on no account must they talk to anybody.'

Then he turned back to the table.

'Right then, gentlemen, if you'll just hang on here for a minute, I'll assemble the lads. OK?'

They murmured their assent and off went the Sergeant Major to brief Miller and Sparks. He ducked into their tent, pleasantly surprised to find them up and dressed – it was only half past nine.

'Want a beer, sir?' asked Miller.

'Later,' replied the Sergeant Major. 'I haven't got much time so listen and listen good.'

They both looked up at him from where they sat on their blankets. The Sergeant Major squatted on his haunches – this was confidential.

'Whether you like it or not, you're heroes,' he began.

Miller raised his eyebrows and looked at Sparks, who shrugged.

'That little upset we had yesterday, it seems the powers that be have blown it up into a second Battle of Waterloo.'

They looked at him uncomprehendingly.

'Never mind why,' went on the Sergeant Major, 'the press is here to interview you. Right now, pay attention. I'll give you the gen.'

They leant forward and the Sergeant Major explained about the enemy aircraft . . . how they shot one down . . . the hand-to-hand fighting . . .

Miller broke in. 'I never laid a finger on him.'

'Don't interrupt,' snapped the Sergeant Major.

When he'd finished, Dusty Miller nodded. 'Oh yes, I remember now. I saw the film – Errol Flynn, wasn't it?'

'Never mind the funnies, Miller, this is serious. Get your tin hats on, button up your shirts and get yourselves over to the Bren pit. Move!'

He didn't wait to see them go; they'd been in the 41st Light Infantry together in the old India days when he was a Corporal. They wouldn't let him down. But all the same, he'd be on hand to make sure they didn't say anything stupid. Partly satisfied, he strode over to the mess tent to collect the eyes and ears of the world.

The press interview with Miller and Sparks was music hall with a dash of party political broadcast.

'How many planes were there?'

'Don't ask me,' said Miller. 'I only had eyes for this one.'

The Sergeant Major breathed a sigh of relief; straight back into their court.

'Was this your first action?'

Miller gazed at the reporter then nudged his oppo. 'Here, Sparks, did you hear that?'

He turned back to the reporter. 'Listen, son,' he said, 'we were in the old 41st Light Infantry and the Sergeant Major and one or two of the other lads there were pulled out of line at Tobruk.' He paused and leant forward. 'At Rommel's personal request.'

Some of the lads sniggered. Another reporter put up his hand. 'What is your full name?' he asked.

'Dusty Miller.'

'That's just a nickname. What's your real name?'

'Ribbentrop,' yelled a wag.

And the cook laughed so much his upper dentures flew out and plopped into the dixie from which he was ladling out the dinner. He fiddled around in the lukewarm stew, and with a grunt of satisfaction popped them back into his mouth. He sucked for a minute then, satisfied, he murmured, 'Mm, it's good today.' Wiping his hand on his apron he found the queue had gone. He shrugged. It was all the same to him: they'd get it warmed up tomorrow.

Sparks took no interest at all in the interview. He just stood in the Bren pit waiting for the fantasy to end. He answered only one question. It came from an elderly war correspondent.

'Being number two on the gun, would you have taken over had Miller been hit?'

Sparks turned away in disgust but another reporter persisted.

'Would you have taken over if Miller caught a packet?'

Sparks cleared his throat and they all waited, pencils poised.

'The only packet he's likely to catch will have twenty fags in it.'

With that he climbed out of the trench and strode away.

The Sergeant Major didn't try to stop him. Sparks was highly flammable and he wasn't about to light the blue touchpaper. They'd got enough, anyway, and some of them were already sidling away towards their trucks for the mad race to the teleprinters in Alexandria. They had enough information, especially with the research that would be carried out on the old 41st Infantry. That alone should be enough to fill the front page.

While all this was going on, in the tent marked CO Jampton was going spare. Almost an hour had elapsed and still no sign of his uniform. What was happening? He certainly couldn't meet the press draped only in an Army blanket. What the dickens was going on out there? Over and over in his mind he'd gone through the interview, how he'd ordered his men to open fire on the German plane and – he was proud of this bit – the fracas with the enemy pilot and his subsequent defection in the fifteen-hundredweight driven by his own driver. He would skip lightly over this, treat it as a joke. It had to be told but they'd understand. We all make mistakes and it's a big man who'll admit them.

For goodness' sake! Corporal Smith should be here by now. Some time ago he'd put his mouth to a gap in the tent flap to order a passing soldier to send her to him immediately. The man hadn't replied, but had signified that he would be back in two minutes. He'd done this by raising two fingers. Then a thought struck Jampton. Good grief, he couldn't possibly have meant two hours!

Not until the second vehicle was a speck on the horizon did the Sergeant Major rap on the tailgate of Corporal Smith's workshop. She opened the canvas flap to see who it was and five minutes later Lieutenant Jampton received his freshly laundered uniform.

* * *

Meanwhile Colonel Brunswick and his Adjutant, having missed the press trucks – which wasn't difficult in a thousand square miles of desert – were approaching the camp from a slightly different direction. Lurching and bumping across the waste land they finally arrived at the Special Ordnance Group in time to see the whole of the camp personnel lined up in front of Second Lieutenant Jampton, who was obviously berating them, tapping his swagger stick on to his hand to emphasise each point. Colonel Brunswick noticed his pressed, clean uniform in direct contrast to those of his charges: some were stripped to the waist, others wore dirty singlets, one of them wore a striped football jersey. It looked more like a badly run prisoner-of-war camp.

The Colonel and his Adjutant got slowly out of the car. Sergeant Major Puller, recognising them, called out 'Parade, atten-*shun*!'. The lads behind him shuffled their feet together in their own time, some of them having a quick drag at cigarettes. The Sergeant Major hadn't missed the blue cloud that had hung over the gathering. It had been the same all through the lecture. Every time the CO looked down for further inspiration many cupped hands went to mouths for quick drags in perfect unison. If this had been a drill movement, it would have shamed the Coldstream Guards.

Second Lieutenant Jampton turned to see what the interruption was, and, seeing his uncle, bounded towards him. Then collecting himself, he marched smartly back to the Sergeant Major.

'You may dismiss the men, Sergeant Major,' he said in a voice he hoped would carry to his uncle.

'Sah!' replied the Sergeant Major, snapping up another salute. He about turned to dismiss the parade but most of them had already gone.

'How are you, Uncle?'

'Dammit, Lieutenant, for as long as this war lasts I'm *not* your uncle. I'm *Colonel* Brunswick.'

Jampton's smile left his face. He stamped to attention and saluted.

'Oh, for God's sake,' said the Colonel, touching the peak of his cap in acknowledgment. Then, slightly ashamed of himself, he said gruffly, 'By the way, this is my Adjutant, Captain Shelley.' This caused another salute from Jampton. The Colonel raised his eyes to heaven.

'You look very well, Uncle,' said Jampton.

The Colonel gave up. His nephew had a skin as thick as a pub doormat.

'The press have been rampaging all over the camp, Uncle.'

Colonel Brunswick suppressed his rage. God almighty, he thought, it's still 'Uncle'. Can't the little bastard see the badges of rank on my shoulder?

The Adjutant stepped in quickly. 'What did they want?'

'Apparently they were here to get first-hand knowledge of the Messerschmitt affair.'

'Apparently?' pressed the Adjutant.

'Yes,' replied Jampton. 'I didn't actually speak to them myself. The Sergeant Major took away my uniform to be cleaned and by the time I got it back they'd gone.'

Colonel Brunswick brightened. 'So you didn't actually speak to them yourself?' he asked hopefully.

'No, sir,' replied Jampton. 'But needless to say I had some harsh words with the Sergeant Major and when you arrived I was laying down the law to the men. In future they will not – I repeat, will *not* ...' He smiled. 'I actually said that to them, sir.'

'Yes, yes,' interrupted the Colonel, not interested in what would be or would not be done. 'Excuse me, I must have a word with Sergeant Major Puller.'

'I'll come with you,' said Jampton.

'I'm afraid not. My Adjutant would like to have a

91

few words with you privately. Nothing serious, just how to make out military reports. A general talk on the responsibilities of command, et cetera.'

And with this he went in search of the Sergeant Major.

Jampton looked after his uncle wistfully, then turned back to the Captain. He cleared his throat and said proudly, 'I'm the Commanding Officer here and Colonel Brunswick is my uncle.'

'So I gathered,' remarked the Adjutant dryly.

'I don't suppose you've met Colonel Brunswick's wife, Aunt Dorothy. She's absolutely wizard. She's the real boss, you know.'

'Really?' said the Adjutant. He didn't want to get involved in domestic issues. 'Now, with regard to your military reports . . .'

'Ah yes,' replied Jampton and they began to walk up and down as they talked.

It was heavy going. Everything that the Adjutant said was interrupted by 'Ah yes, but you don't quite understand . . .' or 'I appreciate what you're saying but . . .' and at one time 'Could it be, Captain, that you're out of touch in Alexandria?'.

The Adjutant gave up. He finished his uphill struggle with 'Please, Lieutenant, please, I beg of you . . .' He paused searching for the right words. 'Just relax and enjoy the sun. Don't start anything until we're *all* ready.'

'Don't worry, sir,' said Jampton, his head wobbling with self-righteousness. 'The next time you visit us you'll find a fighting unit well drilled and eager to go into action.'

The Adjutant sighed. He might just as well have saved his breath. It was like talking to a sand dune. He gazed round and was heartily relieved to see his Colonel approaching.

Again Jampton saluted. Brunswick acknowledged with a nod – he was in a benevolent mood.

'Would you like a pot of tea and something?' asked Jampton.

'No,' replied the Adjutant a shade too quickly. 'I really think we should be making tracks, sir,' he said to the Colonel.

'Oh, aren't you stopping for a while, Uncle? We could have a drink together in the officers' mess.'

'Officers' mess?' enquired the Colonel.

'It's that tent over there,' said Jampton as he pointed.

'No,' replied the Colonel. 'Some other time.' And he made his way towards the car.

Lieutenant Jampton watched as the driver opened the rear door and suddenly remembered he'd meant to ask his Uncle about the blue suitcase he'd left outside the RTO's office on the docks and to remind him that his name 'Lieutenant Jampton' was stencilled on both sides. But it was too late. When the car moved off the Colonel swivelled round to see his nephew standing rigidly at the salute.

'God,' he muttered, 'I wonder who winds him up every morning.'

But it was said in a jocular mood. His conversation with Sergeant Major Puller had been a great relief. Perhaps now the whole petty incident could be put to bed, filed away somewhere deep in Whitehall, forgotten, buried, ciao, finito. He tapped his knee as he hummed a catchy little bit from *The Chocolate Soldier*.

His Adjutant mopped his forehead. 'I think I now understand your antipathy towards Lieutenant Jampton.'

Colonel Brunswick's face clouded. He was silent for a moment, then he said, 'Did I ever tell you about him?'

'No, sir,' replied the Adjutant. It would help to pass the journey.

'Jampton,' began the Colonel, 'is my sister's only child.' He paused to get his words together.

'Poor Emily,' he said. 'You can't imagine what her

93

life must have been like being the mother of that . . .' He jerked his thumb over his shoulder. 'She had two nervous breakdowns, eventually a divorce, and then do you know what she did, Jimmy?' The Adjutant shook his head. 'She got into her car and drove up to Beachy Head, then she got out, locked it, walked smartly to the edge of the cliff, and jumped over.'

The Adjutant whistled sympathetically.

'All from eyewitnesses, you understand, but it's the sort of thing my sister would have done. And the following day young Jampton, only eight mind you, presents himself at my home. And when the butler took him to Her Ladyship she was overjoyed, and she more or less adopted him on the spot.'

He looked out of the car window at a laager of heavy tanks.

'You see, Jimmy,' he went on, 'for a lady in my wife's position her most important function in life is to produce a male heir to carry on the line – and unfortunately she couldn't have children of her own.'

He looked across at his Adjutant, who was fast asleep, and shrugged. He was glad that Captain Shelley hadn't heard the last bit – it wasn't strictly true. He shuddered as he remembered the disastrous coupling on his honeymoon night after which embarrassing episode he'd never insisted on his conjugal rights. She was even uglier with nothing on. For her own part she had been sickened by the whole sordid, disgusting act of copulation. No wonder the poor people did it at the weekend. And so young Wilfred Jampton became the heir apparent, and also, when he was older, he would inherit his own mother's fortune – a little matter that hadn't gone unnoticed.

'Go on, sir,' said the Adjutant.

'Oh, I thought you were asleep, Jimmy.'

'No, sir, I was listening with my eyes closed,' he lied. 'You were telling me how your sister was on holiday at Beachy Head.'

The Colonel stared at him in amusement. 'It's nothing, Jimmy,' he said after a time, all his good humour restored.

In other words he was wide open for the sucker punch that was to be delivered with all the might and power of the press. The battle of the Special Ordnance Group, as it was already being dubbed by headline writers, was beginning to take shape. From the little acorn of Jampton's report, a mighty forest was already begining to bloom, a gem that the media were going to polish far beyond its value. If ever a news item like this was desperately needed, it was now.

In the propaganda war the enemy were having it all their own way. The Germans and Italians were over the moon and they didn't even have to lie about events. In a home movie Eva Braun filmed a jubilant Adolf, a happy smile on his face, doing a Bavarian jig at Berchesgarten. And at a secret indoor riding school just outside Rome, Mussolini, on a heavily sedated white horse, was being led round and round as he prepared to lead the victory parade through Alexandria, and probably Cairo, too, unless he fell off. While in the North African desert, Rommel's High Command excitedly pored over street maps of Alexandria with gleeful anticipation that the battle after next would be over who got the best billet.

So it was hardly surprising that a fracas between the little Special Ordnance Group and the might of the German Afrika Korps was a heaven-sent opportunity in the propaganda war.

The snippet on the nine o'clock news broadcast might have turned out to be a one-day wonder, as Colonel Brunswick fervently hoped, but the press interviews with Sparks and Miller put paid to his optimism. On every front page of every broadsheet and tabloid was a huge picture of Private Sparks glowering over his shoulder at the camera, and Miller, a fatuous grin on his face as he held up his thumb.

Most of the articles were devoted to eulogies – how they were oppos, had served in a front-line infantry regiment in India, and after Dunkirk and their subsequent posting to North Africa had chased the Italians out of the fight, then the rearguard against Rommel and his Afrika Korps, finally ending in Tobruk.

Reading the more colourful writings, it would seem they hadn't had a day off since 1937. It was stirring stuff and it grabbed the nation. Volunteers besieged the recruiting offices; an amateur songwriter came up with a bit of silly doggerel:

> You may have had Attilla
> But now we've got Sparks and Miller.

It swept the country, it was whistled, sung and hummed in factories all over Britain. Huge sacks of fan mail simply addressed to Sparks and Miller were collected at the sorting offices. There was no possibility of sending them overseas – shipping space to North Africa was too tight for that. But all the letters were answered by a staff of civil servants in Shepherds Bush.

Even the politicians jumped on the bandwagon. In Parliament one faction led by the Home Secretary was strongly in favour of bringing Sparks and Miller over to England for a morale-boosting tour of munition factories, training establishments and the like. This proposal, however, was quickly quashed by the Ministry of Production, being of the opinion that, should Sparks and Miller be unleashed on the British public, production could be adversely affected.

Such was their lionisation that munition factories, plants and other industries could shut down as hero-worshippers travelled miles in order to catch a glimpse and perhaps even to touch 'those two brave lads from over there.'

It was resolved, therefore, to keep them where they were, metaphorically patted on the head, and given a toffee sweet. In official parlance they were both awarded the Military Medal and Jampton, as the Commanding Officer, was promoted from Second Lieutenant to First.

In British Military Intelligence Colonel Brunswick was also invited to step up on to the podium. It was hardly surprising: having formed the Special Ordnance Group in the first place he had been commended for his initiative and foresight, so it seemed only natural to award him the OBE. Unfortunately, two weeks later in a directive from the War Office, it was deemed only fitting that he should travel to the camp in order that Sparks and Miller should receive their Military Medals from his own hands.

His first reaction was to refuse on the grounds of urgent intelligence work but on reflection, much as he detested this chore, it was vital that he, and only he, should present the medals. After all, should Winston Churchill, the King or anybody else for that matter take it upon themselves to present the awards personally, the fat would surely be in the fire. God knew what Jampton might come out with.

'Best get it over, Jimmy,' he said. 'Quick trip, in and out, no messing about, back in time for tea.'

And now, once again, they were approaching the Special Ordnance Group. Within five hundred yards of the camp the Adjutant leant forward to look over the driver's shoulder.

'What's up, Jimmy?' asked the Colonel.

The Adjutant pointed. Right across the track and barring their way was a red-and-white-striped pole and from holes in the ground on either side of it four heads popped up.

97

'What the bloody hell's going on?' muttered the Colonel.

One of the soldiers put his head through the driver's open window, turned back to his mates with his thumb up, and they raised the pole in order to let the car move on.

'I don't believe it,' said the Colonel. 'Fifty miles of nothing and he has a striped pole across the entrance.'

Just before they drove into the camp a notice by the track informed them that all visitors must report to the guard tent. And they couldn't miss it: it was neatly bordered by stones. God knew where the little prat had got the stuff from but each stone was painted a glaring white. Looking round him, he noticed that, instead of the one Bren pit where the famous battle of the erroneous Qatari Depression had taken place, there were now four Bren pits, one at each cardinal point round the camp. All were manned but there was, as far as he could see, still only one Bren gun. The rest of the poor sods had to make do with sticks.

Sergeant Major Puller was drilling a squad more or less uniformed, but it was clear his heart wasn't in it. On seeing the Colonel, however, he slammed to attention, called his motley crew to a halt, and saluted. This brought Jampton's head out of the tent and, seeing his distinguished visitors, he leapt forward.

The Colonel half edged behind the Adjutant. From the look on his nephew's face he couldn't be certain the prat wasn't about to embrace him.

After the obligatory salute Jampton said, 'Good to see you, Unc– Colonel.'

The Colonel heaved a sigh of relief. At least Jampton had learnt something. He turned suddenly and said, 'Excuse me, isn't that Sarn't Major Puller over there?'

It wasn't but it didn't matter. He had to get away from this pompous little twat of a nephew before he drew his service revolver and ended Jampton's military career and his own.

Five minutes later he was sitting in the Sergeant Major's tent pouring two healthy libations of Scotch from his hip flask into the two enamel mugs provided by the SM. Puller had reported briefly on events at the camp since Colonel Brunswick's last visit. It was like reading the script of a George Formby film.

'Go on,' said the Colonel.

'Well, and then two days ago one of our three-tonners disappeared.'

The Colonel frowned. 'Disappeared?' he echoed.

'Yes, sir, and so did the two French Legionnaires and six other bods.' The Colonel looked at him searchingly. 'They weren't happy, sir.'

'Did they tell you that, Sergeant Major?'

The Sergeant Major was uneasy. He looked away, stroking his blue chin.

'Come on, man,' snapped the Colonel. 'Why didn't you put a guard on the transport?'

The Sergeant Major straightened. 'I did so, sir – two guards.'

'And I suppose they were both asleep?'

'Oh no, sir,' replied the Sergeant Major. 'They went with 'em. Officially,' he went on, 'we have no jurisdiction over the Legionnaires. They are French nationals. Three of the others are RAF personnel, and the rest . . .' He shrugged. 'Civvies.'

The Colonel nodded. 'And how many of the old 41st Light Infantry are left?'

'Eight, sir, including me.'

The Colonel looked up at the sky, then shook his head sadly. 'Eight,' he mused. Poor bloody infantry, the old 41st. All they wanted was hot food whenever possible, fags, letters from home, but most important, a damn good Commanding Officer. And he had lumbered them with his nephew ... Poor bloody infantry.

Finally he said, 'I appreciate your difficulty, Sergeant Major. But don't worry. I'll have a word with your CO.'

But even as he said it he knew he wouldn't, and despised himself for his cowardice, but, good grief, every man was entitled to his Achilles heel and Jampton was a whole foot.

Later, in the screened-off portion of the medical marquee marked OFFICERS' MESS, the Colonel listened morosely while his Adjutant related his exchange with his nephew.

'Any other requirements?' asked the Colonel.

'Quite a few, sir, but his next item was a padre.'

The Colonel's eyebrows shot up.

'Isn't he well?' he asked hopefully.

His Adjutant smiled. 'It's not that, sir. As from next Sunday he's instigated church parades.'

'Good grief,' exploded the Colonel. 'I hope you told him that padres had better things to do than officiate at church parades.' Unaware of the irony of his remarks, he continued. 'Jampton'll want a military band to go with it, I suppose.'

'Don't worry, sir, I quashed that one. I reminded him that there was a war on.'

'And what did he say to that?'

The Adjutant shrugged. 'He took it well enough, said he understood and would settle for fife and drums.'

The Colonel stared at him for a moment. 'And?' he said finally.

'I told him he could have the drums but Fife was in Scotland.'

The Colonel chuckled and slapped his thigh. 'Did he laugh?'

'No, sir. He stared at me in a peculiar way, than made a note on his pad.'

'What about the medals and stuff?' interrupted the Colonel.

'Ah yes,' replied his Adjutant. 'I've arranged that handing the citations to Sparks and Miller take place in the orderly tent.'

'Good for you, Jimmy,' the Colonel chuckled. 'I'll bet that didn't go down too well.'

'No, sir.' The Adjutant shuddered. 'He was all for a full dress parade formed up in a square with the Sergeant Major in full dress uniform handing you both medals on a cushion.' The Colonel's eyebrows shot up. 'Yes sir,' said the Adjutant. 'I asked him where he was going to get a cushion from and he told me he'd had a pillow dyed purple.'

Brunswick stared at him in disbelief. Jampton was his sister's child and a frightening thought crossed his mind. Could it be that there was insanity in his family?

'Oh don't worry, sir,' went on the Adjutant. 'Like I said, no fuss, and a quick handover in the orderly tent.'

'Brilliant,' said the Colonel. 'A register office as opposed to Westminster Abbey.'

'He took it rather well, sir.'

'Right,' said the Colonel briskly. 'Let's get it over with and then back to Alex. Somebody's got to be there to show Rommel where everything is.'

CHAPTER
FIVE

The following Monday Sergeant Major Puller strode across to the CO's tent. In the last few days there had been six more desertions but it was the two that had gone over the hill this morning that disturbed him most. There was no reply to his knock on the tent pole, so he tentatively pulled back the flap to find that the CO was not at home. He was about to duck out when he caught sight of the manuscript on the table. It was headed 'MILITARY TACTICS' BY WILFRED RONALDSWAY JAMPTON. He was intrigued. Curiously, he flipped through it. CHAPTER 6: HOW TO SALUTE FROM A MOVING VEHICLE. CHAPTER 7: CLAUSEWITZ WAS WRONG, and then BISMARK'S FOLLY. What a load of balls, he thought. How had he managed to get himself lumbered with Lieutenant Wilfred Ronaldsway Jampton, who wasn't old enough to be mad but was certainly retarded? He'd have to be to write this crap.

He turned as the author ducked in through the tent flap. On seeing the Sergeant Major, he looked quickly round to see if he was in the right tent. On being assured that he was, he spoke.

'Been waiting long?' he asked sarcastically.

The Sergeant Major eyed him coolly, not deigning to reply.

Jampton walked round his desk and sat on the chair. 'What's the problem, Sarn't Major?' he asked.

'It's Sparks and Miller, sir.' He paused.

'What about Sparks and Miller?' asked Jampton.

'They've deserted, sir.'

He waited for Jampton's reaction, but he couldn't quite make it out. The CO was smiling with what looked like amusement, the way a man will look after his opponent has just moved a piece on the chessboard that will cost him the game.

'And what makes you think they've deserted?' he asked smoothly.

The Sergeant Major found his anger was rising, but he managed to bring himself under control.

'Because, sir,' he said through gritted teeth, 'they're not here any more. They've gone over the hill, done a bunk.'

He drew a breath; he was sailing dangerously close to the line of insolence and was too well trained to step over it.

'They've taken their small kit with them and one of the wagons is missing,' he added.

The CO regarded him with an enigmatic smile.

'And where d'you think they've deserted to?' he asked.

Good Christ, help me, thought Sergeant Major Puller. Much more of this and I swear I'll bury him up to his neck in sand and let the ants have him.

Jampton leant forward over the table.

'Let me put you out of your misery, Sarn't Major.' He looked at his wristwatch. 'By now they should be halfway to Alexandria.'

The Sergeant Major stared blankly at the pompous little ferret-eyed face.

'Oh yes,' went on Jampton. 'I detailed them to take the three-tonner into Alex to pick up supplies.'

The Sergeant Major couldn't believe his ears. It was as if the prison warden had sent a lifer up to London for a packet of his favourite cigarettes.

'Something troubling you, Sergeant Major?' asked Jampton silkily.

'Yes, sir,' he said resignedly. 'That's the last we'll see of Sparks and Miller and the three-tonner . . .'

Jampton raised his hands and stopped him.

'You're still convinced they've deserted, Sarn't Major?'

'I know these men, sir.'

'You knew these men, Sarn't Major, but this was before they were awarded the Military Medal. If my judgment of human nature is anything to go by, they'll be back in three days, and with more supplies than we indented for, eh?' He winked conspiratorially. But the SM wasn't about to join the conspiracy.

Jampton leant back confidently.

'Listen, Sergeant Major, I'm not a betting man, but I'll wager my wristwatch against your cap badge that I'm right and they'll be back here in three days.'

The Sergeant Major shook his head. 'Right,' he said sadly, 'it's your wristwatch.'

Jampton was flustered. After four more days, sadly, reluctantly and inevitably, he came around to the conclusion that the Sergeant Major was right. Sparks and Miller, military medals and all, were gone for good. The realisation made Jampton cross; he was too young and pampered to understand anger. Whenever something nasty had happened to him in the past it had been swiftly dealt with by his loving, doting and formidable aunt. Even when the young horror set fire to the gardener's cottage there'd been no reprimand, and the old gardener had been dismissed for being stupid enough to leave a box of matches on a shelf by the gas stove, even though young Jampton had had to climb up on a chair to get them.

Sparks and Miller would not have dared to desert if his Aunt Dorothy was here. It wasn't just the actual crime of desertion that bothered him, but he'd given them specific instructions where to find his blue suitcase, its dimensions, and the fact that his name was stencilled all over it; he'd even mentioned the torn label in the bottom corner from a hotel in Eastbourne. He glanced at his wrist and saw only a white band where his watch had been. Exasperated, he threw his copy of *Military Tactics* to the floor and stamped on it.

Seated in the front of the bumping, lurching three-tonner, Sergeant Major Puller dozed. Up to now the journey had been uneventful. It wasn't a safe run, and for that reason the first half was completed under the cover of darkness. This wasn't entirely risk-free. There was always the danger of running into an enemy patrol, or a minefield, but at least there was safety from air attacks.

Now it was beginning to get light and the Sergeant Major yawned and stretched. He was an infantryman and if he wished to sleep he closed his eyes and it was so. He could sleep deeply and quietly until something unusual aroused him – the click of a rifle bolt, the distant soft squeal of heavy tank tracks, or, as it was in this case, first light. He lit two cigarettes and handed one to the driver. They hadn't exchanged much conversation during the journey.

'Want to stop for a minute?' asked the SM.

'No, sir, I'm all right for a bit.'

And as the heat in the cab began to rise, the driver took off his tin hat. Puller looked across at him with interest. The back of his driver's head was flat. It was exraordinarily flat. It reminded the SM of an Easter Island statue. Perhaps he had been born like that, but more than likely his father had fetched him a sharp blow to the back of his head with a shovel during his formative years. He was about to ask idly if this was so but decided against it.

They rumbled on and as the sun began to float from beyond the horizon they noticed a few signs of activity

– not very close and most likely to be British now that they were on the last leg. The Sergeant Major glanced at his watch, and this reminded him. He took the CO's wristwatch from his shirt pocket and examined it. He turned it over and engraved on the back was 'From Aunt Dorothy to Her Little Soldier'. He shuddered. God, he'd have that taken off sharpish. If he caught a packet it wouldn't do to have that on his wrist.

'Got a file?' he asked the driver.

'One in the toolbox, sir. I'll get it out when we stop.'

The Sergeant Major nodded and put the watch on the floor of the cab. The danger now would be from the air. Some lone, predatory Luftwaffe pilot might fancy a bit of target practice and Jampton's wristwatch would be the first thing out of the window.

Suddenly the Sergeant Major leant forward. Ahead of them and to one side of the track were the burnt-out remains of a vehicle. This was not unusual in itself – the desert was littered with sights like this – but something else had caught the SM's eye.

'Pull up,' he ordered.

Then the driver noticed it too, a poignant reminder of the war. Two small, rough crosses topped by two British tin hats. There were no markings but hanging by their string were two identification discs. Slowly the SM bent and took one of them: 'Miller, M. C of E'. The other one was stamped 'Sparks, Agnostic'.

The driver took off his own tin hat in respect. 'Poor bastards,' he muttered.

The Sergeant Major was thoughtful. He wandered over to the burnt-out vehicle. There wasn't too much left of it. He bent to brush the sand from the blackened piece of what was once a radiator, then quickly he straightened.

'In you get, laddie,' he said briskly. 'You'll get your evening in Alex, have no fear.'

The driver was staggered.

'But, sir –' he pointed at the crosses '– what about Sparks and Miller?'

'We're going to pick 'em up.'

The driver stared again at the two crosses, not understanding.

'Oh don't worry about that little bit of pantomime. They're not due for their eternal rest yet, lad. They're in Alex.' The driver wasn't convinced. 'You see that?' The SM pointed to the burnt-out wreck.

'The supply wagon,' said the driver mechanically.

The Sergeant Major snorted. 'And since when have we been driving Mercedes?'

The Sergeant Major had been correct in his assumption. Sparks and Miller had indeed arrived in Alexandria four days ago. It had been just after midnight when they had pulled up behind a line of Bren carriers. As they sat smoking in the cab of their three-tonner they quietly discussed their next move. The first job was to get rid of the truck. This didn't pose much of a problem: they already had a buyer in mind. With this money they would bribe one of the boatmen to take them up the Nile to wherever it took them.

It was a simple strategy and about as watertight as a string vest. Obstacles and unforeseen events were to see to that. However, they settled themselves down for a few hours' sleep with the intention of being on the road at first light. But as sleep was always a luxury to an infantryman, the sun was already halfway up the sky when they finally awoke. But they weren't unduly worried – they felt they had plenty of time in hand. What they hadn't put into their equation was their new-found fame and notoriety.

The *Daily Express* had been first off the mark. Bales of the flimsy overseas editions were flown out to Alexandria and Cairo on the direct orders of the

Minister of Propaganda. It was a morale booster to lift up the flagging spirits of the British and Allied Forces, a desperate attempt to stiffen up the blood in a last-ditch effort to save North Africa. So the privilege of English newspapers, hitherto afforded to only high-ranking officers' messes, was now extended to anybody who could read. And for those who couldn't, there were always the large pictures of Sparks and Miller. In fact, since the newspapers had arrived their faces had become more familiar than Clark Gable and Carole Lombard.

Sparks, who was not driving, was the first to notice the curious stares every time they were forced to slow down in the volume of traffic. A small group of Australians were the first to confirm his fears that, for some unaccountable reason, they were attracting attention. One of the Aussies pointed and yelled, 'Good on ya, Sparks,' and together they whistled, yahooed and waved their one-sided, pinned-up hats.

'Take the next left,' yelled Sparks and they shot down a less-populated side street, and after a few more detours Miller pulled up and stared at Sparks.

'What the bloody hell's going on?'

'Don't ask me,' snapped Sparks.

'I didn't know you knew any Aussies,' said Miller.

'It's not just them,' said Sparks. 'Everybody's been staring at us . . .'

He was about to continue when a well-dressed Egyptian in a linen suit and a fez tapped his fly whisk against Miller's door.

'Yes?' said Miller suspiciously.

The Egyptian looked up at him. 'Welcome to Alexandria, Mr Miller,' he said. Then he craned to one side, standing on tiptoes. 'And Mr Sparks too, I see.'

They looked at each other, baffled.

'Would you do me the greatest honour and sign my newspaper?'

He held up a copy of the *Daily Express* and a pen. Miller snatched the newspaper from him but ignored the pen. Quickly he unfolded the paper.

'Jesus,' he breathed and held the thing across to his oppo.

'Shit and derision,' said Sparks as he glanced at his picture on the front page of the newspaper.

By now a small crowd was beginning to collect.

'It's us,' murmured Miller.

'I know who it is,' snapped Sparks. 'Get this bloody truck moving, now, quick for Christ's sake!'

Miller gunned the engine and the crowd fell back.

'Bloody hell,' said Sparks once they were moving again. 'Have you got any more bright ideas?'

'Me?' protested Miller.

'Let's go up to Alex, you said, and disappear.'

'Well I didn't know, did I?' bleated Miller.

'Look at 'em all staring.'

'Yeh,' said Sparks, 'and these are friendly. They're on our side. What happens when Rommel gets a copy of the *Daily Express*?'

Miller didn't connect for a moment. 'Bloody 'ell,' he shouted slapping the wheel. 'I hope we haven't upset him. One Stuka and half a dozen Hitler youth, that's all he'd need and the camp would be a black patch in the desert. We're better off out of it. Potbelly's place can't be far now.' And his foot went down on the accelerator.

'It's around here some place,' said Sparks, ducking and bobbing his head trying to recognise a landmark. 'Got it!' he shouted slapping his thigh. 'Turn right into that street up there.'

'Which one?'

'By the sign. I'm sure that's Potbelly's place.'

A Sergeant and a Lance Corporal of the Military Police were standing stiffly against a wall, only their eyes moving under the low peaks of their red caps. But they didn't miss much and registered mentally the erratic progress of the three-ton truck speeding dangerously in and out of the traffic.

'Mad bastard,' said the Sergeant out of the corner of his mouth, eyes swivelling to follow its wild dash.

Everybody was in a hurry these days – roll on demob. It was only when the truck, heeling over, took a suicidal dive up one of the side streets that they became animated. That street was out of bounds.

'Come on,' said the Sergeant and together they pushed their way through the strolling mob, most of whom made way, especially anybody in uniform. When redcaps moved quickly it was best to be somewhere else.

Miller swung hard across the road and into the narrow street. The sign read OUT OF BOUNDS TO ALL MILITARY PERSONNEL.

'I've never noticed that before,' said Miller.

'That's because you never bloody well looked where you were going,' yelled Sparks.

The locals were scattering on all sides, cursing and hawking. The lorry wasn't going to slow down and kismet was one thing and 'what is to be will be' was another, but Allah couldn't be every place at once.

'This is it,' shouted Miller and jabbed his foot on the brake.

Sparks lunged across to hammer on the horn. The hostile mob surged round the truck, some beating the canvas side with sticks and screaming in a frenzy of hate. Miller sat petrified while Sparks beat frantically on the horn. A rock splintered the windscreen.

'Come on, come on,' muttered Sparks frantically.

And slowly – bloody hell was it ever slow – the whole shop front swung inward. Panic-stricken, in a series of jerks, Miller turned into the blackness of the car park and immediately behind them the shop front creaked back into place. It was only then that Miller switched off the engine and the two of them sat shakily in the darkness.

By the time the Military Police reached the end of the street they were already too late. The Lance Corporal was about to rush up the street and the Sergeant restrained him. There was a mass of people as far as the eye could see but no truck. Faces cold and hostile turned towards the two military policemen.

'What's happened to the truck, Sarge?'

'What truck?'

The Lance Jack looked at him in amazement.

'The three-tonner.'

'I never saw a three-tonner,' muttered the Sergeant, never taking his eyes off the crowd.

The bustle and anger that had erupted a few minutes ago subsided into a malevolent silence, their attention now directed at the two policemen. It was a page out of the Old Testament.

'Come on, lad.'

The Sergeant was backing slowly towards the main street again. The Lance Corporal was undecided.

'We can make enquiries, Sarge. The truck couldn't have reached the other end, that's for sure.'

He turned to see the Sergeant already rounding the corner into the main drag. Still the locals hadn't moved. He cleared his throat about to speak but his courage left him as a stone whistled past his ear. He turned and ran to catch up with his Sergeant, who was now back in his own patch demanding to see a small soldier's pay book and, while he flicked unseeingly through the pages, the Lance Corporal joined him.

'What about that truck, Sarge?'

The Sergeant handed back the pay book and when the little man had left them he said, out of the corner of his mouth, 'I didn't see any truck, lad. And if you did you should lay off the old . . .' He mimed drinking. Then he added, 'Listen, son, that street is dangerous. I wouldn't go up there in an armoured car with an escort of Royal Marines. I wouldn't even send the missus up there.'

111

He looked beyond the Lance Corporal. 'Where's your cap, soldier?' he barked at a passing soldier.

'Bollocks,' replied the soldier and moved on.

The Sergeant shrugged. 'You can't win 'em all,' he muttered philosophically.

In the cab of their three-tonner Sparks and Miller sat in silence while they collected their jangling nerves.

'What a bastard,' whispered Dusty Miller. He applied a match to his cigarette and the way the flame jumped about and the glowing end of the cigarette trembled it was clear that he still hadn't got over the last half-hour. He took the cigarette from his lips.

'What a bastard,' he muttered again. 'What a lousy, jumped-up, never-come-down bastard.'

There was a silence. Then, 'What if Potbelly won't buy the truck?' asked Sparks.

Miller digested this for a moment. 'He'll have it, don't you worry.'

'He'd better,' replied Sparks. 'I'm not going out there again in this. And he opened the door and jumped down to wait for Abdul. They had a long wait, at least half an hour, but then time wasn't on a watch in this part of the world.

A tiny bulb was switched on and Abdul came mincing down the two steps. Sparks and Miller quietly smoked as they watched him approach.

'My house is yours,' he began, and they all bowed. 'We've been expecting you.'

They looked at each other in astonishment. 'Expecting us?' said Miller. 'How did you know we were coming?'

'Ah,' smiled Abdul coquettishly, 'a little bird, eh? Yes, my friends, a little bird. Now, how can I help you?'

Miller shook himself out of his puzzlement. 'How much?' he said and gestured to the back of the truck.

Abdul peered over the tailgate and shrugged. 'What is this, a joke?'

'No,' replied Miller. 'It's all yours.'

'But there's nothing here.' And he peered over the tailgate again and struck a match in case there was something he had missed.

'The truck, it's all yours, all three tons of it – wheels, good tyres, radiator, the lot; low mileage and the tank's practically full.'

Abdul sucked in his breath and stepped back. 'Oh no, no, no, no, no – is too dangerous.'

Sparks ground out his cigarette. 'Oh come on, Dusty, I told you we should have taken it to One-eyed Ahmed.'

Miller looked at his oppo in amazement. What the hell was he on about? He'd never heard of One-eyed Ahmed.

Abdul was unmoved. 'No, no. A truck is different.'

Sparks snorted. 'Well, that's it then,' he said. 'Come on, Dusty, we'll get a better price from One-eyed Ahmed anyway.' He made to open the passenger door.

'Wait, wait,' implored Abdul. 'Come upstairs. We have a drink and talk, yes?'

Sparks looked to Miller and winked. 'OK, let's hear what he has to say.'

Abdul moved round the bar on the edge of the small dance floor. The place was empty apart from the three of them, which was hardly surprising. It was a nightclub and they didn't do afternoon tea dancing. Miller was satisfied Abdul wanted the truck. All that remained was the price. An hour and three-quarters of a bottle of Scotch later, price was still the only obstacle. Abdul was impassive. He'd kept up, drink for drink, which was hardly surprising as he was only on lemonade.

'All right, then,' said Miller, 'and this is our last offer.'

It was the fourth time it had been his last offer, but he was in the big league and Abdul was a past master.

'I'm listening,' he said quietly.

'Right,' said Miller. 'Two hundred pounds cash, plus room and board for three months.'

Abdul reached for a small bell and shook it delicately, and before he put it down a huge black fella eased from the shadows and bowed. They stared at him. Without a doubt he was the biggest, widest man they'd ever seen. What a monster! The door was easily four feet wide and he still had to come in sideways. His bare arms were bigger than Miller's thighs.

A shiver of fear went through him. Had he blown it? They were up a one-way street. To the military they'd already disappeared and the bits of them floating down the Nile wouldn't be enough to identify. Bloody stupid to leave their rifles in the cab. In any case you'd need an antitank gun to make an impression on this one.

His relief was equalled only by the deep sigh from Sparks as Abdul said, 'Mohammed, my pills.' He leant back, clutching his heart.

'Ain't it marvellous?' breathed Sparks. 'They always have to throw a Sarah Bernhardt.'

Miller looked at him in amazement. Would his oppo realise how close they'd been to the knacker's yard?

Sparks half rose. 'I told you,' he said, 'we should have taken it to One-eyed Ahmed's.'

Miller was puzzled. He dragged his mate back into his chair and, whilst Abdul was washing the pills down with a glass of water, hissed low into Sparks's ear.

'Who the bloody hell is One-eyed Ahmed?'

Sparks shrugged in return; it was enough.

'My friends.' Abdul smiled, spreading his arms. 'My good friends . . . I always help my friends, especially the soldiers who protect us from harm.' He shook his head. 'But three months' room and board, it's impossible.'

Miller knew why three months was too long. The old bastard was expecting Rommel and the Afrika Korps. The last thing he wanted was to be caught harbouring two British soldiers.

But the penny didn't seem to have dropped with Sparks. 'Ah, give him a kick up the arse and let's go.'

But again Miller waved him down. 'Two months then,' he said.

'Two months?' wailed Abdul. 'Two hours you have been here and already one bottle of finest Scotch whisky, zut, gone.' He shook his head sadly. 'My good friends,' he went on. 'Look around you. Am I flocking with customers?' He gestured round the room. 'Nobody ... How can I pay my poor girls? All they do is eat, sleep and get fat. And who has to feed them? I'm a poor man.'

Miller snorted. 'You're breaking my heart,' he said. 'In a couple of hours this place'll be jam-packed and you know it. You had this place put out of bounds 'cos there's more money in civilians, right?'

'Two weeks,' said Abdul suddenly raising his hands in surrender.

Miller looked at Sparks, who yawned. 'Suits me,' he said. He was bored with all the palaver. One week in this place would be more than enough.

'Well, that's settled then,' said Miller. 'Now the money.'

Sparks stood up. 'Sort that out between you. I'm going to get my head down.' He turned to Abdul. 'Which room am I in? Just give me the key and I'll find it.'

'A key?' asked Abdul. A laugh started deep in the fat belly, all the flab quivering like a blancmange in a high wind. 'A key?' he said. 'Yes, my lord, and what time would you like breakfast, my lord?'

Sparks stared down at the man. Miller grabbed the whisky bottle and made to fill his glass. Nobody laughed at Sparks. The bottle was the only weapon within reach.

It didn't seem to bother Abdul. He was wiping tears from his eyes. 'Show Milord to his room,' he ordered.

'But in my humble establishment we cannot afford the luxury of keys.'

This diffused the situation; well that, and the massive Mr Universe standing behind his chair. The enormous monster of a man beckoned and Sparks followed.

Miller relaxed. That could have been nasty. He gulped down his Scotch. Had it been true to its Johnny Walker label he would have been under the table by now, but we all had to make a crust and each bottle was mainly cold tea. At least it was better than gin: half that came straight out of the Nile.

Upstairs Sparks took off his shirt and poured some water out of a cracked jug into the basin. Then he fiddled around in his small kit for a sliver of soap. He worked hard for some lather and finally he managed enough for a wash. The cold water against his face was exhilarating, the best thing that had happened all day. He felt for the jug and poured the rest of the water over his head, then he scooped more water from the basin and repeated the action. He straightened and only then realised there was no towel. He wouldn't open his eyes – his bit of soap had been thinner than a communion wafer but was enough to blind him.

'There's never a bloody towel when you want one,' he muttered stupidly.

'Oh yes there is.'

He stopped dead in his tracks, feeling the roughness of a towel draped over his hands. He liked the sound of that voice. 'Ello, 'ello, he thought, my ship's come in. But when he cleared his vision his face dropped.

'Not you again,' he said. 'How did you know I'd be here?'

'Where else?' said Yasmin.

In the camp it was Corporal Smith and he suspected that Yasmin wasn't her real name, but what the hell! She'd told him that she was half French, half Arab. In any case he called her Yasmin; it wasn't too hard to

116

remember. Up to now he'd only seen her in oversized khaki shirt and shorts, and a few times out of them, but she'd never worn a dress before and he had to admit that the red shoes with high heels did a lot more for her than a pair of Army boots. She sat on the bed and crossed her legs, and, bloody 'ell, they weren't bad either.

He stared at her, perplexed. What kind of a woman was this? She was always several jumps ahead; no wonder Abdul had opened the shop entrance so promptly: they'd been expected. Also, their accommodation was arranged. In all his experience he'd never come across a woman like Yasmin before. Hitherto his women had fallen into two categories – those who would and those who wouldn't. He fancied her but the warning bell in the back of his head jangled. He was the original chauvinist; it was time to lay down a few ground rules.

'You didn't walk here,' asked Sparks, but it wasn't a query.

She smiled. 'No, I've been here for a few days. I got a lift from . . . the other people – the two Legionnaires. We had a very nice journey.'

Sparks was about to remind her that the two Legionnaires had not only stolen a truck but they had deserted. His mouth was open ready to speak when he remembered that that was exactly what he and Miller had done.

She might have been reading his mind.

'I've bought for you a nice shirt and tie and a light suit.'

While she talked she moved over to the old wardrobe and opened the door.

'*Voilà*,' she said with a gesture towards a white suit on a hanger.

He stared in amazement, water dripping off his chin. It wasn't so much the suit – it was the dresses on several

117

other hangers, her dresses. He glanced down at the bed. It would be a tight squeeze. Then he frowned – it was all too organised.

'Listen, Yasmin,' he started. 'How did you know I'd be in this room, this particular one?'

Again she smiled and it made him uneasy. He didn't like being manipulated.

'I told you, Sparks, but you don't listen. Abdul is my uncle. How you say, from far away.'

'Distant,' said Sparks.

'Yes, distant uncle. If it was not for me you would not have been welcome. And even if you come in, you would never have got out again.'

He nodded, then remembered her dresses in the wardrobe.

'Yes, OK, OK,' he said. 'Now listen, Yasmin. It's time we had a talk – let's get it all out in the open.'

He turned to look out of the window, which faced the high whitewashed wall of the building opposite. He wasn't a man of words, and why the hell did she just sit there with that superior smile on her face as if she knew what he was going to say? The wall opposite was easier than having to face her.

'You can't just move in. It's too much like being married.'

She remained silent.

'I told you in the beginning I have to be free.'

Still no response.

'I like you. Yes, I like you a lot, but if I'd known you were going to stick to me like a mustard plaster I would have left you under that pile of rocks back in Tobruk.'

This time she spoke. 'Oh no, you could not do that, it was fate.'

'My eye,' replied Sparks. 'I make my own fate.'

He turned to face her and stopped in surprise. She'd taken off her shoes and was lying, hands behind her head, smiling again. He'd never seen her smile before today.

118

He went on reasonably. 'Now you're a nice bit. I'll give you that, but British blokes are not like other men. They like to be on their tod sometimes. You know, Tod Sloane, alone, by themselves. They like their women . . . well, somewhere else – waiting, like the Arabs. They do it all the time. You ought to understand that, being half Arab.'

Yasmin was angry. 'I am not an Arab. I am French,' she snapped.

'OK, OK,' said Sparks. 'How come old Potbelly's your uncle?'

She snorted derisively. 'Abdul is not my uncle, not a real uncle. It's a courtesy title. I used to work here.'

Sparks's eyebrows went up.

'No, it's not what you're thinking. I wasn't one of the girls. I was the madame, and being Abdul's niece I was under his protection.' Sparks opened his mouth to speak but Yasmin went on. 'And the answer to that is no. Abdul prefers little boys.'

Sparks couldn't help the feeling of relief, but another question entered his mind.

'And Tobruk?'

She waved a hand deprecatingly. 'I was a receptionist at the Hotel Imperial. That's where I was when the roof fell in.'

Sparks nodded. 'You don't half pick some nice places to work.'

He looked down at the towel in his hands, then remembered her dresses in the wardrobe and the way she had taken control of the conversation, the possessiveness of her attitude as if she belonged. He screwed up the towel and flung it into the wash basin.

'As if I haven't got enough problems,' he muttered.

Behind him, swinging her legs off the bed, she began to put her shoes back on, then she stood and made for the door.

'Where you off to?' Sparks said uncertainly.

'What should that matter to you?' she snapped, opening the door.

'Hang on, hang on,' pleaded Sparks. Quickly coming over to her, he closed the door and turned her towards him. They stood for a moment looking into each other's face.

'I love you, Sparks,' she said softly.

'Yeah, yeah,' he replied huskily, and then, with a desperate attempt to regain the high ground, he said, 'All right, then, just this once,' and led her back to the bed.

The following day Sparks and Yasmin were sitting in companionable silence at a table on the pavement in front of Le Chat Noir, a popular restaurant at the corner of Saad Zaghioul Street. They were idly watching the colourful panorama of many different races passing up and down – Egyptians in djellabas, uniforms of many nations, black-robed, masked ladies carrying baskets, pots, suitcases on their heads. Some of the tenseness was leaving Sparks. Passers-by had looked towards them but without recognition. Most of the military ignored him altogether and had eyes only for Yasmin. It was hardly surprising. His off-white suit wasn't a bad fit and his light hair dyed black was now supplemented by a Ronald Colman moustache. He was satisfied his disguise had passed the test. In fact, when he had seen himself in the fly-specked mirror over the wash basin, he'd half ducked, wondering who the bloody hell it was. He smiled at the recollection and beckoned a waiter over. 'Two beers,' he said.

'*Bien.*' The waiter bowed and was about to leave when Yasmin spoke to him in French.

'My friend is a joker. Cancel the two beers and make it two pastis.'

'*Bien, madame.*' The waiter bowed again and left.

Sparks watched him go then turned to Yasmin. 'What was all that about?' he hissed.

Yasmin leant towards him and said softly, 'A rich young Egyptian does not order beer, and most certainly not for his girlfriend.'

Sparks was about to argue, then realised the logic in this and decided to ignore the girlfriend bit.

'*Voilà*,' said the waiter placing the two glasses and a jug of water on the table.

'*Merci*,' replied Yasmin dismissively.

And the waiter bowed and left, disappointed not to have poured the water, which would have given him a bird's-eye view down her cleavage. Yasmin did the honours, turning the yellow liquid into a milky whiteness.

'What's this?' asked Sparks dubiously.

'Pernod,' she said, and added mischievously, 'It's good for your sex life.'

Clinking her glass with his, they drank. Sparks nodded appreciatively and relaxed even more. He was about to take out a packet of cigarettes when suddenly he stiffened. Yasmin followed his gaze quickly. Two military policemen, redcaps, blancoed webbing, boots that shone like a new gramophone record, were about twenty yards away, walking in step unhurriedly. But surely they would pass the table. Yasmin squeezed his hand but it didn't reassure him. He appreciated all the work she'd done on dying his hair and stuff but these bastards had X-ray eyes.

He looked round him searching frantically for a quick exit when his eyes fell on a newspaper discarded on the next table. Snatching it up, he held it open to hide his face. It looked for all the world as if he was reading the bottom line on one of the centre pages, but in reality he was watching the black shiny boots and white gaiters approaching from underneath the paper. Slowly and inevitably they drew level, then they stopped and moved towards the table. Sparks's heart was beating faster than it had ever done, even before an

121

attack. At least in battle he knew what to expect. He closed his eyes, desperately trying to stop his hands from shaking, when one of the redcaps spoke.

'That one's Sparks isn't it, the light-haired geezer?'

Sparks was baffled. Could they see through the newspaper? Then Yasmin leant forward and looked at the front page of the old edition of the *Daily Express*.

'Ah yes,' she said, 'and the other one is Miller, yes?'

'Yes,' said one of them, and the boots turned away from the table and the voice spoke again to his mate. 'I've seen those two somewhere.'

There was a pause and then the other voice replied, 'I think everybody in the world has seen them two. I wouldn't be surprised if they were on the front of *Time* magazine.'

Again there was a pause and the first voice spoke. 'I can't help feeling I've seen them recently, here in Alexandria.'

There was a silence once more. 'It'll come to me,' said the voice. And the boots moved off.

Yasmin took the newspaper from Sparks's trembling fingers and turned it round to show him the front page and the photos of himself and Dusty Miller.

Sparks sagged back in his chair, sweat pouring down his face. He pushed his glass away.

'Bugger that for a lark. I need a proper drink.' And he sent the waiter inside for a large Scotch.

Yasmin patted his hand. 'Relax,' she whispered. 'You are not Sparks now. You look more like an unsuccessful Egyptian tax collector.'

A tumbler full of doubtful whisky was set before him and he was about to drink when he felt a tug on his sleeve. His nerves were still ragged and he yelped, throwing most of his drink over the table. He turned his head to see an Egyptian wearing dark glasses, fez and striped djellaba.

'You buy postcard, yes?'

Ignoring the singsong sales pitch, he turned back to his reading.

'Hello, sir, you like dirty postcard?'

'Piss off,' he muttered out of the corner of his mouth.

'Many positions, yes?'

Sparks's fists bunched on the table. The Arab leant forward quickly and whispered in his ear. 'It's me, you pillock.'

Sparks was dumbstruck. It was Miller all right and he really had some postcards.

'Pretend to be going through 'em,' he hissed.

Sparks took the pictures. They weren't dirty postcards, just the crap tourists bought showing 'Pompeii's Pillar', 'The Catacombs of Kom al-Shqafa' and other places to visit in Alexandria.

Yasmin turned away in disgust. An unsuccessful Egyptian tax collector would certainly not be buying dirty postcards at the corner of Saad Zaghioul Street. An unsuccessful Egyptian tax collector would most likely be selling them himself.

Miller, who had nodded to Yasmin, whispered in Sparks's ear pointing to the postcards as he did so. 'Some time next week a felucca going up the Nile. Cost a bit but it's the best I can do. OK?'

'Your Gestapo is back,' whispered Yasmin, and Sparks looked up to see the two military policemen returning along their beat. Miller snatched the photographs and disappeared. But the military policemen, showing no interest at all, carried on past the table.

Sparks drained what was left of his whisky. His nerves couldn't stand much more of this but the news from Dusty Miller was good. In a few days they'd be on a boat going up the Nile, and then what? He didn't care. Any boat, anywhere, as long as they didn't end up in a convoy to Russia.

* * *

Three days later another one of the Special Ordnance vehicles pulled up in the commercial part of the city on Salah Salem Street and Sergeant Major Puller jumped down. Turning, he looked up at the driver. 'I'll see you at the Allied Services Club at nine o'clock.'

'Where's that, sir?'

'It's two blocks up from here.' He turned and pointed. 'You can't miss it. It's opposite the Egyptian Officers' Club.'

'OK, sir, I'll find it.' He put the lorry into gear and was gone.

Sergeant Major Puller watched as the Bedford rejoined the disorderly stream of traffic, then he made his way into the building marked MINISTRY OF AG & FISH. He asked a Corporal at the enquiry desk for Colonel Brunswick and within ten minutes, a tumbler of Dimple Haig in his hand, he sat facing his old CO.

'You're quite right,' said Colonel Brunswick softly. 'They're in Alex – but God knows where. But they're here all right. You can't plaster their ugly mugs all over the front pages of the newspaper without some bright Charlie recognising them.'

The Sergeant Major nodded into his whisky. 'In that case, they shouldn't be too hard to find, sir.'

'Don't be too sure,' said the Colonel. 'I've had several eyewitness reports. On Monday they were seen driving along the main boulevard then they turned up a side street, and that's it, bingo. According to the Military Police, they just disappeared up their own exhaust pipe. I don't know how they do it,' he went on, 'but they're going the right way to be bigger than Lawrence of Arabia.'

The Sergeant Major nodded. 'Well me and my driver will be doing the rounds tonight, sir, all the usual watering places.'

'That's no good, old friend. They won't be there. They'd be recognised.'

'I agree, sir. But if I ask a few questions, somebody may come up with something.'

Colonel Brunswick shook his head sadly.

'You'll have to tread warily, Sergeant Major,' he said. 'If this ever gets out that they've done a bunk, my head will be on the block. You can't paint them up one minute to be the lily-white saviours of our civilisation, and the next as common deserters. It wouldn't look good and you know the form as well as I do. It doesn't matter how tall the pile of crap is as long as it doesn't fall on you.'

He poured them another drink and his next question was right off at a tangent.

'How many other desertions did you say you'd had?' asked the Colonel looking out of the window.

'Eighteen, counting Sparks and Miller, sir,' replied the Sergeant Major.

There was a pause.

'Eighteen,' murmured the Colonel, 'and all of them since Lieutenant Jampton took command?'

Sergeant Major Puller squirmed uneasily in his chair but before he could speak the Colonel swivelled back to the desk.

'I'm sorry, Sergeant Major. I shouldn't have asked you that.'

The Colonel was embarrassed. It was a tactless question and he was out of order. God Almighty, Puller was the glue that had held the SOG together, but he wasn't there now: he was here, in Alex, while his nephew Jampton was loose in the camp. Christopher Columbus! There could be a mass breakout and when the Sergeant Major returned he could find all the men and vehicles gone while that young pillock of a First Lieutenant was marching up and down by himself. It would have been funny if they weren't related.

The Sergeant Major finished his drink and rose from his seat. 'Well, the sooner I get started the better, sir.'

'Good man,' said Colonel Brunswick and led him to the door. 'You know where I am if anything turns up. Good luck,' he said, extending his hand.

'Thank you, sir, I'll be in touch.' And with that he left the office.

The Colonel closed the door softly. He was on the horns of a dilemma; in fact, one of the points was in a very uncomfortable place. All the trouble had started since he'd appointed Lieutenant Jampton to take command of the Special Ordnance Group.

Had it been any other young officer, the answer would be simple: a quick posting to one of the farthest corners of the Empire where he could parade, salute and march to his heart's content. But unfortunately Lieutenant Jampton was not just any other officer: he was his nephew, and it was his wife Dorothy who had engineered his posting. If the truth be known, he feared Dorothy more than all the brass hats in Whitehall, and didn't those mandarins look upon Jampton as some sort of a hero? And hadn't the Colonel himself been honoured with the OBE for appointing Lieutenant Jampton to the command of the Special Ordnance Group?

A huge sigh escaped him. Damn and blast, he'd had enough of his nephew, Sparks and Miller. Fur was going to fly when he got his hands on them; they'd disappear all right and so would Lieutenant Jampton. And they'd be heroes again and decorated no doubt, but posthumously this time – he'd see to that. There were ways and means – having them parachuted behind the German lines was the first idea that sprang to mind. They wouldn't walk away from that, even if he had to pack the parachutes himself. There was a war on, goddammit!

Three minutes after nine o'clock that evening Sergeant Major Puller arrived at the Allied Forces Club ignoring the curious hostile stares as he entered. It was understandable – it wasn't the place for officers and senior NCOs. To his left a great mob shuffled round the dance floor paying no attention to the efforts of the sweating musicians. It was too hot for dancing anyway but this wasn't dancing: this was mobile coupling. Those that weren't part of the slow gyrations on the dance floor were eyeing the crumpet from the sidelines.

The Sergeant Major looked across to where the tables were; most of them were unoccupied. But one table was busy: a soldier with his back to him. It was his driver all right – he'd recognise that flat head anywhere. Seated opposite him were three girls hanging on to his every word. Whatever he was saying must be a great line. One of the girls turned towards the door, catching sight of the Sergeant Major. The SM pointed to the soldier at the table and the girl patted his arm. He looked over his shoulder, then stood up and hurried across.

'Any luck?' asked the Sergeant Major.

'Yeah,' said his driver. 'That one in the green dress, she's panting for it.'

The Sergeant Major passed his hand across his eyes in exasperation. 'I'm sure she is,' he said, 'but what about our lads?'

The driver was puzzled for a moment. 'Oh,' he said, 'Sparks and Miller.' He became confidential. 'Tell you what, Sergeant Major. I only had to mention they were mates of mine and the birds are round me like flies round a corned-beef tin.'

The Sergeant Major glanced over the driver's shoulder at the girls, heads together and now in animated, excited conversation.

'So it's obvious that Sparks and Miller aren't here.'

'No, sir. Bloody hell, if they were here nobody else would get a look-in. They could have their pick.'

'Right lad,' said the Sergeant Major, 'we'll go somewhere else.'

127

The driver was stricken. 'What about the birds, sir?'

'Say goodnight,' said the Sergeant Major gently, 'and I'll see you outside in one minute.'

'But, sir,' wailed the driver to the disappearing Sergeant Major. He turned to the table but the girls were still wrapped up in each other.

'Ah bollocks,' he muttered and went out to join his governor.

They visited two more places but, like the first, they were hopeless. Sergeant Major Puller came to the conclusion that there was no way Sparks and Miller would flaunt themselves in public but he felt in his bones they were still hidden away in deep cover somewhere in Alexandria. He dismissed his driver, who couldn't believe his luck and hurried back to the Allied Forces' dance to rejoin his fan club. Sergeant Major Puller smiled and made steps to the senior NCOs' mess for some serious drinking.

In Abdul's nightclub the volume of noise was lower than in the dancing places of the Allied troops. But there was the same frenetic atmosphere, that undercurrent of excitement that presages a typhoon, a plague of locusts, or imminent takeover by Rommel and his Afrika Korps. In one corner of the room a grand piano was played softly by the usual black man, strikingly handsome with a smile that flashed round the room like a second-hand lighthouse. Four drinks were lined up on the piano before him, testimony to his expertise and popularity.

On a table by the small dance floor Sparks and Yasmin faced each other. He ran his finger round his collar. The shirt seemed fine that morning but the heat must have shrunk it, he thought. He was still wearing the cheap off-white linen suit.

Most of the other tables were occupied, but because it was out of bounds to all troops there were no uniforms and probably no wives. It wasn't that kind of a place. There were enough girls to go round and, being professionals, they were wearing happy smiling faces behind which mental tills were pinging softly.

Dances had always fascinated Sparks: a herd of wildebeest scenting lion; too far away for immediate concern but close enough to stop them eating. He watched the dancers. No room for actual dancing, just enough for moving slowly in a one-way shuffle. It would be easier to make the floor go round and save everybody the trouble of having to move at all.

Yasmin looked at Sparks, thoughtfully twiddling the stem of her glass. 'What do you mean when you say "over the wall"?'

Sparks shrugged. 'Take off, disappear, scarper.'

'You mean desert?' asked Yasmin.

'If you like,' he said.

She was silent for a moment, then: 'Don't they shoot you for that?'

'They'll have to catch me first,' he added sardonically. It was time to change tack. 'How the hell did we get on to this subject anyway?' But she wouldn't let go.

'But you're not a coward, *mon cher*.'

He flinched at the endearment – it was getting too cosy.

'Don't you believe it, gel,' he said. 'I don't want to go home on a stretcher with a fag in me mouth and me thumb in the air. I'm a coward all right. Most of the heroes I knew are six feet under in a war grave.'

She reached across the table and put her hand in his. He thought for a second, then his hand stayed where it was. Bloody hell, what was happening to him? He'd been running off at the mouth like a lovesick teenager. He'd said more in the last few hours than he'd said all year and it was July, for God's sake. He could feel the shackles going on, and worse, he didn't dislike the sensation. It must be the Scotch. He looked into her eyes, though, and he knew it wasn't.

129

A well-dressed European approached their table and, ignoring Sparks, he addressed the girl.

'May I introduce myself? I am Hans Gruber. Good evening,' he said with a slight foreign accent. 'I am sure we have met,' he said, 'but the place eludes me.'

'I live in Paris,' replied Yasmin coolly.

'Ah Paris,' he said softly. 'I know it well.'

Sparks was getting restless, his fingers drummed on the table but the man went on as if he wasn't there.

'And that is where we have met; the George Cinq perhaps.'

Yasmin didn't reply. The man held out a gold cigarette case. She shook her head and he took one for himself and lit it. He blew smoke to the ceiling, then asked.

'And what brought you to Alexandria?'

Sparks had had a bellyful. 'Look, mate,' he said softly, 'that's enough questions for one night. Go and drink your sherbet.'

The man looked at him disdainfully. 'I'm sorry, forgive me.' He bowed stiffly and walked away.

Yasmin followed his departure with cold eyes, then turned to Sparks. 'I know that one,' she said. 'He claims to be Dutch but he's German.'

Sparks raised his eyebrows. 'Probably doing a bunk, same as me. Still, if we all did that there wouldn't be a war, eh?'

The pianist arpeggioed into a popular hit tune and couples started to gyrate slowly around the floor again. Yasmin smiled at Sparks, rose and pulled him to his feet. Good grief, he hadn't been on a dance floor since before the war and now here he was shuffling round like the rest of 'em.

Christ, he thought, better go easy on the Johnny Walker.

Yasmin was talking. 'Pardon?' he said.

'But you are a regular soldier, you enlisted.' She was back on that tack again.

'Yeah, that's right,' he said. 'Back in 1936 I was out of work and I was waiting in the pouring rain for a bus when I saw this poster. "Join the Army" it said and underneath it showed a laughing great pillock by a palm tree with a tennis racket in his hand. Well that was it. I always fancied meself at Wimbledon; I signed up the next day, but I didn't know there was going to be a war, did I?'

'But surely the Army fed you and clothed you; surely you mustn't complain if they ask you to fight in return.'

'I've been fighting,' said Sparks, bored with the topic now. 'They've had their four pennyworth out of me. Listen,' he went on, 'I'm starting to hate our officers now more than I do the Germans so I think it's time to move on.'

'But you can't beat the Army, Sparks. It's too big, too powerful.'

'I know,' he said, 'but you have to try, don't you?' He took her hand. 'Come on, let's sit down. I'm thirsty.'

As they came back to their table Abdul was waiting for them. Dry-washing his hands, he was in a bit of a state. Next to him was the tall German who claimed to be Dutch and knew Paris. Sparks pulled out the chair for Yasmin, then moved round and sat opposite. It was his turn to ignore the visitors.

'What'll you have to drink?' he asked Yasmin. She shook her head. Sparks snapped his fingers at Abdul. 'I'll have a large Scotch,' he said.

Abdul was unhappy and worried. 'Please,' he said, 'this gentleman here would like to buy the lady a drink.'

'She doesn't want a drink but I'll have a large Scotch, OK?'

'Please,' wailed Abdul bouncing from one foot to the other, 'this gentleman is an old and valued customer.'

'What about me?' said Sparks. 'I'm a founder member.'

131

The German broke in swiftly and smoothly. 'In that case you must be aware that it is against the rules to monopolise one of the girls unless, of course, you are willing to pay for the pleasure.'

'Are you willing to pay for the pleasure?' asked Sparks, matching the German's even tones.

'But of course,' said the German, bowing to Yasmin.

Sparks stood. 'As you wish,' he said and hit the German full in the face, knocking him arse over tit across the next two tables, scattering glasses and ashtrays. He was out cold. For a second there was a stunned silence, then pandemonium broke out as dancers surged round the table to see what was going on. Some people stood on chairs to get a better view and the pianist thumped into 'An Apple for the Teacher'. Waiters pushed their way through to clean up the broken glass and bits of food.

Abdul gazed horrified at the slack form of his old and valued customer.

'He's paid for it,' said Sparks coolly, then behind him he heard an urgent tinkling. 'Hurry it up,' he said to Yasmin. 'Abdul's little bell is a direct line to his muscle-bound minder and this room isn't big enough for both of us; it's hardly big enough for him.' He took her arm.

Yasmin was white and trembling. 'You said that nothing was ever settled by force.'

'Who says it's settled?' replied Sparks drily. 'He and I might get together again one day.' And with that he hustled her through the bead curtains, took hold of her hand and dragged her upstairs to their room. He stopped outside the door, listening.

'For God's sake, Sparks,' began Yasmin, but he silenced her with a finger to his lips. Cautiously he looked over the balustrade but there was no sign of pursuit. Satisfied, he entered his room quickly and quietly.

Yasmin shrugged and, as she was about to follow him, he returned to the door with a bundle of silk.

'Take your nightie somewhere else,' he whispered urgently. 'I'm expecting company.'

Before she could speak he pushed her into the corridor and slammed the door shut. Once inside he jammed a chair under the door handle. It was pathetic. Sickeningly, he thought of Abdul's great monster of a minder, those huge hands that could easily strangle a water buffalo, making his way purposefully up the stairs.

In a panic he dragged the chest of drawers behind the chair. It wasn't much but at least he'd have fair warning. Taking his rifle from the top of the wardrobe, he slapped in a magazine and pushed the bolt, levering a bullet up the spout. Fear gripped him as he thought of the monster again.

It was in this ready position that he awoke with a start. Sunlight was streaming through the window, so at least he'd got through the night. Quickly he looked to the door, but the chair and dresser were still in place. He stretched and smiled ruefully about his fears the night before. They had been unfounded.

This was what he thought and he couldn't have been more wrong. This was just a reprieve.

After another fruitless day of search, Sergeant Major Puller decided it would be easier to find a wandering yeti than Sparks and Miller. It was hopeless, and now, after a shower and a quick shave, he was in the senior NCOs' mess seated comfortably at a brass table littered with bottles of Stella beer, the chasers. It was the hard stuff in Dimple Haig bottles that did the damage. He was in the company of his old mate, Quartermaster Sergeant Docherty.

It was his last night in Alex and he was determined to hang one on. Soon he'd be back with the Special

Ordnance Group, and, if there was anybody left, they would be short on water now. He cleared his throat.

'My driver will be round at your place at first light for supplies, Doc,' he said.

'Aye, that's OK, Sam, just take what you want. I'll not be there myself but Sergeant Cockerell will attend to you.'

'Thanks, Doc.'

They downed two shorts, then reached for the Stella. It was a grand life. After a time the Quartermaster leant forward and tapped the Sergeant Major's knee.

'Any luck with that blue suitcase you were enquiring about?'

'Nah,' replied Puller. 'I've seen the RTO and he reckons that if it was left on the dockside it would probably be loaded back on the ship. He says my best bet is to write to Southampton – but bugger that for a lark. I have enough trouble just writing home.'

They sat together for another few minutes smoking quietly; it was good to be with your mates. A mess Corporal came up to the table. 'Sergeant Major Puller?' he enquired.

'That's me, laddie,' said Puller.

He took a folded note. It was a memo – he was to report soonest to Military Police barracks; information received regarding two lost lambs. He stood wearily. It always bloody happens when you're having fun.

'Problems?' asked the Quartermaster.

'Could be. If I'm not back in an hour, there're problems.'

He gulped down one of the glasses of Scotch. 'Well, if I don't see you again this time, I'll be back.'

'Sure you will, Sam.'

Puller took a deep breath to get himself in order. 'Just starting to hang one on, too.'

'Always the same,' said Doc. 'Be seeing you, so long.'

'Yes,' said Puller making his way to the door.

In the Military Police barracks an incident room had been set up and three Sergeants and an officer were poring over a street map when Sergeant Major Puller walked in. They turned and nodded a greeting. The Captain beamed.

'That was quick, Sergeant Major. Thanks for letting us know where you would be.'

Sergeant Major Puller nodded. Even he was not quite at ease in a Military Police barracks.

The Captain went on. 'The situation is this. We've had an anonymous telephone call and we think it's genuine. Sergeant Bailey here reports that he identified a three-ton Bedford truck turn into this street.' He tapped the map with a pencil. 'This street, by the way, is out of bounds to all military personnel. That's why it stuck in Bailey's mind. Somewhere up this street the truck vanished and as you can see it's a helluva long street. If we started a house-to-house search it would take forever and our birds would certainly get wind of it and fly the coop.'

Puller waited. It sounded good so far.

'Right, then,' said the Captain briskly. 'We make a dawn raid. Not too many people about and light enough to see what we're doing, OK?' He looked at the Sergeant Major.

'Sounds all right to me, sir, but which house are we raiding?'

'Ah well,' said the Captain shaking his head, 'that's where we have to rely on our mystery phone caller. If he's genuine, he'll be in the street and will point us to our objective.'

'What if he's not there, sir?'

The Captain shrugged. 'In that case we carry on up the street and come out the other end.'

Sergeant Major Puller nodded. Under the influence of the whisky, he thought this seemed a reasonable assumption.

135

The Captain went on. 'But from that moment both ends of the street will be kept under a strict surveillance. If they're there, they'll have to come out sometime. And make no mistake – once they've got wind of our slow patrol up the street they'll be spooked all right. They'll try to break cover sooner rather than later.'

'Right, sir. When do you want me at the start line?'

The Captain looked at his watch. 'Let's say four thirty a.m. That'll give us time for a final briefing and a cup of black coffee, I hope.' He laughed loudly. Who said a policeman's lot was not a happy one?

Some hours later as the streets were beginning to lighten, Sergeant Major Puller was sitting alongside the Captain in the lead jeep. He shivered from the cold of the morning air. A shower and several mugs of black coffee were clearing the whisky fumes from his brain and, with the adrenalin coursing through his blood, he was almost at maximum readiness.

Stealthily the six vehicles crawled up the deserted street. They hadn't gone more than eighty yards when a white-sleeved arm shot out from a dark doorway pointing across the street. This done, the arm disappeared just as quickly. The Captain and Sergeant Major Puller looked curiously at each other and back to the doorway. This time a man emerged and repeated his pointing to an import-and-export firm. He was uneasy at being out in the open and, having pointed again, hurried back into the shadow of his doorway.

The redcaps alighted and looked blankly at the shutters and then at the Captain. How the bloody hell were they going to get in? There was no entrance, a real weird setup. They turned to look for their informant and one of the Sergeants went across to the doorway and dragged out the man, who shook off the Sergeant's hand and hissed, 'I thought you would come in the dark.'

He wasn't a pretty sight: he had two enormous black eyes and a plaster over the bridge of his nose. Then quickly he looked sharply up and down the street, and reached up to press a part of the wood surrounding the shutters. Immediately the façade began slowly to move inwards and, as it did so, Hans Gruber scuttled back to the opposite dark doorway. The dark-haired Englishman would be paid in full for his moment of brutality.

Some of the redcaps remained outside to apprehend anybody making a bolt for it. But the main body entered the cavernous maw quickly and by the light of their torches they picked out the three-ton Bedford.

'Bull's-eye,' whispered the Captain and swiftly they moved up the two steps that led to the empty nightclub and above that the bedrooms. Whistles shrilled and they fanned out along the corridors. There was no need for stealth now. The idea was to create bedlam and panic and they certainly achieved this. Doors opened and worried faces peered out. Somewhere a woman screamed. But not having the full layout, the MPs had underestimated the extent of the honeycombed building. It sprawled out from the original façade over several shops on either side and they would have needed three times the manpower to cover the place.

The Captain came to a quick decision: search from the lower floor up making sure that nobody slipped through the net. This afforded rooms on the top floor breathing space.

And the rooms upstairs, being the smallest and cheapest, were where Sparks and Miller were billeted. Yasmin, organised and cool, pushed into Miller's room and shook him awake.

'Put this on,' she said and thrust a long black wig in his hands.

'What's up?' he said. 'What's all the racket?'

'Just put this on,' she spat. 'Ali will join you in a minute. He knows what to do.' And she was gone.

137

On the floor beneath, the redcaps systematically entered and searched every room. It was quite an experience. In one room a woman crouched on the floor, mother-naked, while behind her a tall man in white tuxedo jacket and holding an enormous feather looked round dispassionately as the Military Police hurried in, opening the wardrobe, looking under the bed, then, apparently satisfied, hurrying out and closing the door behind them. One of them, a Sergeant, let out a great breath.

'By the balls of St George,' he exclaimed, 'it takes all sorts.'

'I know, Sarge,' said his colleague still in a state of shock. 'But what does he do with the feather?'

The Sergeant looked at him in astonishment. 'I'll have a fatherly talk to you later,' he said, and they pushed into the next room.

A fat woman lay alone in bed. 'Get out of here, you pigs,' she said. 'Is my day off.' And when they looked under the bed she said, 'Is not there; there's one at little door at the end of corridor.' Then she heaved herself over and before they'd left she was snoring.

On the top floor now Yasmin hurried along the corridor followed by Sparks.

'In here, quickly.' There was one door that had a keyhole and Yasmin had the key. Quickly she opened the door and pushed Sparks into the room, slipping in behind him and locking the door.

'Bloody hell,' said Sparks. 'This room's a bit of all right.'

'Yes,' said Yasmin quickly. 'This is Hans Gruber's room, the man you hit in the face. Luckily he's away tonight.'

She hurried over to a large wardrobe. 'Quickly now,' she said, 'help me push this.' And between them they manoeuvred the piece out of the way. Behind it was a narrow opening and, squeezing through, Yasmin held out her hand to Sparks.

'*Vite, vite,*' she hissed, 'in here.'

With a little more difficulty he was through. What met his gaze stopped him dead in his tracks. The whole room was a mass of electrical equipment. On one side a huge wireless transmitter occupied the entire wall and smaller sets stood on a bench at the back.

'Blimey,' he muttered, completely awestruck. 'Well I'm damn sure this isn't just for *Forces Favourites.*'

He turned to Yasmin but she wasn't there. From the other room came a gasp and a strangled '*Merde!*'. Quickly he stepped through the narrow opening and saw her struggling to move the heavy wardrobe back into place. He pushed her away but before he could get his shoulder behind it Yasmin dragged him away and hissed, 'Don't be such a fool.' She tugged him to one side and pushed him back into the wireless room. 'I'm as big a fool as you,' she gabbled hurriedly. 'It was my intention to hide you in here. I'd forgotten the weight of the wardrobe.'

A whistle pierced the silence. Yasmin bit her lip in frustration – she had to think faster than she'd ever done in her life. Sparks took a step towards her but she angrily waved him away. Then suddenly she snapped her fingers. 'We have about three minutes so listen and do not interrupt.' She motioned towards the huge wireless transmitter. 'This is the centre of espionage of German Intelligence.'

Sparks was about to speak.

'Shut up and listen,' she said. 'This is what you will do.' And quickly she explained the plan.

In the corridor below Sergeant Major Puller flung open a door of the last room on that floor. Two redcaps followed him. In the bed a woman lay with her back towards them. Facing her, leaning on one elbow with his other arm round her, lay a middle-aged Egyptian. He was angry and hurled abuse at them in some language or other, but his meaning was clear.

'Won't be a minute,' said the Sergeant Major. 'Keep your hair on.'

They'd done under the bed and the wardrobe and as they made to leave the SM turned. 'Carry on smoking,' he said and closed the door behind him.

The 'woman' on the bed turned and breathed a sigh of relief. It was Dusty Miller in a wig. 'Cor, that was close,' he whispered. 'Thanks, mate.'

He turned to the man, who was looking at him in a strange way. Enlightenment dawned. He was out of bed like a flash, backing away clad only in his khaki underpants.

'Let's not get carried away, mister,' he said shakily.

The man fluttered his eyelashes. 'I help you, now you help me, yes? We can be nice to each other,' he simpered. 'I show you ecstasy, yes.'

Miller backed away. 'Don't let's be hasty. I'm warning you, mate.'

Outside in the corridor the Sergeant Major stopped as he heard the commotion, then with an almighty crash the Arab came flying through the closed door, wood and plaster flying everywhere. The Sergeant Major advanced cautiously. Stepping over the prostrate body, he stared through the hovering dust and the splintered remains of the door. A broad smile creased his face as he gazed upon Dusty Miller, still wearing the wig.

'Well, I didn't know he was ginger,' said Miller.

Puller pushed open what was left of the shattered door and beamed at him. 'You know,' he said, 'in that wig I could fancy you myself.'

Miller snatched off the wig and slung it on to the bed.

'Now come on, lad,' said the SM gently. 'Where's your mate?'

'Isn't he with you?' said Miller all innocent. 'I thought he was with you lot back at the camp.'

The MP slipped on the handcuffs, one round Miller's

140

wrist and the other he snapped round the bed rail. They still had one more room to search. The MP gave a blast on his whistle. It was the signal that one of them was in the bag. More MPs dashed up the stairs led by the Sergeant Major, who tried the handle of the first door they came to.

'This looks interesting,' he said, 'the only door that's locked.'

The MP, a sturdy lad from Newcastle, stood back and with one mighty thrust of his size twelves the door crashed open and in ten seconds the room was full of redcaps.

The Military Police Captain pushed his way through and stared at Sparks and Yasmin seated at the console.

'What's all this then?' he asked.

Sparks flung down a pencil in disgust. 'You've really messed it up this time,' he said. 'Another day and I'd have had the lot of 'em.'

On being taken to the Military Police barracks, Sparks, still feigning anger and frustration, insisted on making a statement. Miller looked on in disbelief. He had never heard his mate speak for so long nor with such fluency, calling into question the legitimate births of all Military Police, General Auchinleck and the Army and insisting that, given another two days, he would, without a doubt, have rounded up all the German agents in Alexandria, Cairo and possibly Lisbon. All this would not now be accomplished because of the bumbling of the British Army machine. This done, they were marched into a cell in the Military Police barracks, given a huge breakfast of bacon and eggs, and for the rest of the day nobody came near them.

It was a mistake. This gave them more than enough time to cobble up a plausible story. The reason they'd been left alone was a typical Army balls-up. Nobody knew who was to press charges. The MPs had a strong

141

case: Sparks and Miller had been picked up in an out-of-bounds area. But the Special Ordnance Group wanted to charge them as deserters.

Colonel Brunswick arrived and questioned Sparks and Miller in one of the debriefing rooms. They were questioned separately but by now had had plenty of time to get their stories together on what had transpired. This time they both made and signed statements. But after perusing them the Military Police were reluctant to charge them at all. Naturally, they didn't want to put themselves in the firing line by accusing two legends who quite possibly were sincere in their assertion that they were following a lead that had uncovered the German espionage network.

But Colonel Brunswick was also in a quandary. After all the adulation and canonisation of our two heroes, it wouldn't do. He, himself, had joined in the applause so now it was incongruous that he should denounce them as common deserters.

As for Sergeant Major Puller, he could see which way the wind was blowing. 'I knew it,' he muttered to himself. 'It's all going to end up smelling of bloody roses again.' And he left the building to get some fresh air.

Back at the Special Ordnance Group, it hadn't been a good day for Lieutenant Jampton either. For a start, the man he'd assigned as his batman forgot to wake him with an early-morning cup of tea, the result being he'd slept in till the sun was well into the sky. He hurriedly dressed and stepped out of his tent – and his heart nearly stopped. The place was deserted. Surely they hadn't all decamped during the night. He glanced at his wrist and realisation hit him. His watch wasn't there. He remembered he had lost it in a foolish bet with Sergeant Major Puller. He shaded his eyes and looked towards the sun, but he was no nearer judging the time.

His only conclusion was that it was daylight. Carefully, heart in his mouth, he approached the first tent and was greatly relieved when he heard steady snoring. He poked his head through the tent flap. The two lads were blissfully sleeping and, judging from the smiles on their faces, in a better world. Jampton's little mouth tightened and he kicked one of them not too gently. The sleeper came from wherever he'd been and rubbed his eyes.

' 'Ere, what's goin' on?' he said.

Jampton was beside himself. 'D'you know what time it is?' he snapped. It was meant as a rebuke but by now the whole camp knew about the CO's watch.

'Hang on a minute, sir,' said the man, helpfully fiddling in a boot for his watch. He stared at it, not fully awake yet, and said, 'It's a quarter past nine, sir.' Then he smiled and settled back in his blankets again.

For a moment Jampton was spellbound and then he found his voice. 'Get up! Get up, the pair of you!' he shrieked.

'Yes, sir,' they mumbled and scrambled to their feet.

Jampton was about to speak again when he noticed that one of them wore only a short singlet and socks. But Jampton's horrified stare was taken by the man's wherewithal: it was enormous. He seemed to recognise the scruffy short singlet. Could it be the pseudo-matador who'd greeted him on his first arrival at the camp? He'd been shocked then by the white hairy backside, but this was worse: it was a frontal view. Embarrassed, Jampton tore his eyes away and staggered outside into the hot sun. Good grief! Was the man deformed? Or perhaps it was some tropical disease. He didn't enter any other tents but strode back to his own for his swagger stick. From there he went from tent to tent, banging on the canvas, shouting, 'Out you get, rise and shine!' The cook hadn't even started breakfast.

'It's after nine o'clock, man,' shouted Jampton.

'I'm sorry, sir, I thought it was Sunday.'

It was three tents further on before the inanity of that remark hit Jampton. Sunday was a day like all the rest – the war didn't stop on the Sabbath. The camp was now crawling back to life but even so it was half past eleven before he mustered them all for roll call. When the Sergeant Major was here this was all taken care of and out of the way by eight o'clock. But dammit, wasn't he the Commanding Officer? He'd show them. And as a punishment, before they entered the mess tent for breakfast, he'd have them jogging around the camp perimeter three times. Oh yes, he'd show them who was boss all right.

Having explained all this to them he gave the order to 'Right turn' and smiled pompously as he watched them double out of the camp. This done, he strode over to the mess tent for a steaming mug of tea but when he entered it was deserted. 'Good Christmas,' he muttered. The cook was sweating round the perimeter with the rest of 'em.

Someone else came in behind him. He whirled in relief, but it was only Captain Witherspoon, the MO, holding a large mugful of gin. 'I saw all that,' he said. 'You're a hard man. Yes, sir. They'll know better next time.' And he strolled back to his own little world leaving Jampton mollified. And yes, the MO was right: he did have a way with the men.

Time passed and still no sign of his joggers. A new fear gripped him. Suppose they kept on running till they reached Alexandria? It was a stupid thought but then thinking wasn't his strong point. He heaved a sigh of relief when they finally appeared, still jogging. It never occurred to him they were returning the same way they had left; nor that the escarpment on the side of the camp could conceal so many men. Had he decided to take a stroll round the rocks, he might have wondered where all the cigarette butts had come from. He waved

144

his hands above his head. 'All right,' he yelled, 'that's enough.' And gratefully they wheeled abruptly and trotted sweating into the mess tent.

As they passed him he spotted Jackson, his new batman.

'Jackson,' he squeaked, 'fall out and come here.'

Jackson did as he was told and stood to attention.

'What happened to my early-morning cup of tea?' asked Jampton wishing he'd chosen a smaller batman. It wasn't dignified to have to look upward every time he gave him an order, even less dignified to carry a box round with him. He wished he still had his fifteen-hundredweight. That was always a good platform. He realised that Jackson hadn't replied.

'All right, then, I'll let it go this time but any more of it and you're on a charge.'

'Yes, sir,' replied Jackson stiffly.

'Good. Now a cup of tea and whatever else is going, in my tent, now! Is that clear?' And before Jackson could reply he swung on his heel and marched to his tent. Suddenly he stopped and turned again.

'Jackson,' he yelled.

'Sir,' Jackson yelled back.

'What time is it?'

Jackson looked at his wrist watch. 'Ten past twelve, sir.'

'Thank you,' replied Jampton, and ducked into his tent.

The first thing he noticed was the letter he'd been writing the night before. He sat down and picked it up.

Regimental Transport Officer
c/o Alexandria Docks.

Dear Sir,
  We met some time ago in your office where you handed me my movement orders. I was the first to

disembark and I would like to thank you for the help you gave me with directions to this location, etc.

I am now here – but unfortunately my suitcase is not. It was inadvertently left just outside your office – a large blue suitcase – and my name, rank and number is stencilled on both back and front . . .

An idea struck him. It might be easier if the RTO delivered it to his uncle, and, yes, Colonel Brunswick would carry some weight. After all, he did outrank the man. His thoughts were interrupted when Jackson bowed into the tent with a mug of lukewarm tea and a mess tin full of hard biscuits. Jampton's face fell.

'I'm sorry, sir, but that's what we're down to until Sparks and Miller get back with the rations.'

Jampton stared at him and what added insult to injury was the great blob of powdered egg on Jackson's chin.

'Well,' said Jampton, 'let me know the minute they get back.'

'Very good, sir.' And, pushing the tent flap to one side, Jackson ducked out.

Sparks and Miller spent their eighth day under close arrest in the Military Police barracks. Close arrest is probably too harsh a term. Eight days in a five-star luxury hotel would have been more appropriate, and they enjoyed their holiday. Too many people knew who they were and inevitably tongues were beginning to wag. Fan letters started to arrive at the barracks, boxes of chocolates, books, Havana cigars, and hundreds of cigarettes, all of which Sparks and Miller were happy to share with their gaolers who, in return, put carpets and white linen sheets in the cell and served breakfast in bed. They were even provided with a wireless so they could listen to Vera Lynn – they were exemplary prisoners.

However, investigations and discussions were still flying backward and forward between Whitehall and North Africa in an effort to decide what should be done with them.

Colonel Brunswick was summoned to the British Consulate and was immediately shown into the large ornate office of the Consul.

'Ah, Colonel Brunswick.' A tall, smartly dressed, grey-haired man rose from his chair and extended a hand across the desk.

The Colonel shook it, then placed his hat and baton on the desk before settling himself in a black leather chair. Then he noticed the bleak stare of the Consul and realised he hadn't been invited to sit. Surely he hadn't been expected to stand to attention throughout the interview. After all, he was a Colonel. He returned the baleful look and tried to regain some composure.

The Consul sat and cleared his throat. 'Tell me, Colonel Brunswick,' he began, 'Sparks and Miller.' He leant back in his chair and looked keenly at the Colonel, awaiting an answer.

Brunswick stared back. What was he supposed to say, and why had he been summoned so peremptorily? Sparks and Miller were strictly military, so why was he in the Consulate? His first thought had been wildly exciting. Was he to be asked to consider the acceptance of a knighthood? But the frostiness of his reception kicked this heady thought well over the grandstand.

'Sparks and Miller,' he returned as if he wasn't quite sure he should be discussing the matter.

The man leant his elbows on the desk and thrust his head forward. 'Colonel Brunswick, I would like you to understand that I am speaking on behalf of the Government at the very highest level . . .'

The Colonel felt a cold trickle of sweat from his armpit. He didn't like what he was hearing, nor the tone with which it was delivered. He could definitely forget his knighthood for a start. They might even ask him to return his OBE.

'Now,' went on the Consul, 'having cleared the decks as it were, I am authorised to acquaint you with a few details.' He looked steadily at the Colonel as if expecting a reply.

'May I smoke?' he said, and before the man could respond he was already patting his pockets, only to find he'd forgotten his pipe and cigarettes. He had only matches and he could hardly smoke one of them.

The Consul coolly pushed over a silver cigarette box and Colonel Brunswick gratefully helped himself. They were Turkish, cork-tipped, and in his confusion he lit the wrong end. Doggedly he drew on the cigarette hoping his clumsiness had gone unnoticed, which was highly improbable. Sparks were flying all over the place and he was frantically patting his thighs to avoid going up in flames.

The Consul rose diplomatically and walked over to the window. 'Colonel Brunswick,' he said to the view outside, 'your two heroes claim that owing to overhearing a suspicious conversation they followed a man to a notorious night spot and stumbled inadvertently upon the centre of German Espionage.' He turned from the window. 'Those are the facts?'

The Colonel, having stubbed out his flaming cigarette, nodded weakly. 'Broadly speaking, yes,' he coughed.

The Consul smiled sardonically and resumed his seat. 'Bullshit,' he snapped explosively.

The Colonel jerked bolt upright in his chair. Coming so unexpectedly from the lips of this cultured, sophisticated man, it was as if he had suddenly dropped his trousers and shouted, 'Anyone for tennis?' Pulling himself together, the Colonel replied.

'I tend to agree, sir,' he said lamely. 'I must admit, some of their testimony is extraordinarily coincidental and, er, fanciful.' He broke off as a pinprick of pain stabbed his thigh, and he thought he smelt burning.

'My dear Colonel,' said the Consul silkily, 'you don't believe their story any more than I do, and neither do my superiors in Whitehall.'

The Colonel bristled. He wasn't some day boy being carpeted by his form master: he was the Director of Military Intelligence, for God's sake. But even as the thought crossed his mind he dismissed it. He might be one of the bigger fish in Alex but in the corridors of Westminster he wasn't even plankton bait and the Consul was merely voicing the instructions of the War Cabinet. But then again, wasn't this purely a military matter?

As if reading his thoughts the Consul went on. 'In the normal course of events it would be dealt with summarily by one of your courts martial, but I'm afraid the whole situation has now become political dynamite between us and the French.'

'Us and the French?' repeated the Colonel stupidly.

'Yes,' replied the Consul. 'The search for the enemy transmitter was a joint Anglo-French operation, was it not?'

Brunswick nodded, then enlightenment dawned. 'I see it all now, sir. Typical French. They're squealing like stuck pigs because we got there first.'

'Hardly,' said the Consul, 'the French apparently uncovered the transmitter seven months ago.'

Brunswick's mouth fell open in astonishment. He was absolutely dumbfounded. How could this be? He and his French counterpart held meetings at least once a week to compare notes. He stared incredulously at the Consul. 'Seven months?' he gasped.

'I'm afraid so,' said the Consul.

Colonel Brunswick rose slowly to his feet and began

pacing thoughtfully up and down the carpet. It was all becoming clear now – the number of abortive raids based mainly on French Intelligence, and the number of times he'd been assured that the area around Abdul ben Hussein's establishment had been swept clean by French agents.

'The bastards,' he muttered.

'I tend to agree with you, Colonel,' said the Consul. 'Churchill and de Gaulle have been at each other's throats and the entente cordiale is in a very parlous state.'

Colonel Brunswick stopped his walkabout and slumped back in his chair. He shook his head disbelievingly, still unable to take it in. 'But the transmitter was in operation right up to the time we closed it down last week.'

'Of course,' said the Consul, 'when the French agent penetrated their source of transmission, the code books were photographed.' He shrugged his shoulders. 'Naturally this enabled the French to decipher all communications between Rommel's Headquarters and the Abwehr.'

Brunswick screwed up his eyes. While his backroom boys were going spare trying desperately to break the code, their French counterparts had been going through the motions. 'But goddammit,' he blurted, 'why didn't they let us know?'

The Consul smiled wryly and spread his hands. 'They didn't trust us not to blow the whistle and have the station shut down.' He paused. 'Exactly as you did. However, the good news is that the French double-cross in withholding information is Winston's strong card and de Gaulle will have to climb down and toe the line.'

After a time the Colonel rose. 'And what about Sparks and Miller?' he asked.

'Ah yes,' said the Consul, 'Sparks and Miller.' He cleared his throat. 'We come now to the crux of the matter and the reason for our meeting.'

Colonel Brunswick sighed. He'd already had the crux. Was there more, for God's sake?'

The Consul cleared his throat. 'The popularity of Sparks and Miller is such that Whitehall was about to have them taken out of the battle zone for a personal tour of the British Isles.' He paused. 'However, this latest escapade has put the tin lid firmly on their triumphal tour of Blighty, and this is the scenario I am instructed to pass on to you.'

The Colonel craned forward eagerly.

'First of all,' said the Consul, 'it must be fully understood that no meeting at any level has been convened to discuss this matter. In fact, the whole of this suggestion is entirely your own idea.'

Brunswick nodded weakly. He knew the form. If it all went wrong he'd be the one with the black hood over his head standing on the trapdoor.

The Consul continued. 'On your own initiative you approached Sparks and Miller with a proposal and on acceptance you clandestinely enrolled them in the Intelligence Service.'

Colonel Brunswick's eyes widened in disbelief.

The Consul nodded. 'I know,' he said, 'but this is what I am instructed to pass on to you. I am merely the messenger.'

He went on: 'As their superior you ordered them to make their way to Alexandria and thence to the address of Abdul ben Hussein and see what they could uncover.' He looked directly at the Colonel. 'Are you with me so far?'

Brunswick nodded. It was getting better by the minute. After all, it had had a successful outcome; why shouldn't he be the instigator? He decided to elaborate a little. 'Ah yes, the reason we couldn't send in any of our regular agents –' he shrugged and spread his hands '– it would have created a breach of confidence with our French allies.'

151

The Consul couldn't believe his ears. After all, he was merely passing on a face-saving formula cobbled up in London and this idiot sounded like he was starting to believe it. 'Yes, well,' he said, 'be that as it may . . .'

He desperately wanted to terminate this interview. 'Naturally,' he went on, 'none of this will reach the news media. The discovery of this transmitter is classified material and in this case *especially* classified.'

'I understand,' agreed the Colonel.

'I believe,' concluded the Consul, 'I have passed on all the information supplied to me by my superiors, and I do not have to tell you that this conversation never took place.' He looked for a moment at the Colonel and sighed. 'Have I made myself clear or is there anything you would like me to clarify?'

The Colonel, recognising the bum's rush, rose to his feet with dignity. 'As this conversation never took place,' he said coldly, 'I would like to remind you that I am not a fool and I resent your treating me as one.'

The Consul regarded him steadily while he digested the outburst. The first part was debatable, and as for the second half, how else did you treat a man who believed the trumped-up poppycock constructed in this elaborate cover-up? Not only that, he'd almost set fire to himself before this conversation never took place.

Colonel Brunswick wriggled uneasily in the silence. Had he said too much? Ah well, bugger the knighthood and roll on peacetime, when he could carry on his soldiering in a more leisurely fashion.

The Consul rose to terminate the meeting.

'Incidentally,' he said, 'you are to promote Sparks and Miller to the rank of Sergeant. After all, they are to be rewarded for their services to British Military Intelligence and are to be returned to their unit forthwith and with God's help that will be the end of the matter.'

'Very good,' muttered the Colonel looking as if he

had been hit by a steam hammer. 'I'll inform Lieutenant Jampton.'

'Ah yes,' said the Consul, 'Lieutenant Jampton ... would naturally have to be a party to this. He is upgraded to the rank of Captain.'

Brunswick reeled back. What comic opera was he in? At this rate in a few months he'd be standing before Jampton's desk calling *him* sir. He waited for a moment or two, hoping to hear some good news about his own career prospects, but then as the Consul took some papers from a drawer in his desk he realised this was a sign of dismissal. So he picked up his cap and baton and made his way towards the door.

The Consul spoke. 'By the way, Colonel, did you ever come across a French woman by the name of Estelle Chambertin?'

Brunswick looked at the floor. 'Estelle Chambertin?' he repeated.

'A young society beauty in Alexandria before the war.'

'Ah,' said Brunswick, straightening his shoulders, 'before the war I was a serving officer in India.' Then as an afterthought he asked, 'Should I have known her, sir?'

'It's of no importance,' said the Consul. 'Only she was one of the best agents in French intelligence. It was she who cracked the location of the enemy transmitter and who photographed the code books.'

The Colonel whistled softly. 'Estelle Chambertin,' he muttered.

The Consul nodded. 'Her cover name, however, was Yasmin.'

The Colonel nodded again. 'I'd like to meet her one day,' he said and opened the door.

'That won't be possible,' said the Consul. 'According to the French Intelligence she was killed in Tobruk when the Germans took it.'

'I'm sorry,' said the Colonel, and let himself out.

As soon as he left the building he let out a long sigh of relief, recollecting the interview as he pushed his way through the crowded thoroughfare. Well, interview wasn't exactly the right word – it was more of a bollocking, really. This thought rushed to the surface of his mind, dragging anger with it. Sparks and Miller would pay for this, by God they would. It was obvious their main objective had been to desert and in defending their attempt to cover up, he'd been made to look a right nana. The passers-by parted to give him passage when they saw the look on his face. It was the same look in any language – 'Get out of my way or I'll kill you.'

He almost broke into a run but stopped himself just in time. Colonels didn't run, they had other ranks to do that for them. Slowing his pace had a calming effect on him and by the time he'd reached the Ministry of Ag and Fish he was in a more rational frame of mind.

CHAPTER
SIX

When Sergeant Major Puller and his flat-headed driver rolled into camp followed by the second three-tonner and two water bowsers, Lieutenant Jampton shot out of his tent as if he'd been spat out of a peashooter and he could hardly conceal his relief when Sparks and Miller alighted and stopped before him bringing up two fine military salutes. But there was something different about them and it wasn't just Miller's haircut. Then he suddenly tumbled: they both sported the white chevrons of Sergeants so whatever they'd been up to in Alex had been successful enough to gain them promotion. Then an awful thought struck him. If they had made Sergeant, what heights must Sergeant Major Puller have reached? He hoped to God he still outranked him.

The Sergeant Major jumped down from the cab wearily and saluted his Commanding Officer. Thank God, thought Jampton, I'm still in charge.

As the trucks were unloaded, Jampton's eyes gleamed with suppressed excitement – crates of rifles and light machine guns were offloaded. He hadn't expected to receive these, but the truth of the matter was that the RAOC in Alexandria would have supplied anybody with whole arsenals of bombs, land mines, high-explosive shells – in fact anything to clear the decks before Rommel could get his hands on them.

For the young Lieutenant it was Christmas morning, especially when the Sergeant Major handed him a package marked 'Private and Confidential'. He slit it open and a handful of cloth pips fell out on to the ground and, reaching in, he pulled out the citation informing him that he was now promoted to the rank of Captain.

Sergeant Major Puller couldn't believe his eyes as he looked round the camp. Small changes had been made during their adventures in Alexandria. The guy ropes on the CO's tent had been painted white, many new stones had been found and painted white also and these formed dinky little paths criss-crossing the camp. All they were short of was a wishing well, half a dozen donkeys and a model railway and they could have run day trips for the poor kids of Alexandria.

Besides all this reorganisation, Jampton had been working on a scheme for a night exercise. It was brilliant in its simplicity – a convoy of trucks with himself at the head. They would travel fifteen miles southeast under cover of darkness, returning to encircle the camp. They would then break into two sections just before first light and with a pincer movement execute a mock attack from two sides. Umpires with white armbands stationed at various points around the perimeter would judge the successes. He couldn't wait to pass on his plan to his three senior NCOs – but first things first. He had to get his extra pips sewn on to his epaulettes.

The lads would be pleased. He felt that he was making great progress with them. As two of the lads had walked past his tent one night he'd heard himself referred to as 'Hugh'. It wasn't a bad nickname. It had a warm familiarity about it and he was not displeased.

If only he had known that Hampton Wick was Cockney rhyming slang alluding to a man's anatomy and Hugh Jampton denoted one of great size.

On 7 August the brand-new Captain Jampton was strutting busily inspecting various parts of his camp, head swinging from side to side, eyes down in order to keep them on his new Captain's pips. He hadn't the foggiest idea how he'd come by this promotion. Naturally he'd interrogated the Sergeant Major and Sergeants Sparks and Miller but to his every question they had replied 'Classified'. They were as close-mouthed as a suffragette on a hunger strike.

He had acquainted the three of them of his night exercise and they hadn't exactly demurred. However, he wasn't taking any chances and for the last two evenings had had the rotor arms from all the vehicles brought to him. So if they wanted to desert again, they were welcome to walk.

It was an uncomfortably hot morning and he decided that a lemonade was in order, so he made his way back to his tent, and while he sat sipping his drink his heart beat fast with excitement as he thought of this evening's exercise. What fun! Quickly he erased this last thought from his mind. It wasn't fun, it was war. His jaw set firmly and he had a steely glint in his eye; to be more exact he thought he had. He decided to check this out. Rising quickly from his chair he stepped towards the mirror but as he bent to look into it he recoiled in horror: a large squashed fly was smeared over the glass.

At that moment his batman, Jackson, entered with Jampton's afternoon tea. Jackson put the cup and saucer down reverently. Only the common soldier drank out of enamel mugs. He was about to leave when his CO called him back. Jackson turned with a sigh of exasperation.

'Yes, sir?'

Jampton eyed him coldly. 'Your job,' he said in biting tones, 'is to keep my billet clean and tidy.'

Jackson frowned. 'Well with due respect, sir, it's not in bad shape for a tent in the desert.'

'Oh really?' replied his CO. 'Then may I ask what that fly is doing on my shaving mirror?'

Jackson craned his head round the tent pole, then he looked across at Jampton. 'Not a lot, sir. He's dead.'

'I can see that,' snapped Jampton waspishly. 'I am a soldier.' He said this with heavy sarcasm, although it was the first dead thing he'd seen in his short military career. Then even he realised the stupidity of his remark. 'Clean it up at once.'

Jackson took a dirty khaki handkerchief from his pocket and spat on the mirror. Jampton's stomach lurched. 'Not in here, man, take it to the mess tent and wash it thoroughly in boiling water and disinfectant.'

Jackson lifted the small round mirror from its nail, and as he was about to leave the tent Jampton called after him, 'And kindly inform Sergeants Sparks and Miller I'm ready for them now.'

'Yes, sir,' replied Jackson, and when he was outside he turned back towards the tent and curtsied.

In a tent marked SENIOR NCOs Sergeants Sparks and Miller sat cross-legged on a blanket facing each other. 'Yours and up twenty,' said Sparks and pushed a pile of matches into the centre. Miller looked at his cards, panic-stricken. He wasn't a good poker player – if he was dealt a handful of rubbish he'd groan and moan, and if ever he was dealt a full house or a royal flush he'd most likely faint. Sparks took a long swig from a bottle of Stella. He was unconcerned; they were only playing for matches, for God's sake. Still it passed the time.

Miller, in an agony of indecision, glared at his cards. At that moment Jackson stuck his head through the tent flap. 'Hugh wants to see you pronto,' he said.

Sparks and Miller ignored him and after a couple of minutes Miller tore his eyes from the cards and spoke to Jackson, who was still there. 'All right,' he said, 'we got the message.'

Jackson didn't move. He was probably hoping to be offered a bottle of beer, but Miller wasn't having any.

'What are you waiting for,' he said, 'a twenty-one-gun salute?'

Jackson withdrew his head.

Throwing down his hand, Sparks said, 'Come on, let's make tracks.'

Greatly relieved, Miller threw his own hand down and rose.

'I hope it's not tonight,' muttered Sparks.

'What's wrong with tonight?' asked Miller.

'Have you seen the weather?'

'Yeah,' replied Miller enthusiastically and ducked out of the tent.

Sparks stood thoughtfully for a moment. He knew his oppo and he didn't trust the eager way he'd said yeah. Hurriedly he ducked out into the hot furnace of the afternoon. There was no sun, however, just a brassy sky. He caught up with Miller and grabbed his arm.

'All right, arsehole,' he said. 'What d'you have in mind?'

'Me?' asked Miller, innocent as a first-year choirboy.

And before Sparks could tap him further they were joined by Sergeant Major Puller and wordlessly they made their way on to the CO's tent and ducked inside.

'Make yourselves comfortable, gentlemen,' said Jampton, gesturing to the three upturned beer crates.

When they'd entered his head was bent over the maps on the table so he couldn't be sure if they'd saluted. No matter – there were more important things to discuss. He glanced round at the blank respectful faces.

'It's tonight gentlemen,' he said dramatically and waited eagerly for their reaction.

It wasn't exactly exuberant. To be more accurate it was received with bored indifference, so he pressed on. He turned towards the blackboard, on which was pinned a large map of the North African Desert. Over this large yellow area Jampton had pencilled lots of circles, triangles and thousands of arrows pointing every which way, rather reminiscent of the Bayeux Tapestries depicting the Battle of Hastings. With his pointer he rapped on the map to emphasise his words – speed of the convoy, supplies, the blackening of faces, passwords, and general tactics. After twenty minutes he turned from his blackboard to his audience.

'Any questions?' he beamed.

Sergeant Major Puller, who had been sitting with his arms on his knees, head down, eyes closed, raised his head wearily and said, 'Pardon, sir?'

Jampton, brought down to earth, repeated lamely, 'Any questions?'

They looked at one another, then after a time Miller put up his hand and asked, 'Any mail for us while we were away?'

Jampton sighed in exasperation. 'Let me reiterate,' he said, 'and go over the salient points again. The convoy will consist of eight three-tonners. I will be leading in my fifteen-hundredweight; you Sergeant Major, in the fourth vehicle and Sergeants Sparks and Miller in the second fifteen-hundredweight will take up the rear. Questions, gentlemen?'

Sergeant Major Puller looked across at Miller, who returned the stare with an expression too innocent to be honest. Puller turned towards the CO.

'You did say Sergeants Sparks and Miller would take up the rear, sir?' he asked.

'I did, Sergeant Major.' He shrugged his thin shoulders. 'I had no choice; Sergeant Miller volunteered.'

Half to himself, the Sergeant Major muttered, 'Yes, I'd a feeling he might.'

God almighty, placing these two at the rear of the convoy was like putting juicy beefsteak in front of a hungry dog and telling it to sit.

Miller jumped in. 'I know it's a risky placement, sir,' he said earnestly in his best Errol Flynn impersonation, 'but the lads would feel easier knowing we were backup.'

'Jesus,' breathed Sparks and turned away, only to find himself staring at a portrait of the King and Queen hanging from the ridge pole. It's a madhouse, he thought. His gaze swept over the neatly folded blankets on the bed. A bed, for God's sake. Where the hell had Hugh come by that? He craned slowly forward to see if there was a pisspot underneath.

'Well, the order of march is settled then,' chirped Jampton.

'It seems to me,' said the Sergeant Major, 'this is all academic. We won't be going out tonight, sir.'

Jampton was thunderstruck. This sounded dangerously like mutiny. 'May I ask why not?' He must remember this for the court martial.

'Weather conditions,' replied the Sergeant Major.

Jampton relaxed. 'The weather,' he snorted. 'I know it's hot now, of course it's hot.' He leant forward. 'But you seem to have forgotten that this is a night exercise. It'll be bl–' He stopped himself. He almost said bloody cold but not in front of the men. Next thing they'd be calling him Wilfred.

The Sergeant Major sighed. 'I don't think you quite understood, sir. There's a dark band along the horizon on the south, sir, a khamsin, and if my guess is right, it's going to be the daddy of all sandstorms and it's heading our way.'

Jampton's mouth opened and his eyes stared ahead as if trying to see through the canvas to the south. He gulped noisily. 'A sandstorm,' he muttered stupidly.

'Yes, sir,' said Puller relentlessly. 'And in a sandstorm nothing moves except the desert. Even the camels hunker down until it's blown itself out.'

Jampton looked as if he would burst into tears. It wasn't fair. He couldn't go out to bat because it had started to rain. He was saved, however, when Sergeant Miller intervened.

'With due respect to Sarn't Major Puller, sir,' he began, 'we're a fighting unit and war does not wait for weather conditions. This would be a test of our combat efficiency in the worst of all climatic conditions.'

Jampton brightened and metaphorically he put his pads back on.

Miller continued: 'And to go out on this night we will be stretched to the limits of our endurance.'

With this, he leant back, remembering just in time that he was seated on an upturned beer crate and to topple to the floor would have taken the gloss from his morale-boosting speech.

Sparks stared aghast, especially when he saw the relief on Jampton's face.

'My thoughts entirely,' snapped the little CO, jabbing the point of a pair of compasses into the map so hard that when he tried to pull them out the table rose slightly and his cup of tea slid gently to the edge and crashed to the floor.

Sparks gazed down at the smashed crockery and watched the tea disappearing down a crack in the floorboards. Good Christmas, he thought. Floorboards, for God's sake! I wonder what the bathroom's like.

The meeting lasted another two hours, during which Jampton lectured on the history of the British Army going back to Henry V, Part II, through the Crimea and up to the present day. Sergeant Major Puller, watching him with glazed eyes, hadn't uttered a word and Sparks had slowly fallen sideways off his packing case fast asleep. Miller sprang forward, helped him to his feet and explained to his Commanding Officer it was a recurring bout of malaria and Sparks had obviously forgotten to take his medication. And with that he helped Sparks out of the tent, presumably to visit the MO.

As soon as they left, Sergeant Major Puller deemed it a good opportunity to change Jampton's mind. Deep

African darkness had fallen outside and outriders of the khamsin were beginning to cause the tent to billow and wriggle. Vainly, Sergeant Major Puller tried to point out the dangers of the coming exercise. In weather like this they could drive blindly into an enemy stronghold, drive arse over tit into a deep wadi, get bogged down in the Qatari Depression.

'That's fifty miles off our course,' Jampton replied.

The Sergeant Major shook his head. Fifty miles off track was quite likely with Jampton navigating. The Sergeant Major had then persevered. There were also the marshlands, and he had to explain that marshland was the desert jargon for minefield.

But no matter what objections the Sergeant Major had come up with, they fell on deaf ears. The little prat jocularly enquired if the Sergeant Major was getting cold feet. Jampton seemed to revel in the elements. Mind you, he didn't look so cocksure when he stepped out of the tent and the wind blew him back in again. The Sergeant Major gave it up as a bad job. It was like talking to a deaf camel. Disgustedly he made his way back to his own billet.

At 2300 hours the convoy was lined up rocking furiously under the onslaught of shrieking sand. All the crews were aboard and waiting patiently for their Commanding Officer. An ironic cheer went up as Jampton emerged from his tent. Sergeant Major Puller, from the cab of his three-tonner, watched the dim figure approaching. He was no match for the wind. It was like watching a wounded dung beetle struggling to its last resting place, one step forward and two steps back. Exasperated, the Sergeant Major heaved the door of the cab open and let himself down to assist the pathetic figure. Grabbing his arm, he dragged him to the lee of the nearest vehicle. It wasn't much better but at least they could stand, provided they held on to the tailgate.

Puller made a last plea for common sense. Putting his

mouth to Jampton's ear he shouted, 'Abort this exercise, sir. Tomorrow night will be better.'

Jampton could see that this was the only sensible course and was about to agree when, with some odd freak of nature, the ferocity of the storm lessened as if the wind itself wanted to hear the verdict.

Jampton's head came up as he noticed the lull and he had a vision of his Aunt Dorothy at the dinner table: 'Wilfred may not look as strong as other boys but he has a backbone of pure British steel.'

It was enough. Jampton straightened. 'The exercise will proceed as planned,' he piped, and with that he left the shelter of the wagon.

It was a mistake. The desert storm, angry at his decision, picked him up and hurled him backwards into the arms of the Sergeant Major. But the die was cast – Puller struggled with him and with the help of the driver managed to manhandle him into his fifteen-hundredweight at the head of the column.

Once inside the security of the cab, protected against the maniacal screaming of the khamsin, Jampton felt better. He'd show his men that he wasn't just their Commanding Officer, he was a leader. Hadn't they all laughed at Hannibal when he took his elephants over the Alps. He gazed along the faint beams of the headlights as the bits of sand and grit flew towards him, glistening as they hurled themselves at the windscreen at fantastic speed. Shaking himself out of his hypnosis, he picked up his handset.

'Point to rear, do you read me? Over.'

He waited a moment. Through the static he faintly heard Miller's voice. 'Rear to point, Strength two. Out.'

Jampton flicked his switch again. 'Point to all vehicles, advance.' And the convoy lurched slowly into the teeth of one of the worst storms in living memory.

The Sergeant Major, in the passenger seat of his three-ton Bedford, swayed as the vehicle lurched over the uneven terrain. He was an angry man. He'd served under many useless officers during his military career but Jampton took first prize. The sheer arrogance and stupidity of the little prat beggared belief. The Sergeant Major regretted the promise he'd made to Colonel Brunswick, a promise that he would keep an eye on his nephew and guide him in the hopes that one day he may prove himself. It was becoming an impossible task – like trying to train a tsetse fly to be a vegetarian. And like tonight's lunatic episode the tsetse fly had the capacity to kill.

The convoy struggled into the storm. They were grinding into the teeth of it and it was awe-inspiring. Jampton, in the lead vehicle, was scared out of his wits. He'd had the headlight covers removed in order to give him better night vision, but all he had was about three yards. A normal CO would have aborted the exercise, but this was Jampton, and wasn't he at the front?

Sergeant Major Puller, only a yard or so from the vehicle they were following, glanced across at the dark figure of his driver, Old Flathead, who was desperately trying to keep in view the two faint rear lights of the vehicle in front.

'Bloody 'ell,' he said, 'we want our 'eads examined. I wouldn't send 'Itler out on a night like this.'

It was horrendous. The winscreen wipers were useless, smearing the glass in the all-too-infrequent lulls. It was so bad that some of the lads had left letters with their mates at the camp to be posted in case they didn't return.

Jampton's voice crackled over the intercom. 'Point to rear, everything all right?' There was a rush of static, then a faint voice: 'OK, sir. No problem. Over and out.'

Sergeant Major Puller listened to this exchange, as did all the convoy. His mouth was gritted with sand. It was sheer lunacy.

Another burst of static and the CO's piping voice

enquiring as to the welfare of the convoy. The Sergeant Major groaned. He had a feeling the CO was enjoying the challenge. The radio squawked again. 'God blimey,' ejaculated the Sergeant Major. If the prat had a gramophone in his cab, he'd be playing record requests.

Slowly and ponderously the convoy forced its cumbersome trek through the howling sand. Every five minutes or so point-to-rear communications were issued. The Sergeant Major smiled grimly. At least the little arsehole was now beginning to have doubts as to the wisdom of having Sparks and Miller at the back end.

At the rear end of the convoy Sparks and Miller were in the middle of a heated argument.

'Major Crawley?' exploded Sparks.

'Yes, Major Crawley. He was the best officer we ever had.'

'Bollocks.'

'It's not bollocks,' yelled Miller. His voice was raised not so much in anger, but rather to make himself audible above the shrieking madness of the storm.

'Creepy Crawley was an arsehole,' insisted Sparks. 'He was a forty-year-old Jampton.'

'Jampton wasn't killed at Tobruk, was he?'

Sparks looked across at the dark, hunched shape of his passenger.

'What are you on about?' he said finally. 'Neither was Creepy Crawley.'

'Course he was, I'm telling you he was.'

'Well, you're bloody wrong, mate.'

Sparks slapped the wheel in exasperation. 'A week before Tobruk he went up to Alex for a conference.'

It slowly sunk into Miller's mind that Sparks was right. Major Crawley had been at a high-level conference in Alexandria but he wasn't going to admit he was wrong.

'All right,' he said. 'He may have left for Alex but nobody's seen him since.'

Sparks slapped his forehead in exasperation. 'He's in the base hospital at Alexandria, you great steaming pillock.'

There was silence for quite a few moments, then Miller said, 'Where was he wounded?'

'He wasn't wounded, either,' said Sparks, beating the wheel to emphasise each word. 'He went to a high-level conference and pissed as a fart he fell out of a gharry and broke his leg.'

Sparks waited for a reply but there wasn't one.

Miller was hunched forward, nose to the windscreen.

'What've you seen?' asked Sparks.

'Nothing,' said Miller.

Sparks relaxed, then Miller thumped him on the arm. 'Didn't you hear me?' he yelled. 'Where's the bloody rear lights?'

Instantly Sparks put his foot down and the fifteen-hundredweight shot forward, but, strain as they might, there were no two red pinpricks of light ahead.

'Get on the blower to Hugh.'

Miller took up the microphone. 'What shall I tell him?'

'Just contact him, you useless pillock. Tell him we've got a puncture, the engine's packed in ... I dunno ... We've stopped for a picnic.'

Miller was already trying to raise the convoy but it was hopeless and with a sickening feeling they realised that they were utterly lost in a wild, screaming frenzy of a world gone mad.

Sparks eased up on the accelerator.

'Go on, go on!' urged Miller.

And so they bumped, lurched and lolloped into the ever-increasing maelstrom. But they had no chance of catching up with the convoy – they might just as well have tried to cross the Atlantic on foot.

Miles ahead, Sergeant Major Puller groaned as the wireless clicked again.

Jampton's voice squeaked through but this time it wasn't the usual enquiry about his rear guard. 'Point to all transport, ten minutes' halt. Out.'

Thank God and little apples for that, thought the Sergeant Major. Now was the time to have a word in private with his CO. The amount of wireless traffic emanating from his fifteen-hundredweight during the journey would have been picked up by every listening post within a twenty-five-mile radius, and could have been interpreted as anything from the convoy they were to a tank battalion moving to their start lines in preparation for a full-scale attack. Even in this weather German units could already be standing to on red alert.

He struggled to force his door open. The strength and scream of the wind fought him as he pulled himself alongside the vehicles to Jampton's fifteen-hundred-weight. The twenty yards or so by the side of the dim line of vehicles was the longest twenty yards of his life.

He clambered into the back breathing as if he had run all the way from Cairo. He tapped his CO on the shoulder. Jampton gave a startled yelp and whirled to the dark hulk leaning over him. The Sergeant Major put his mouth to the CO's ear. 'Your wireless trans-missions, sir.'

'Pardon?' yelled Jampton.

'Cut down on your wireless transmission – easy for an enemy to pinpoint.'

'Oh,' shouted Jampton, 'transmission.' He snatched up the mouthpiece and put it to his lips. 'Point to rear. Over.'

Puller shook his head, exasperated. He was about to repeat his warning when he stopped suddenly. On the wireless there was only static. Jampton was unpertur-bed, however, and again he pressed his transmit button. 'Point to rear, I say again, do you read me? Over.' And once more there was no reply.

After a few moments the Sergeant Major shook his

head, and then: 'The crafty bastards,' he muttered. They'd hopped it again. He was sure, now, and reluctantly he had to admire their single-mindedness. This time they'd get away with it. The stupidity of a night exercise with conditions like this ... They'd be lucky if the whole convoy didn't disappear as well.

Jampton pressed the transmit button again, but the Sergeant Major gently took the instrument from him. 'May I suggest something, sir?'

Jampton nodded eagerly. He was near to panic. It was enough that he'd lost Sparks and Miller again and any help from whatever quarter was more than welcome.

The Sergeant Major continued. 'I suggest, sir, we head back for camp,' he shouted, and paused as the demoniacal wind rose to a shriek. When the screaming died to an acceptable level he pressed on: 'This way we have every chance of running into Sparks and Miller if they've broken down somewhere, in which case –'

But here Jampton interrupted. 'I've got a better idea,' he shouted. 'We'll make our way back to camp and with any luck we may come across Sparks and Miller.'

The Sergeant Major added sarcastically, 'I was about to suggest something like that.'

He turned to leave Jampton's fifteen-hundredweight when a hand restrained him. He looked back to the shape of his CO.

'Sergeant Major,' shouted Jampton, 'I want you to lead us back to camp.'

Puller eyed him suspiciously.

Jampton craned towards his ear. 'It'll be good experience for you and should anything happen to me in actual combat it would be your responsibility anyway.' And before the Sergeant Major could reply, he'd forced himself out of the door in order to make his way to the Sergeant Major's vehicle in the middle of the convoy.

The Sergeant Major clambered over and took the CO's vacant seat. But before he'd settled the radio crackled and he heard the tinny voice of his CO: 'Wagons Roll!' There was a click as communication was broken off.

'Bloody 'ell,' breathed the Sergeant Major, 'that was quick.'

Jampton had obviously been blown four vehicles' length in three seconds. He nodded to the driver, who turned his ignition key, and after some heart-stopping moments the engine roared into life.

The journey back was a doddle; the storm was now at their backs and, sensing victory, eased, finally dying out. And when the convoy arrived back at base, the desert several miles north of its previous location had rearranged itself and lay, docile, to greet the sun appearing over the eastern rim.

Sergeant Major Puller sighed with relief as his battered convoy halted at the storm-vandalised camp that was once the Special Ordnance Group. Hardly surprisingly, there was no one to greet them. Wisely, as the last red tail-lights had disappeared into the gloom at 23.00 hours, there had been a concerted rush – defence force, umpires alike – to the safety of the mess tent, which was shielded by an escarpment of rock.

It hadn't been a holiday for them either. Several of the tents had been blown away and were conceivably swinging gently from some lamppost or other in Alexandria's main street. The white stones were in disarray all over the place and from the air it must have looked like a poison toadstool.

The lads who'd been out all night in the convoy dropped red-eyed and bone-weary out of their trucks and made their way to the mess tent, striding over the sleeping defence force for a mug of char and something solid. Others, too far gone to eat, moved like zombies

170

to some of the tents left standing and fell into a deep sleep, too tired even to snore.

Captain Jampton, however, sat proudly at his table. He wasn't too tired, having slept most of the way back. Now refreshed, he was mentally composing a letter to his Aunt Dorothy. After all, his convoy was probably the only living thing that had moved last night. Even the war had come to a standstill whilst friend and foe alike cowered hugging themselves while the storm raged. But hadn't he led them through the worst of the elements? It was leadership above and beyond the call of duty equalling Scott's expedition to the Antarctic. Still fantasising, he reached for an airmail form, but his train of thought was broken as Sergeant Major Puller entered the tent.

Jampton looked up at the weary figure and his thoughts of the gallant Captain Oates sprang to mind, the only difference being that Captain Oates was leaving the tent whilst Puller was coming in.

The Sergeant Major, eyes red-rimmed, spoke through dry cracked lips. 'I've checked the men and equipment, sir. All present and correct.' He paused for a moment, then added with relish, 'Except the loss of Sergeants Sparks and Miller and one fifteen-hundredweight vehicle.'

Jampton's heart sank. He'd almost forgotten about those two. 'Tell me, Sergeant Major, is it your belief they've deserted?'

Puller shrugged. Good grief, thought Jampton, what is the Army coming to when in answer to a question from the Commanding Officer an NCO, a senior one at that, just shrugs? And come to think of it, when he entered the tent he'd omitted to salute. Wisely he ignored the lack of discipline. There'd be time for a quiet reprimand later. Finally he said, 'Thank you, Sergeant Major, that will be all.'

'Just one more thing, sir. We've lost another three-tonner and eight men.'

Jampton stared at him aghast. 'But you said apart from Sergeants Sparks and Miller all the convoy was present and correct.'

'This three-tonner wasn't in the convoy, sir. At first light this morning they left camp.'

Jampton was stricken. On the verge of panic he could see his command crumbling and being decimated and the only German he'd seen so far was the pilot of the Messerschmitt. Not a lot for his future memoirs.

'Didn't anyone try to stop them?' he blurted. 'The guards?'

Again the SM shrugged. How could he explain to this incompetent that the guards, like any other sensible human beings, had hunkered down and in all probability were fast asleep when the truck left? In fact, the truck had been dispatched with a rousing send-off, some of the lads handing letters over the tailgate to be posted in Alexandria.

Captain Jampton stared up at his Sergeant Major, aghast. Then after a moment he remembered who he was, sprang to his feet and snapped, 'Right, Sergeant Major, I want everybody on parade in ten minutes.' But as he looked into Puller's face, a shiver ran through him. Had he had a few more marbles he would have recognised Puller's expression as that of a man about to commit murder. Involuntarily he took a step back, his chair crashing to the floor, and hurriedly cancelled his last order.

'I'd forgotten about the convoy, Sergeant Major. Let the men sleep for a while.'

The Sergeant Major nodded and let the anger flow out of him as he left the tent.

When he'd gone, Captain Jampton shakily poured himself a glass of lemonade. God, how he needed that! He righted his chair and sat down to compose a report to his uncle, but what could he say? He pushed the paper to one side. Sparks and Miller wouldn't have deserted; it was unbelievable. No, they'd walk into camp in the next few days, sand-encrusted and sheep-faced at having lost the end of the convoy. If only he could have realised how near he was to the truth.

Sergeant Sparks struggled to open his eyes. It wasn't easy – sweat and sand made it difficult. He tried to lick his lips but there was no moisture. As he gradually came to his senses his first impression was that he was being roasted. Through half-open eyelids he tried to identify his surroundings. Everything was bathed in a sickly yellow light. It was only when he saw the dashboard that he realised he was in the cab of his fifteen-hundredweight. The windscreen and side windows had been blasted with sand and the truck itself was listing at an alarming angle. With an effort he managed to haul himself behind the steering wheel.

He looked across to his left and saw that his mate was sleeping like a pig in a rubbish tip, his sandy and sweat-plastered face poking out from a balaclava – not a pretty sight. Stale ciagarette smoke, the stink of sweat and the odour of rotting feet pervaded the atmosphere.

The door swung slowly open letting in a shaft of bright sunlight. Sparks heaved himself out on to the soft sand and yawned. He stretched his arms above his head. The heat was ferocious but infinitely more enjoyable than the malodorous atmosphere inside the cab. He fiddled for his fly buttons and faced the truck – when it hit him like a sackful of All Bran. He hadn't touched the door and it hadn't opened by itself. He whirled round to see an Arab woman in the traditional black chador, one arm holding the material to cover her nose and mouth. Sparks stared at her for a moment, then gazed all around him. Nothing but the high mounds of the sand dunes. He turned back to the woman. Where the hell had she come from? The woman bowed.

'Good morning, my heroic Sergeant Sparks. I hope you slept well.'

Sparks was dumbfounded. 'Yasmin,' he croaked.

'Of course,' she said calmly.

Sparks was baffled. 'Yes, but how did you ...' He stopped. 'Oh bloody 'ell, you were in the back.' She nodded. 'I might have known,' he said. He slapped the top of the cab in exasperation, then yelped as the hot metal burnt his palm.

Yasmin lowered her head to hide her laughter. Sparks whirled round but the head of Miller came between them as he sought to disembark.

'What's all this bloody racket?' he demanded peevishly. 'I was having a lovely dream then – I was a chicken and the cook was just taking me out of the oven.'

He turned to Yasmin. 'Good trip?' he asked.

Sparks's eyes blazed, 'You knew she was in the back?' he hissed incredulously.

'Well, yeh,' said Miller easing himself out of arm's reach. He wasn't afraid of his oppo but neither was he in the mood for a punch-up, not before breakfast.

'Listen, old son,' he said. 'If I'd told you she was on board, I know you. In that bloody awful sandstorm you would have turned round and dropped her back at the camp.'

Sparks snorted. 'That's where you're wrong. I would have turfed her out and let her walk back.'

Yasmin's eyes flashed but she said nothing.

'All right,' said Miller, 'let me ask you something. Where are we? Go on, answer me that. Where are we?'

'How the hell should I know?' blurted Sparks. They glared at each other, fists clenched, but just as the bell was about to go for Round One Yasmin spoke. 'Would anyone like a grape?'

Quarrel forgotten for the moment, they stared at her in bewilderment. Slowly, from the folds of her chador,

174

she drew out a bunch of luscious green grapes. She broke the bunch into two halves, handed one to Miller and tossed the other contemptuously to Sparks. He grabbed them clumsily and several fell to the ground. Miller was stuffing his face with a look of rapture, juice rolling down his chin.

Sparks tossed his lot disdainfully on to his seat in the cab. 'Where did you get these?' he asked quietly.

'From the oasis,' replied Yasmin coolly.

Miller, sucking juice from his hand, looked at the grapes on the seat. 'They'll dry out there,' he said and scooped them up to his joyful mouth.

Ignoring him, Sparks continued. 'So you know where we are?' he said.

'Yes, I do.' Then with some asperity, she added, 'You are both like children. This isn't your East End of London. This is the desert and without me you would not last a week.'

Sparks looked down as he scuffed sand over the grapes. 'OK, OK, I'm sorry. It's just that ...' He stopped and looked at her. 'Oh bollocks.'

Yasmin smiled. She was happy again. 'Bollocks' was Sparks's way of making an apology.

Miller smiled too. 'See what I mean? She knows the desert, speaks Arabic like a native, and she's got you taped.'

Sparks wasn't listening. He was leaning in the cab for his water bottle. Miller turned to Yasmin and winked at her with a thumbs-up sign. Sparks guzzled the tepid water, swilled it around his mouth, then he had a proper drink and snapped back the cork.

'OK,' he said, 'let's get mobile. It'll take us half an hour to dig this heap out of the sand.'

Miller looked at Yasmin. 'How far is this oasis then?'

Yasmin smiled. 'Not very far. As I said I was there first thing. That's where I got the grapes.' She paused then, coyly: 'I hope you don't mind, Mr Miller. To get the grapes I traded your spare shirt.'

Miller pretended to be aghast. 'Bloody 'ell, I was saving that for church parade.'

Sparks was already busy with a spade. The wheels on one side of the truck were axle-deep in sand.

'Never mind that,' said Miller. 'If she can walk it, so can we.'

'Oh yes,' said Yasmin. 'Just over this large dune and you can see the oasis.'

Miller snatched off his balaclava and combed his hair. 'Must make a good impression,' he said and started off up the dune.

Sparks eyed the large humped sand hill and watched his mate scrabbling up to the top. He squinted as Miller reached his point of vantage. Miller, a small figure now, stood for a moment, then in a panic-stricken rush tumbled and rolled, slithering back to Sparks's feet. He grabbed Sparks's leg, then hauled himself up, struggling to regain his breath.

'It's an oasis all right,' he panted, 'but it's full of troops.'

'Ours?' asked Sparks urgently.

'I don't think so. They've got a flag up but it's not the Union Jack.'

They both looked questioningly at the girl. 'Oh yes,' she said, 'it's an Italian base . . . but it's up to you.' She shrugged. 'The next oasis on this track is two hundred kilometres away.'

Sparks grunted as he resumed his digging. 'I knew there'd be a catch in it somewhere.'

Miller grabbed a second shovel and was already furiously trying to extricate the other wheel.

Yasmin spoke softly. 'I do not think you have much choice.'

They both stopped attacking the sand and followed her gaze. A line of dots shimmering in the heat was approaching slowly.

'What is it?' asked Miller.

No one answered; they watched in silence as the shapes shimmered into recognition. Twenty or thirty Arabs mounted on camels, in line, plodded towards them.

'Friendly?' asked Sparks.

There was a pause, then Yasmin said, 'If they continue as now towards us they may be friendly, but on the other hand if they stop . . .'

It was at that moment the cavalcade stopped. They were about two hundred yards away. Two other riders jogged up to join the leader.

'The rifles,' hissed Sparks.

Yasmin steadied him. 'Do not move suddenly. They will be upon you before you can open the cab door.'

Miller gulped. His bowels were turning to water and it wasn't just the grapes. He muttered, 'God Almighty! They stake you out naked, cut your balls off and stuff 'em in your mouth.'

'Yea?' said Sparks quietly. 'They wouldn't get all yours in.'

Yasmin spoke softly. 'They are undecided. Walk up the dune and surrender to the Italians.'

Miller wasn't so sure. 'They'll pick us off before we get halfway up.'

'I do not think so,' said Yasmin. 'I think they are more interested in your vehicle. They will be puzzled as to why you walk away and leave it and while they make up their minds you will be over the top and protected by the Italians.'

The two Sergeants looked at each other, then dropping their spades moved as casually as they could up the treacherous sliding sand. Halfway up, without stopping, Miller clasped his hands over his head.

'What's that for?' gasped Sparks.

'We're surrendering. When we get to the top we'll be in full view of the Itis and I don't want to be shot by them either.'

Sparks said nothing but slowly raised his hands to clasp them as Miller had done. Only a few more yards. It was heavy going and not easy with hands clasped over their heads. They daren't look down to see what the Arabs were up to. Each slithering step was a nightmare. Any moment could bring that sledgehammer blow from a bullet between the shoulder blades. Only the lucky ones heard the crack of a rifle that followed.

They hadn't much further to go when a strange thing happened. From the opposite side of the dune a white topi came into view over a red face, then the rest of whoever it was appeared as he breasted the rise, sun sparkling on his bemedalled chest. He was obviously an officer of some nationality or other. The two soldiers' eyebrows shot up in unison as a long line of men came into view following him. But the strangest thing of all was that every man had his hands clasped firmly on top of his head.

Sparks and Miller, hands clasped over their heads, stared uncomprehendingly as the General, or whatever he was, stopped a pace in front of them. He was a pathetic figure for all his medals and highly polished boots with his hands clasped over his topi showing the black sweat patches under his armpits. For a few seconds they stood facing each other and Miller began to see the ludicrousness of the situation. Here in an unmapped piece of desert in North Africa, this hands-on-head charade was at an impasse. Ships were being torpedoed and sunk off the west coast of Africa; the Luftwaffe patrolled the skies with the arrogance of victors; tank battles were being fought; men were dying on the hot dusty desert; and whilst all this carnage was going on, this ludicrous comedy was taking place on top of a sand dune.

Miller felt an urge to giggle; it was on the tip of his tongue to blurt out, 'O'Grady says hands down', an old

178

childhood game. But then some soldiers never really grew up.

The 'General' was the first to speak. '*Bon Giorno*,' he said, 'I am Capitano Carlo Abruzzi and I have the honour to surrender my command.'

Sparks and Miller stared at him in complete bafflement and, fearing he had not been understood, the Italian went on. 'We are your prisoners.' He gestured to his troops with his elbows.

The two Sergeants looked at each other. 'No, no,' said Miller, '*niente*. We are *your* prisoners.' He smiled ingratiatingly, pointing in turn to the officer with his elbow.

Sparks was fed up with the whole thing. 'Listen, Capitano,' he muttered, 'I don't know how many lads you have, but there's only two of us.'

The Italian Officer eyed him suspiciously. 'Then you are not forward reconnaissance for more British troops?' he asked.

'You must be joking.' Sparks unclasped his hands and fished a cigarette out of his shirt pocket and lit it, blowing a plume of blue smoke into the hot still air.

The spell was broken. The Italian troops were already scrambling back down their side of the dune. Some then shouted back in a tone that didn't sound exactly complimentary. Their officer shrugged and took his hands from his head. He gestured at his disappearing troops.

'You must understand. We have been here for a long, long time and they are a little sand crazy, *comprendi*?' He turned and followed his command down to the oasis.

'Got any more bright ideas?' asked Sparks when the officer had gone.

Miller shrugged. 'We'll see what Yasmin says.'

Sparks thought for a moment, then nodded, and they made their way back across the dune. As they neared the edge they looked down on to the fifteen-hundredweight, but there was no sign of Yasmin.

After a moment's silence Miller glanced at his mate. 'Where is she?' he whispered.

Sparks indicated her tracks in the direction of and around the side of another large pile of sand. Miller nodded and was about to slither down the dune to the truck when Sparks restrained him. Miller looked up enquiringly but Sparks was looking past him and down the track. Two hundred yards to their right the Arabs were exactly as they had been, still and motionless high on their camel saddles.

Miller came to a sudden decision. 'Sod this for a game of skittles,' he said. 'I'm going to collect my gear and follow Yasmin's trail.'

He was about to move forward when he noticed that Sparks had turned and was walking in the opposite direction in the wake of the Italians. Miller struggled after him and caught his arm. 'What about our gear?' he asked.

Sparks eyed him curiously for a moment. 'If you make a move to that truck, I wouldn't bet a penny on you coming back alive.'

Miller scoffed. 'You're getting jumpy in your old age.'

Sparks nodded. 'You go if you want. I can just see you at the Pearly Gates and when St Peter says "Who're you?" you won't be able to tell him because you'll have a mouth full of bollocks.'

He turned and strode away and, after a moment's hesitation, Miller scrambled after him – he was convinced.

The oasis was a pleasant surprise. When they first caught sight of it below them they stopped dead in their tracks and gazed in wonderment at the spectacle. They weren't the first people to be enchanted at their first view of the El Waddim Oasis.

Before the war the El Waddim Oasis was described in Thomas Cook's travel book as 'The Jewel in the North African Desert' and visitors to Alexandria were urged to take advantage of a three-day trip to where native caravans from the four corners of Africa exchanged goods, craftware and gossip. For tourists in Alexandria it was a visit not to be missed. Accommodation was available at the El Waddim Hotel and the cuisine was European under the direction of a French chef.

Sparks and Miller would have agreed wholeheartedly with this description. They could hardly believe their eyes. Below them was a wonderland, palm trees fringing a glittering lake surrounded by a sprawl of whitewashed huts. Some of them were two-storeyed and, like a duck shepherding its brood to the water, there was a larger building which could have been a picture palace or a mosque but was, in fact, a hotel or, to be more exact, a hotel in happier, more tranquil days.

After a time Miller turned to Sparks and asked in a hushed voice, 'Is this for real or are they making a film?'

Sparks didn't reply but Miller could see that he was impressed. In a sort of daze they made their way towards a trestle table in the shade of a copse of palm trees.

'Please be seated,' welcomed the Capitano, and a white-coated steward placed a large jug of beer before them and two glasses.

Miller filled his glass and raised it to the Italian in a toast of comradeship. Then he glanced around him and sighed happily. If this was being a prisoner of war so be it – he could put up with the hardships.

After a few more bottles of beer the stiffness and formality of the occasion disappeared and euphoria began to take its place.

The Capitano was now relaxed, his tunic unbuttoned

and a soft damp cloth on his head. His white topi had been removed by his batman and placed reverently in a hatbox.

'Nice place you have here, Capitano.'

The Italian waved his hand deprecatingly. 'Please not to call me Capitano – I am not a soldier and I'll be happy for you to call me Carlo.'

'Thank you,' said Miller, 'and you can call me Dusty if you like.'

They shook hands solemnly and then clinked glasses as they toasted each other, and they sat together in easy silence for a few moments. Then Miller shaded his eyes.

'What's all that lot down there?' he asked, indicating a cluster of native tents shimmering in the heat about a half mile away. There were camels, goats and lots of tiny children running around.

'Ach,' said Carlo, 'that is the native Bedouin encampment. They were all the staff at this hotel before the war. They were moved out to accommodate us, but obviously they didn't go far.'

Miller sighed, taking in the general scene. 'This is better than Blackpool,' he muttered.

Sparks smiled sardonically. 'All we need is a few fish-and-chip shops. I can live without the candy floss.' And feeling that he'd already said too much for one day he downed another bottle of Stella.

Carlo nodded. 'It's not too bad for a week or two,' he said, 'but we are here more than one year. We are a little *fou*, you understand. How you say, sand crazy?' He belched softly. 'I think Il Duce has forgotten us. When Hitler beckoned, Mussolini rolled over on his back to have his belly tickled – and *phutt* – we are in the big war.' He slapped his biceps and gave an impressive uppercut in the air in an Italian gesture of contempt.

'Tough tits,' muttered Sparks, but nobody seemed to have heard.

Carlo took a sip of wine and continued. 'Straight away I am constipated into the Army.'

Miller choked on his beer.

'This isa notta fonni,' snapped the Italian.

Miller held up his hands placatingly. 'No, no,' he said, 'I think you mean conscripted into the Army.'

'I said that,' snapped the Italian.

'No,' said Miller, 'you said constipated into the Army.'

Carlo looked puzzled. 'What is constipated?'

'Well, it's, er, it's when you can't go.'

'Go where?' asked Carlo.

'Leave it,' said Sparks. 'Don't take any notice of him.' He nodded at his mate. 'He's been out here too long as well.'

Carlo recovered his good humour. 'I will never understand your English language.' He laughed and Miller joined him and they toasted each other again.

Sparks leant across the table. 'You sound as if you don't like the Army,' he said.

Carlo snorted. 'I hate the Army. I am not a soldier. I am the best head waiter in Roma.' He stared gloomily into his glass for a moment, then struck the table with his fist. 'Everybody who was anybody dined at the Hotel Excelsior on the beautiful Via Vittorio Veneto to sample the magnificent cuisine – and to see me.' He thumped his chest and coughed slightly.

He smiled sadly at his reminiscences.

'Once we were patronised by Mussolini's son, Count Ciano, a party of six. What beauty, aah!' He kissed his fingers. 'That lunch went on for three days.'

'I'll bet that cost a packet,' said Miller enviously.

Carlo stared at him for a moment, then his face cleared and his hand waved dismissively. 'We did not speak of money – it was Mussolini's son.' It was said casually but it was obvious that it hurt.

'Not even a tip?' asked Miller guilelessly.

Immediately Carlo's mood changed. 'Oh yes, I get a tip. Do you know what it was?'

They both shook their heads dutifully.

Carlo continued, 'A week later an envelope is coming from the Ministry of War, and me –' he thumped his chest, '– the greatest head waiter in Italy, instructed to pack and report to the Stazione Centrale Roma Termini immediately and shortly after I become Capitano Carlo Abruzzi in this godforsaken place. That was my tip.'

A mess waiter in a shabby off-white jacket brought two more jugs to the table. Miller smiled his thanks and gazed round with a sigh of satisfaction.

'Where is everybody?' he asked.

'Everybody?' asked Carlo, puzzled.

'The troops, you know, soldiers.'

'Ah,' Carlo said, dismissing them contemptuously. 'As I told you before, they are not soldiers, they are waiters, fruit sellers, wine producers. Soldiers!' He sniffed. 'We are not fighting men, we are supply and catering.'

'Oh,' said Miller, not quite understanding.

At that moment Yasmin joined them. She sat next to Sparks and an agitated Italian followed her, gesticulating but not brave enough to touch her. He bowed to his CO and in a flood of Italian apologised for the intrusion of the Arab woman. The CO dismissed him with a wave of his hand and stared coldly at Yasmin. Coolly she removed her head covering and the change in the Italian was electric. This was no Arab woman. Suddenly he was the head waiter again. Rising with supreme politeness, he leant over the table, took her hand and kissed it. She bowed her head graciously and in fluent Italian proceeded to introduce herself.

Sparks and Miller listened open-mouthed. They heard her mention their names and when she had finished Carlo beamed at Sparks. 'You are a very lucky man indeed.'

'Yeh,' said Sparks and took a long pull at his beer.

Miller was lost in admiration. 'She's full of surprises,' he said. 'She's got Italian as well.'

Carlo clapped his hands and his batman emerged from the large building with the hatbox. The Capitano glared at it, then rattled off in Italian sending the man back inside to return with another wineglass. After it was filled, Carlo stood, raising his own glass. He bowed to Sparks. 'A toast to your beautiful signorina.'

Yasmin looked at Sparks with a half-smile on her face. Sparks hesitated for a moment, then raised his glass of Stella and drank.

'Lovely here, isn't it?' said Miller, making an all-round gesture with his glass. He stopped as two men approached, hand in hand, dressed in long flowing djellabas and obviously enjoying each other's company. They sat down at the table and nodded to the company, eyeing the two Sergeants curiously. Performing his duty as the host, Carlo introduced the new arrivals as Eeny and Meany. The slighter of the two, in a broad Lancashire accent, said, 'I'm Eeny.' Then with a giggle said, 'He's the Meany.'

Miller stood up, bowed his head and offered his hand, which they shook delicately. 'I'm Dusty Miller and this is my friend and comrade, Sergeant Sparks.'

He clicked his heels and sat. Already he was under the Italian influence. Sparks looked away in disgust; he wasn't fully reconciled to the ludicrous situation. Any minute now, he thought, I'm going to wake up in an Army mental section.

Carlo rose. 'If you will excuse me, I have some work to do.' He bowed to the table and was gone.

A soldier with a serviette over his arm brought fresh glasses and poured the wine for Eeny and Meany and discreetly backed away. Miller took a long swig of his beer while Eeny and Meany clinked glasses and sipped.

'This is the life.' Miller smiled expansively, and then said pensively, 'I wonder if they sell postcards.'

'Just arrived?' asked Meany.

'A couple of hours ago,' said Miller.

'You'll like it here,' said the other one and added, 'How did you find this place?'

Miller chuckled. 'We were on a night exercise in all that bloody muck and sand and somehow we got detached from the others and ended up here.'

'What mob are you with?' asked Eeny.

'Special Ordnance Group,' said Miller.

Meany stiffened and Eeny spluttered in his wineglass. They all looked at each other, all joy gone now.

'Did I say something wrong?' asked Miller. He looked at Sparks, who burst out laughing.

Miller was shocked. He hadn't seen Sparks laugh like that since the cook backed on to the stove and set his trousers on fire.

'What's so funny?' asked Miller.

Sparks wiped his eyes. 'Have another look,' he said. 'It's that bloody Jerry pilot you shot down and the little fella's Hugh's driver.'

Miller was still perplexed.

'You shot him down,' said Sparks. 'He forced what's his name to drive him back to his unit.'

'Oh yeah,' gasped Miller as enlightenment dawned. Then he brightened and a broad grin spread across his face. 'How are you both?' He reached over the table with his hand outstretched.

For a moment the German pilot stared at him, then he also laughed and eagerly shook Miller's hand. 'Allow me to introduce myself – I am der Fliegerhauptmann Rudolph von Bosch. You may call me Rudy.'

The slight man leant forward. 'And I'm Driver Gratwick.'

'And how is Deadshot Dick?' Rudy asked laughing. 'I didn't recognise you at first because when we had our little contretemps your face was covered with a balaclava helmet.'

For the next few minutes they toasted one another, then Carlo, then the British and the Germans, and for some obscure reason Tito got a mention.

Rudy filled them in on how he had known of this oasis having overflown it as a test pilot and how Carlo had welcomed them with open arms, thirsty for news of the outside world and the state of the war. He went on to explain that, although Carlo had a highly functional wireless transmitter/receiver, the news in both Italian and German was heavily biased.

'Where's your transport?' asked Gratwick.

'It's over the other side of that dune,' said Miller pointing. There was a moment's silence while Rudy and Gratwick stared at him aghast. Miller looked from face to face. 'What's up?' he asked finally.

'You left your truck unguarded?' gasped Rudy and they both rose and hurried towards the dune, Miller trying to keep up with them, wondering what all the fuss was about. Perhaps he was in Carlo's parking space. They wallowed frantically up the soft sand of the dune and with sweat pouring down their faces they finally staggered across the top and gazed down the other side. The German pilot wiped the sweat away with the back of his hand and shrugged.

'The bastards,' gasped Miller.

He couldn't believe his eyes. The fifteen-hundred-weight had been there – a patch of oil testified to that – and the truck hadn't been driven away. The tyre tracks stopped at the patch of oil. The pilot pointed along the scuffed tracks of the camels, leading straight and inexorably into the distance. Miller shook his head in bewilderment. He'd served long enough in India to have witnessed and heard tales of events that bore no rational explanation. And here in the Middle East, set an Arab down anywhere in the desert and he would unerringly make his way to Cairo, Alexandria, or anywhere he decided to go.

As if reading his thoughts, Gratwick chimed, 'I suppose they dismantle the truck, distribute the load and just carry on.'

Sparks nodded and squinted towards the sun. 'They'd had a few hours' start,' he murmured.

Miller was still mystified, unable to grasp the situation. 'Blimey,' he burst out. 'I must remember to write to the motor-racing authorities. Those lads would be a godsend in the pits at Brooklands.'

'Our truck went like that,' said Gratwick as they started back to the oasis. 'Parked outside our hut it was and when we got up in the morning – *phhhh* – it had vanished into the air.' He paused, then after a moment: 'I've still got the rotor arm.'

'We're not the only victims,' said Rudy. 'What about poor old Carlo?'

'What about him?' asked Miller.

'When he first arrived here he had a half-track and eight Dovunque 35 trucks. After only two days the half-track was gone. The rest soon followed.'

'Yes,' Gratwick broke in. 'And can you imagine how much one of them would weigh? This wasn't like one of our Bren carriers. This was more like a medium-sized tank.'

'Bloody hell,' said Miller automatically. It was scorching hot now and he didn't want to hang about chitchatting. He began to move forward to the distant shade of the oasis.

'No, wait,' chuckled Rudy. 'You haven't heard the best bit.'

Miller groaned inwardly and blew a bead of sweat off the end of his nose.

'The following night,' the pilot went on, 'Carlo mounted a four-man guard but of course not being soldiers they climbed into the back of one of the trucks with a few bottles of wine and a pack of cards.'

Miller laughed. 'I get it, and in the morning all the

other trucks had gone.' It was a good yarn but not worth getting sunstroke for.

'No, no, you're wrong,' put in Gratwick. 'That's what we thought at first.' He nudged his companion. 'Go on, Rudy,' he whispered.

Rudy smiled fondly at him and continued. 'The funny part was, well not funny really, but the trucks were still there in the morning except for the one containing the guards that had completely disappeared. How do you like that? A truck and four guards vanished into thin air.'

Miller stopped, now intrigued. 'How d'you know they were in the back playing cards?'

'Ah,' he said, 'that is the interesting part.'

Now Miller was hooked and even Sparks, who had been a short distance away, came to join the group.

'Go on,' he said. 'I've been listening.'

'Well,' continued Rudy, 'Carlo naturally took a patrol down to the native village to search for clues and just outside the Bedouin tents they found the Four of Hearts half buried in the sand.'

'So that's how you know they're the villains?' Sparks nodded to the distant sprawl of the native camp.

'Yes,' said Gratwick, 'but you haven't heard the best bit.' He glanced shyly at his companion. 'You tell it best, Rudy.'

The German pilot smiled and stroked the back of his fingers down the boy's cheek. Behind them Miller looked quickly at Sparks and blew him a kiss. Sparks glowered, then addressed the German. 'Go on, then,' he said. 'What's the best bit?'

Tearing his gaze from Gratwick's face, Rudy turned to them. 'Naturally,' he began, 'Carlo reported the loss and within a few hours a Fiat G12 transport plane landed and a company from a crack Italian regiment entered the camp and began to search with probing rods. They had the Arabs digging all over the place.

Mine detectors were used. But after two days of turning the place upside down, nix.' He made a sweeping gesture with his hands to emphasise the nix. 'It was only when the elite force was boarding the plane to return that one of them discovered his wristwatch had gone, then another looked at the white band on his wrist where *his* watch should have been.

'Frantically the troops checked their personal belongings – five wristwatches, three wallets and even two of the mine detectors. They were angry and it was all their CO could do to shepherd them into the plane. No way were they going to enter that camp again. He couldn't afford to lose a dozen members of a crack Italian regiment.'

At the end of the anecdote, Rudy and Gratwick laughed uproariously. Miller laughed with them, although he thought the story about as funny as an amputation. Still chuckling he led the slither down the soft sand of the dune. At the bottom his good humour returned. 'Well, we're stuck here now. We'll have to make the best of it,' he chirped.

His euphoria was short-lived. When they arrived at the table under the palms, Carlo greeted them morosely. He rose from his chair and as he turned to go he looked over his shoulder and growled, 'The Germans are coming.' Then he entered the shadowy doorway of the hotel.

Miller stared after him, unable to digest the words; the scent of roses was fading fast. 'The Germans are coming,' he muttered to himself in a strangled voice. He'd heard these words many times as an infantryman but this time it didn't seem fair. He jerked his head round to Sparks, who merely shrugged.

'Did you hear that?' gasped Miller.

Sparks nodded and straddled a chair. 'You didn't expect it to last for ever, did you?' he said laconically, helping himself to a bottle of Stella.

Miller turned to Rudy and Gratwick for enlightenment but they didn't seem to be too bothered. He knew they were good mates but then so were he and Sparks, but they didn't sit leaning towards each other like that, foreheads touching while they looked into each other's eyes. You might do that with a bird, but not two men.

But there were more immediate matters on his mind and whirling around he made his way to the hotel to seek clarification from Carlo. He'd never been in the hotel and as he reached the door it was as if he'd stepped out of the war into the Grand Hotel, Bournemouth. He was dumbstruck. In the middle of the floor, Carlo was supervising his staff while they busied themselves spreading table cloths and arranging cutlery, candlesticks, wineglasses and ice buckets. Miller was flabbergasted. This had nothing to do with the Army: this was a poncy hotel and he was suitably impressed.

He wandered over to Carlo. 'Got a wedding this afternoon, have you?' he asked, gesturing towards the tables. Carlo ignored him as he straightened a napkin.

Miller stared round him. What was going on? His brain would accommodate only so much and he'd had enough input for one day. He was about to speak when he heard the sound of a piano coming from the gallery and he looked up to see a string quartet tuning their instruments. He cleared his throat.

'Is this all for the Germans?'

Carlo nodded abstractedly while he studied a menu. The quartet broke into 'The Merry Widow Waltz'.

Miller shook his head in disbelief. 'Will there be dancing as well?'

Carlo handed the menu to one of his staff, then turned towards the chubby, sweating Britisher. He sighed. 'Let me explain, my friend,' he began. 'Twice a week a German supply plane flies in with our rations. They arrive after dark and return before first light – a pilot, a navigator and a Feldwebel.' He drew his thumb down his cheek and blew a soft raspberry. 'A pig of a man, even for a German.'

Miller nodded sagely. 'All this for the German flight crew?'

Carlo shook his head and tapped his finger along the side of his nose and quietly he said, 'Sometimes they bring with them besides a ration a Very Important Person ... We are not told, you understand, the name of our guest but at the end of the message informing us of the arrival of the supply plane there are the words "Grade I". And so tonight we are expecting a Very Important Person, whoever it may be.'

'Ah,' said Miller, but although he could not for the life of him comprehend any of it, and more for the want of something to say, he asked, 'What table am I on?'

The Commandant placed a hand on his shoulder in fatherly fashion and said, 'You, my friend, along with your comrades will be locked away in your hut until they have gone.'

Then his manner changed abruptly. 'Do you play chess?' he said.

'No,' replied Miller.

'Pity,' sighed Carlo. 'Then you'll have to find something else to do, won't you, because I'm busy.' And with that he disappeared into the kitchen.

CHAPTER

SEVEN

The letter, as usual, came via diplomatic pouch, delivered by dispatch rider to the Ministry of Ag and Fish, to be accepted and signed for by Colonel Brunswick. He sighed, not for the first time, at all this official rigmarole for what was, after all, only a letter from his wife. But then for people in the stratospheric heights of the Social Register, objects such as postboxes were for ordinary people. In any event they could hardly be termed letters. A more accurate description would be documents containing vital information. In fact, had they been intercepted by the enemy intelligence service, Hitler would most certainly have his feet up in Buckingham Palace by now.
He read on:

> At dinner the other night Winston, looking remarkably fit after his trip to Cairo, was scathing (as only he can be) when he referred to General Auchinleck, and by the time you receive this Auchinleck will be on his way to India under a cloud.

Colonel Brunswick put the letter down and sat back in his chair, took off his glasses, and pinched the bridge of his nose to digest this. He wasn't totally surprised at Auchinleck getting the boot, but shouldn't he, as Director of British Military Intelligence, have been privy to this information before now? He hadn't even been aware of Churchill's visit to Cairo, and that was only up the road, for God's sake. Shaking his head, he readjusted his glasses and continued to read:

> His replacement is almost certain to be a General Bernard Montgomery – a bit of a dark horse. But Max (Lord Beaverbrook) was in favour, saying Montgomery may yet surprise everybody. If it is to be Montgomery, your assessment of him would be appreciated.
> As ever –
> D.
> P.S. I understand the pressures of your work but it seems that you have made no headway at all in the matter of Wilfred's missing suitcase. Surely in your position you have agents in the dock area. It does not appear to me to be an insurmountable task to recover it. After all it is a fairly large blue suitcase with 'Jampton' stencilled all over it.

Exactly as his wife had forecast, seven days later, on 18 August, General Bernard Montgomery took over command of the Eighth Army.

Colonel Brunswick was neither elated nor depressed by the news. Morale was low and it seemed obvious that the new Commander had only been appointed to hand over Alexandria to the Afrika Korps. However, he would present his credentials. It never occurred to him that General Montgomery was himself planning to visit the headquarters of British Intelligence, and soon – the following day to be exact.

The headquarters of British Miliary Intelligence in Alexandria bustled with frenzied activity. Every day brought its new crisis and this Wednesday was no exception. Colonel Brunswick paced up and down in a muck sweat. At 1800 hours precisely General Montgomery would walk through the door. Ordinarily this would not have thrown him in such a panic. At worst he would have been mildly apprehensive. But the General had engineered the meeting for the express purpose of making the aquaintance of Sergeants Sparks and Miller. It was a get-together that must be avoided at all costs – but his options were few. He couldn't think. Short of blowing up the building, there didn't seem a way out.

The General had even dispatched a light plane to the Special Ordnance Group to bring them in – a plane, for God's sake. They were only Sergeants, whilst he, a Colonel, had to make trips out there in a clapped-out staff car, the only consolation being that had the General taken it into his head to fly down to meet them, it would be catastrophic – 'goodnight Vienna'.

In five minutes he would realise that his heroes, and his nephew, were only human. At least Sparks and Miller were. He groaned. Jampton would surely blow the gaff on what really happened during his battle with the Messerschmitt and that would trigger off a chain reaction that would end up with him running a recruiting office in Outer Mongolia.

'Bloody Montgomery,' he muttered, 'he's only arrived in the country five minutes ago, hasn't even had time to get his knees brown, and his first priority is to meet Sparks and Miller. You'd think he'd have more important things on his mind.'

Brunswick poured himself a large whisky, downing it in one. He was about to replenish his drink when suddenly he slammed the bottle down on his desk as if it had burnt his hand. From all he'd heard, General Montgomery was a strict teetotaller and could smell alcohol across the length of a moderately sized parade ground.

Hurriedly the Colonel locked the bottle in a drawer and searched around frantically for his bag of Mint

Imperials. In his panic he didn't hear the knock on the door but couldn't stifle a yelp as he saw his Adjutant standing before the desk.

'Bloody hell, Jimmy,' he gasped. 'Must you creep around like the Holy Ghost? And whatever happened to knocking?'

Captain Shelley was unflustered as he handed over a large bag of mints. 'Managed to locate some from one of the cypher clerks.'

The Colonel looked at him in amazement.

'You asked me some time ago, sir, and *voilà*.' He put the paper bag on the desk.

'Ah yes, I remember,' said the Colonel, helping himself to a sizable handful.

Captain Shelley coughed discreetly and was about to speak when the Colonel raised his hand. Whatever his Adjutant had to say would have to wait until he finished the burning mess of mint in his mouth, which was bringing tears to his eyes. He was chomping hurriedly like a man eating hot chips on a cold night.

Finally with a great gulp he belched softly and began. 'First of all, Jimmy,' he started, pausing while his tongue cleared the last remnants from his teeth.

Again the Adjutant cleared his throat.

'No, hear me out first, Jimmy,' said the Colonel. 'When Sergeants Sparks and Miller get here I want you to spirit them away and brief them before they meet the General.'

This time Captain Shelley didn't bother to clear his throat. He leapt straight in: 'But, sir –'

'Don't interrupt me,' snapped the Colonel, slamming his fist on the desk. 'In an hour or two they will be here. It doesn't take that long by air.'

Judging his moment, the Adjutant said softly, 'Sergeants Sparks and Miller aren't coming, sir.'

Brunswick's jaw fell open, his expression that of a man just discovering he's incontinent. The Adjutant

196

watched him curiously; the healthy brown tan of the Colonel's face changed to a sickly yellow, then, like the sun going down over Mandalay, it became bright red.

'Go on,' said Colonel Brunswick in a small clenched voice.

'The plane returned empty-handed, sir, and according to the pilot the two Sergeants are missing.'

'Missing?' echoed the Colonel reaching for the keys that opened the drawer to his Dimple Haig.

'Yes, sir,' said the Adjutant. 'Apparently they were all out on a night exercise when they became detached from the convoy, which is hardly surprising in that sandstorm.'

The Colonel stared at his Adjutant. Then with trembling hands he unlocked the drawer and slammed the bottle of whisky on the desk. Out of the heap of garbage that raced in his head, he came up with a question. 'Why weren't we informed immediately?' he snapped.

The Adjutant shrugged. 'The pilot said that a Sergeant Major told him that Captain Jampton has held up his report in the hope that Sergeants Sparks and Miller would return to camp in the next day or so and no harm would be done.'

He swivelled his chair viciously. What a king-sized cock-up, attaching Jampton to the Special Ordnance Group. Why the hell hadn't he posted him to set up a listening post or something in the back end of Sudan? He thought about this for a moment and then he brightened. Yes, why not? Yes, why bloody not? He had only to sign the movement order and his nephew would be out of his hair for good.

He stood up. 'Let's go to the wireless room, Jimmy,' he hissed. 'I want to speak personally to that jumped-up, never-come-down arsehole of a nephew of mine.'

The Adjutant didn't move and the Colonel looked at

him enquiringly, feeling that his crisis hadn't quite come to the boil.

'It's no good contacting the Special Ordnance Group, sir,' he said. 'I did that half an hour ago and Captain Jampton has just left, leading a patrol to search for the two Sergeants.' The Colonel dropped back into his seat. There was only so much a man could take. He poured himself a large drink. There wasn't going to be a meeting anyway, so first things first.

'Jimmy,' he said, 'I want you to put me in contact with General Montgomery in person. There's no point in meeting now, right?'

'Have you any idea where I might locate him, sir?'

Brunswick lost control for a moment. 'How the hell should I know? I'm not Nostradamus – I'm just the poor humble Director of British Military Intelligence.'

The Adjutant turned to leave but the Colonel hadn't quite finished. 'Get in touch with my wife in England,' he said. 'She's the most likely person to know the whereabouts of Montgomery. Pass on my regards and while you're at it ask her how Rommel is.' He chuckled at his last sally.

The Adjutant smiled briefly and the Colonel, now restored to good humour, relaxed. 'Now seriously, Jimmy,' he went on, 'let's find a way out of this present disaster.' He poured himself a large whisky and invited his Adjutant to pull up a chair and join him. For a time they sipped and thought, staring down at the carpet. Finally the Colonel broke the silence.

'Whatever possessed that stupid nephew of mine to take his men out on a night exercise in a sandstorm?'

His Adjutant nodded slowly. 'Not just a sandstorm, sir, the worst in living memory. A large chunk of South Africa is now in the war zone.'

The Colonel stared at him, then after a time he said, 'Hardly a night for deserting.'

The Adjutant shrugged. 'I wouldn't put anything past

Sparks and Miller, sir, but to break off from the convoy would have been sheer lunacy. It certainly couldn't have been premeditated.' He went on: 'No, sir, if you want my opinion I believe Sparks and Miller genuinely lost contact with the convoy.'

Colonel Brunswick swivelled in his chair and stared out of the window. 'Let's hope they have enough fuel and water to find their way back.' He raised his glass. He'd had just enough to make him maudlin. He took a large drink and added, 'Poor sods.'

EIGHT

The poor sods at that precise moment were enjoying a glass of after-lunch Courvoisier at the table under the shade of the palms. 'I could put up with this life for ever.' Miller beamed expansively, drumming his hands on his tight belly.

Carlo nodded sadly. 'And I, my friends, would gladly exchange this life for a daily bowl of watery soup in a POW camp.'

Miller's eyes widened. 'You're joking,' he said.

Rudy smiled sadly from the other side of the table. 'I fear the good Commandant is quite serious,' he said. 'You are ex-Infantry men, you live rough, share hardship and danger, and to be alive at the end of each day is a bonus. So to you, this oasis is a bed of roses.' He looked into his glass and sighed. 'For myself, after only a few weeks here sometimes I yearn to be back in the sky.' He turned towards Gratwick and patted his hand. 'It is only you, *mein schatz*, who keeps me sane and happy.'

A gloom settled over the assembly and after a few moments Carlo drained his glass, rose and said, '*Scusi*, but I have to look after the arrangements to receive our guests.'

They watched as he disappeared into the hotel. 'Ah well,' sighed Miller, 'I hope somebody turns up this time. He ponced the place up on Tuesday but nobody important arrived – just the flight crews. I'll bet they thought it was Carlo's birthday or something.'

'It must be somebody very special,' said Gratwick nodding towards the hotel. 'They've been at it since dawn.' He shook his head and smiled. 'You should have seen Carlo in his dressing gown, strutting about, clicking his fingers, tasting the wine, and the flowers.' He held up his hands. 'It looks like Lenin's funeral in there.'

Two Italians, soaked to the skin, emerged from the hotel carrying buckets.

'Any luck?' shouted Gratwick.

One of the Italians stopped. '*Si, signor*,' he said. '*Manifico!*'

'*Bene*,' replied Gratwick and the two Italians bowed and hurried off.

Miller stared at Gratwick in amazement. 'Where did you learn to speak Italian?' he said. Gratwick bowed his head modestly. 'Well go on,' said Miller, 'what was that all about?'

Gratwick giggled. 'You're not going to believe this,' he said, 'but they're rigging up a fountain in the middle of the floor.'

'Blimey,' whispered Miller. 'Who're they expecting, Reich Marschall Goering?'

Rudy sipped his wine. 'Hardly,' he said. 'Not fat Hermann. He wouldn't come this close to the fighting and if he did he'd have two Staffels of Messerschmitts escorting him.'

He was interrupted by the reappearance of Carlo, uniform sodden, lank black hair plastered over his face. 'Is not quite right, this fountain. One time little water.' He held forward his thumb and forefinger to indicate a two-inch jet. 'I go to look, and whoosh!' He made an extravagant gesture with his arms. 'Water everywhere, all the candles phutt.' He shrugged. 'Ah,' he said philosophically, 'there is still time.' He sat there, a forlorn heap of Italiano, then two tears ran down his already wet face.

'Don't let it get you down,' said Miller. 'If you haven't got it fixed by the time they arrive, how about a regatta?' It was a vain attempt to lighten the atmosphere.

'*Scusi*,' said Carlo wiping his eyes. 'This place makes me unhappy.' He dragged out a handkerchief as more tears poured down his face. Then he raised his head to the sky and wailed, 'I want to go home.'

There was an embarrassed silence round the table, as all tried to avoid looking at him. The moment was so tinged with sadness that even Sparks began to feel homesick, although he could never remember having had a home.

Gratwick broke the gloomy silence. 'Cheer up, Carlo, it'll soon be over.' There was a pause, then he added, 'One way or another.' He glanced covertly at Rudy and immediately tears welled in his eyes. Rudy put a protective arm round him, too full to speak.

Miller looked round the table. 'Bloody hell,' he said, 'what time is the reading of the will?' He turned to Carlo. 'Look, mate, if it's that bad why don't you form up your lads and march out into the blue and give yourselves up to the first patrol you come across?'

'Oh yes,' replied Carlo. 'I'm not a lucky man. The first patrol will be German and what then?'

'Well,' replied Miller with a shrug, but that was all. He couldn't answer that.

In the silence that followed Yasmin moved round the table and poured Carlo a glass of wine. He didn't seem to notice.

Then Sparks with a sardonic grin said, 'There's a camp maybe ten to fifteen miles from here, northwest. They're British. They'll be glad to have you.'

Miller looked at him, puzzled. Then his face cleared. 'Yes,' he said, 'the Special Ordnance Group. We know the CO very well: Captain Jampton.'

Then suddenly he stopped as if hit by a tube train,

realising with horror the consequences of what was being proposed. It was all very well to walk into camp with a bunch of Italian prisoners – they'd be heroes again – but the prospect of giving up this life of Reilly to return to the ramblings of the asylum didn't bear thinking about.

'Well, I'm not going for one,' snapped Gratwick in a voice they hadn't heard before. 'I'd sooner take my chance with Rudy and his mob.'

Carlo looked from one to the other. 'What is this Special Ordnance Group?' he asked.

Miller shook his head. 'No, Grat's right. It wouldn't work. Captain Jampton, the CO, is a funny bloke. He'll most likely lock all your lads up in a wire cage. And, blimey, he'd peg you out in the desert somewhere and let the ants have breakfast.'

Carlo shuddered. 'There is the Geneva Convention,' he muttered.

'Jampton won't give a bugger about that,' said Miller. 'He's a hard man.'

He was desperately trying to think of something to put the cork back in the bottle of the SOG when inspiration struck him. He slapped the table, eyes wide. They all turned towards him curiously. 'How's this for a top-of-me-head suggestion?'

They were all expectant now. Miller leant forward conspiratorially, glancing over his shoulder to assure himself there was no one within earshot. 'That supply plane, when it lands, why don't we commandeer it? We'll all nip on board and in a few hours we'll be in Alexandria.'

'*Mio dio*,' exploded Carlo in disgust and made to rise.

'No, hear me out,' said Miller tugging him back into his chair.

But Carlo snorted derisively. 'I see it now. Sixty or seventy of us crammed into the plane, some more on the wing and the rest strapped to the tail.' He looked sternly at Miller. 'If I were you, my friend, I'd take more water with it.'

Miller stared at him, his brain racing like a tortoise with a bad leg. 'We can't take everybody on one flight,' he said. 'That stands to reason. We just take a plane load to Alexandria, then we come back and take some more of them, like a bus service.'

He knew he was babbling a load of rubbish but it was necessary; anything to divert Carlo's happy thoughts of sanctuary with the Special Ordnance Group.

Carlo rose, shaking his head. 'I think is better we forget it. I apologise for my weakness and is good of you all for your kind suggestions.' With that he went back into the hotel.

Instantly Miller whirled round at Sparks. 'Why don't you keep your big mouth shut?'

Sparks lit a cigarette. 'What's the matter?' he said. 'Can't you take a joke?'

'A joke?' spluttered Miller. 'Didn't you see his eyes light up for a minute? Ten-mile march. Good Christ, he was thinking about it. If I hadn't stepped in they'd be getting their small kit together now ready for off.'

Gratwick shook his head. 'Carlo would be mad to give all this up,' he said.

'No, *leibchen*, you do not understand,' said Rudy. 'This, to them, is a prison without bars and they have served a sentence of more than a year; same sun, same faces, every day the same. At least as prisoners of war there would be other Italians. Probably they would meet old friends.'

Gratwick looked at him sadly. 'You want to be flying again, don't you, Rudy?'

Rudy laughed. 'Of course I do, but here I am enjoying a wonderful holiday. No, not holiday – what was the word you used?'

Gratwick blushed. 'Honeymoon,' he whispered softly.

There was a moment's silence. Then Sparks rose and stretched. 'Come on, Yasmin,' he said. 'It's time for my Italian lesson.'

Yasmin stared at him, puzzled.

Sparks shrugged. 'Forget it,' he said and started towards the huts.

He hadn't gone more than a few paces when Carlo hurried out to the table and called him back. And when he had their full attention he said, 'As Commandant I couldn't possibly go on that plane. It would not be honourable.'

They looked at each other with 'what's he on about?' expressions. 'The German plane,' said Carlo, as if this explained everything. 'I have spoken with my second in command and two senior members of my staff.'

Miller made to speak but the Italian waved him to silence.

Carlo chuckled. 'It would appear that such a plan as yours has been discussed many times but they were afraid to speak with me, uncertain of my, er, et . . .' He struggled but the word 'reaction' escaped him. So he ended lamely, 'They do not trust how I will feel.'

He rang a small bell on the table and immediately from the shaded doorway of the hotel three figures joined them – presumably the second in command and two of the seniors. Carlo didn't bother with introductions.

'Now, gentlemen, we have only about four hours before Junkers lands.'

Miller gulped and thought, Is the man serious? But a look at the four earnest Italian faces convinced him that the plan was not only afoot but was at the eight-furlong marker.

Carlo gestured for his second in command to take the floor.

'My English very bad, *capiche?*' They nodded, wondering what was to come. 'It lands, yes,' started the man, demonstrating his words with a motion of his hand descending slowly on to the table, even to the bumps as it landed. ' "Allo," says Fat Fritz.' He spat and flicked his thumbnail against his front teeth. ' "Come," we say, "we have girl for you in hut." And when in, *poof.*' He made a motion turning a key in a lock. And to make sure he'd been understood he added, 'We make prisoner, yes?'

And making the identical mime he locked up one of the officers. 'We all on plane, yes?' Two of the Italians nodded eagerly and the second carried on. 'We keep pilot, yes?' He struggled for the words and pointed two fingers saying, 'Bam bam.'

'Gun?' said Miller helpfully.

'*Si*, gun to pilot head and we say "Alexandria, *subito*".' He sat back exhausted.

It was all too simple. It was more than that – it was lunacy! Several moments passed in appalled silence then all the 'buts' came tumbling out.

The Luftwaffe wouldn't just sit back when their supply plane failed to return.

Did they intend to shoot the two Germans locked in the huts?

Would the pilot know where Alexandria was? After all, it wasn't signposted; and four hours was hardly enough time to make preparations. And wouldn't it be wiser to leave this until the next trip?

At this the second in command shook his head violently and slapped the table. 'No! No! No!' he said. 'It must be tonight. We wait next trip, then next trip, and next trip, another year has gone.'

Carlo sadly nodded his head. 'He is right, of course. After all, what is there to do? The Germans are taken prisoner and that is all. My second in command has explained to me that the plane will not leave before one o'clock in the morning. So they fly through the darkness for protection and arrive in Alexandria at first light. Simple, no?' But it was far from that.

There were enough doubts and questions to fill the *Encyclopaedia Britannica*. But after another half-hour of discussion two things became clear: one, come hell or high water they were going tonight; and two, Sergeants Sparks and Miller were to deliver them to the provos in Alexandria. Miller added a silent codicil to this – at a price.

Sparks shook his head in disbelief. The enormity of the enterprise was beyond credulity. It was outrageous, fraught with booby traps, and he knew for a certainty that he, for one, would not be going – but a glance at his oppo's face was enough. With a sinking heart he knew he would be on that plane.

Inside the hotel preparations for the enterprise were already well in hand. Weeks ago a list of aspiring POWs had been drawn up and the second in command was already apprising the lucky few of their good fortune.

Carlo was back in command but with more urgency. He was beginning to believe that the plan was his own. There was no doubt that it was common knowledge. He had to remonstrate with some of the men who began singing as they worked, and with a final look around he ordered his second in command to oversee the preparations whilst he went to his hut to arrange the seating plan.

Everyone nodded happily; it was a well-known fact that the seating plan was an excuse – it was time for the siesta of Capitano Carlo Abruzzi and nothing short of the Armistice was going to deprive him of his happy hour.

Yasmin rose from the table and made her way to her billet. She entered swiftly, locking the door behind her. Then she took down a piece of paper and wrote out a message. Thankfully, it was short and the encoding of it didn't take too long. In fact, in less than ten minutes she was making her way round the back of another larger hut and, looking round to make sure she was unobserved, she raised her hand to knock quietly.

Inside Carlo was about to climb into bed when he was interrupted by the discreet knock at the door.

'*Prego! Comme esta*?' he shouted peevishly.

'Yasmin,' came a small voice.

'*Momento*,' he called, but it was five minutes before he opened the door letting out a cloud of expensive perfume.

Quickly she slipped inside.

'This is indeed a pleasure,' said Carlo, gallantly. He was glad he'd had time to snatch off his hairnet and put in his teeth. 'Would you like a glass of wine?' he asked.

'Thank you, no,' she replied. 'This is not a social visit. It concerns the plane going to Alexandria.'

Carlo's smile vanished when he took in the serious look on Yasmin's face. He was surprised to realise that, from their very first meeting when her beauty had lit up the future, he hadn't seen much of her. She'd become almost invisible in the anonymity of her black Arab chador. And now as she turned back her headscarf he was startled with a realisation that he'd almost forgotten her as a woman.

'Capitano Abruzzi,' she began urgently, 'you must stop this madness. You must not let this nonsense take place.'

Carlo was speechless. The whole enormity of the exploit flooded him with instant panic. If his second in command or even one of his men uttered these words he would have agreed at once. But the enthusiasm, and the speed at which all the discussions had taken place, had taken the matter out of his hands. He'd been swept along like a cigarette butt in the Tiber.

'One word from you,' she urged.

'You don't understand,' he said helplessly.

But he knew she did. He was weak. He wasn't Capitano Abruzzi – he was Carlo, a head waiter. *Mamma mia*, what could he do? The express was already racing towards the buffers without brakes.

Yasmin regarded him helplessly with those soulful dark eyes.

Immediately he stiffened. Like all good Italians he became a man again. 'You are right, my dear,' he said in a commanding voice. 'It is madness.'

But even as he took down the hanger containing his tunic his shoulders slumped. He turned slowly to face her, raising his arms aside in a useless gesture of defeat. With his tunic on the hanger he could have been a matador, apologising to the bull for what he was about to do.

Yasmin knew in that moment that further appeals would be a waste of time. She sighed. 'As the outcome appears to be inevitable, Carlo, I would ask you to do one thing for me.'

Carlo returned his tunic to the wardrobe and walked towards her. 'What would you have me do?' he said.

'Listen to me carefully,' she said. 'What I have to say is official.'

He straightened and his eyes took on a new wariness, 'official' being the trigger word. 'I am listening,' he said and eyed her gravely.

Yasmin handed him the sheet of paper consisting of five figure cyphers. He glanced at it, then looked at her enquiringly.

Yasmin went on. 'I want you to instruct your wireless operator to send this message.' She paused. 'Below I have put in the frequency he must use.'

He stared at her for a moment, then said, 'Am I permitted to ask what the message is and to whom it is addressed?'

'It's addressed to British Military Intelligence and it gives the ETA of the plane that is to leave tonight.'

Carlo stared at her, a million questions roaring inside his head. 'But this is impossible, my dear,' he spluttered. 'The success of the flight is totally dependent on secrecy.'

She smiled. 'What is secret about an unarmed enemy plane flying over British airspace? It would be an easy target for every anti-aircraft battery within fifty miles of Alexandria, not to mention the fighter planes of the Royal Air Force.'

Carlo nodded slowly. They had naturally discussed this possibility, but it had been glossed over as one of the hazards of war. But now, in the cold light of reason, Carlo had to accept that it would indeed be suicide.

As if reading his thoughts, Yasmin continued. 'This message will guarantee safe passage and a landing at Aboukir.

Carlo pondered this at length and after a time he nodded again. 'Yes, I see.' He rose and paced the room as if measuring it for a carpet.

'Who are you?' he finally asked.

'Yasmin.'

He came over to the table and leant towards her.

'And who is Yasmin?' His face was a few inches from hers.

'That is information you do not need to know,' she replied coolly.

'Are you with British Military Intelligence?'

'No, I am not connected in any way with British Military Intelligence. I can only repeat that unless you send the message you will be responsible for the deaths of many of your compatriots, not to mention the British contingent.'

They looked at each other, then after a time Carlo capitulated. 'Very well, I will see that this is transmitted.'

'Thank you,' said Yasmin. 'This message must be sent immediately and repeated until an acknowledgement is received.'

He turned to take his topi from its hatbox and when he looked round she was gone. She was halfway across the compound as he raced towards the wireless hut. Yasmin let out a sigh of relief and walked over to rejoin the rest of the company, stopping suddenly when she caught sight of Sparks and Miller. A smile of amusement crossed her face and she shook her head in reluctant admiration.

Dusty Miller never missed a trick! 'All aboard for the *Skylark*,' he greeted her. And she smiled again at the neat stack of papers and the large empty biscuit tin. This mystified her and Miller winked. It had been a hard wrangle with the second in command but Miller had finally won the day. First, they required paper and a rubber stamp. These requests didn't create any difficulty but the sticking point had been when Miller insisted that all the would-be prisoners would have to pay their fare with gold wristwatches, bangles or money if there was any. This was when tempers flared.

Sparks stepped forward and was about to hang one on the second in command, who stepped back quickly, but there was a knife in his hand. Miller jumped between them and calmed matters down with a soothing, brilliant explanation. There had been a misunderstanding. The fares charged to the prisoners would be needed to grease the palms of the British authorities in Alexandria in order to ensure special treatment for the POWs. It seemed reasonable enough to the Italian way of life and with acquiescent nods they all shook hands and the day was saved.

The Italians wouldn't have capitulated so easily had they known the truth. No British official was going to get his hot, sticky little hands on this pile of joy. It would barely cover the expenses of a safe passage down the Nile. Disappearing from the airfield was the hard part; they already knew of a boat.

Yasmin was intrigued as a straggling line of POWs

approached the table. Miller put out his hand to receive a gold wristwatch from the first man in the queue and after a cursory examination he put it into the biscuit tin. The man then passed on to Sparks, who briskly banged down a rubber stamp on to a piece of paper, which he solemnly handed over. The man stared joyfully at his boarding pass and the date, 23 December. He didn't mind. He'd worked in the office and 23 December was the only date on the rubber stamp.

The next in line took his place in front of Miller with his worldly goods, and so on until all the passengers had been booked in. Miller's eyes gleamed as he looked into the biscuit tin. He could hardly get the lid on. To hell with the boat – there was enough here to hire a light plane.

In the rest of the camp, excitement was now at fever pitch. Letters were being written hurriedly to be posted in Alexandria and for some unknown reason everybody seemed to be talking in whispers. The lucky prisoners of war were embraced many times and tears were shed all over the place. The tension was unbearable and when the African night came down like a heavy velvet curtain whisked over a lighted window, hearts were beating faster and mouths were becoming drier – they were committed.

In the blackness of the night the side of the runway was seething with watchers, but nobody spoke. Eyes scanned the dark sky as if they were waiting for the end of the world, ears straining for the uneven beat of the approaching supply plane. Way over in the Bedouin encampment a camel coughed and all heads jerked in that direction, but on identifying the sound there was a general relaxation. It broke the almost unbearable suspense.

But the quiet mutterings ceased immediately when in the distance came the sound they had all been waiting for: badly synchronised engines getting louder as the plane neared its destination. As if this was a signal, the dark shapes awaiting its arrival evaporated into their huts. It was vital that this was to be a normal, ordinary, scheduled flight. A command was issued and the kerosene lamps on either side of the runway were lit as the plane made its final approach. It wasn't a bad landing considering the unevenness of the flight path.

When the plane came to a final stop Carlo minced nervously forward, resplendent in his full dress uniform, complete with medals, just in time to reach the plane as der Oberst der Luftwaffe ducked out of the door. Carlo saluted and then escorted him towards the hotel. During the fifty yards of darkness Carlo was proud of himself – cool, urbane and gracious – but immediately they stepped into the lights of the hotel his bottle went. Sweat poured from his face and he was trembling so violently he had to explain to his honoured guest that it was an illness which ran in the family.

He turned to summon the wine waiter. He snapped his fingers but they didn't seem to work, so he clapped his hands. And at the signal one of his minions hurried over with a glass of champagne on a silver salver. Unfortunately he, too, was gripped by nerves and by the time he reached der Oberst, there wasn't much champagne in the glass but his tray was awash.

The situation was saved at that moment when a huge jet of water erupted from the rockery in the centre of the floor, drenching both Carlo and his honoured guest. Carlo was mortified, ineffectively dabbing der Oberst der Luftwaffe's uniform with his handkerchief and babbling apologies. Der Oberst, however, seemed to take it all in good part. In fact, he was envisaging a humorous anecdote at the dinner table when he returned to his mess. Carlo's second in command, assessing the situation at a glance, came forward and ushered the great man to his suite on the first floor . . .

And Phase I of Plan Junkers was already in operation.

The plane itself was still on the runway and in the back the Feldwebel, a large, pimply faced Bavarian, sat on a crate watching the Italians at work, but he was uneasy. He wasn't too thick to notice that as the Italians carried the supplies down the ramp they seemed to be avoiding looking at him. Something was afoot, but when another Italian sidled up to him with a much-thumbed, creased photo of an undressed female, he relaxed, feeling that this must be the reason for their unusual behaviour.

He waved the man away scornfully. But the man was persistent. He pointed at the picture and then towards a camp. The Feldwebel took the picture from him and had another look. He hoped it wasn't *this* woman – if the photo was anything to go by she must be over eighty by now.

The Italian, sensing interest, sketched the shape of the woman with his hands, pointed at the German and said 'jigga-jig'. He stepped back out of the plane and beckoned to him. The German was intrigued; at least it was a change from the dull routine of his flight. Looking round he ascertained that he could safely leave the unloading to the Italians and jumped down to follow the pimp.

When they reached a hut the Italian knocked lightly on the door and cooed softly, 'Here is Fritz.' Then, pushing the door open, he stood aside to let the German enter. Immediately the door slammed shut, Fritz whirled round to hear a heavy key turning in the lock. Wildly he looked round him but there were no windows at all, no furniture either. He wasn't very bright but he had sense enough not to hammer on the door with his fists. Shrugging his shoulders he sat on the floor and waited for developments.

The German navigator was as easy as his comrade. Going through the hotel he went to the washrooms at the back and stripped off for his customary shower before the return trip. Refreshed and cleansed, he donned his uniform, but when he tried the door handle he found he was locked in. Puzzled and angered, he hammered on the door. Somebody was going to suffer for this! It never occurred to him that it might be himself.

The pilot was a different matter altogether. Sometimes he would go into the hotel for a shower but this could not be guaranteed. More often than not he stayed with the plane until it was time to take off. This was one of those occasions. He was sitting in his seat making routine checks and as he bent over his instruments he felt the cold muzzle of a revolver against his neck. Two Italians sprang forward, pinning his arms while they tied his wrists behind his back. It was all done so expertly and so quickly he hadn't even time to say "Gott in Himmel". The pressure of the revolver eased and Miller said, 'That didn't hurt, did it?'

The pilot was bewildered. He couldn't understand English, far less the situation he was in. He only knew that something was definitely wrong. He was escorted to the rear of the plane and forced to sit on the floor. Miller strode over and crouched before him. He was about to speak, but instead he rose and staggered back a pace, holding a handkerchief to his face. 'Bloody hell,' he muttered, 'he's crapped himself.' At least this one wasn't going to be a problem. '*Sprecken sie* English?' he said.

'*Ja*,' squeaked the man, frightened now.

'Good,' said Miller. 'Well, just sit quietly while I collect the rest of your mates . . . *comprendez*?'

The young pilot nodded quickly and Miller signalled to a couple of the Italians to keep their eye on him. He backed away and jumped down from the plane where the air was fresher.

At the same time in the VIP suite at the hotel, der Oberst der Luftwaffe was a happy man. It was his first visit and tales of this fabulous oasis had not been exaggerated. This suite would not have disgraced the Adler Hotel in the Wilhelmstrasse.

Clouds of steam emanated from the bathroom as the General, wrapping a towel round his waist, walked into the bedroom and felt the softness of the bed, marvelling at the clean white sheets and the soft eiderdown. It was tempting but there would be plenty of time for a good night's sleep when he had eaten. And again, tales of the fabulous chef were already making his mouth water.

He frowned as his eye fell upon his discarded uniform on the floor. It was where he had left it on the understanding that, by the time he had bathed, it would be pressed and ironed for the banquet. Anger began to replace his euphoria. He snatched up the soiled garments, then whirled as a voice from the doorway said quietly, 'Get dressed.' Der Oberst der Luftwaffe was at first startled, then bewildered. Surely his eyes were playing him tricks. It was a British Sergeant pointing a Luger pistol at him.

Sparks strode forward, snatched the uniform from the General and flung it back at him. 'Put it on!' snapped Sparks, cocking the pistol.

And Phase I of the plan was complete.

Outside the plane the Italian prisoners waited nervously for their orders to board. It had all seemed rosy during the planning stages of the day but now when all was inevitable the future didn't look too bright. The German flight crew were already sitting dejectedly at the back end of the plane while Miller, standing at the door screwing up his eyes, peered hard into the blackness, wondering what had happened to Sparks and der Oberst der Luftwaffe and his part in the exercise. Impatiently he was about to jump down and investigate when out of the gloom stepped his last passenger, followed by Sparks.

'Where the hell have you been?' snapped Miller. 'It'll

216

soon be daylight.' And he wasn't far wrong, it was now nearly 3 a.m.

Sparks didn't reply but ushered der Oberst der Luftwaffe to sit on the floor with his colleagues. They all sat at attention looking straight ahead in deference to the high rank of their senior officer. And then Sparks noticed the fat Feldwebel who sat glowering, his eyes a purplish black and closed, and there was an ugly bruise on his cheek. Sparks looked at him, then turned to Miller. 'Walk into the propeller did he?'

Miller replied, 'Nah, he was going to board the plane and on the top step he suddenly turns and shouts "*Heil* Hitler".'

Sparks smiled.

Miller went on. 'Well, I was on the bottom step and the only place I could reach was his bollocks so I gave him an uppercut and as he doubled forward his face caught my knee. He's a lucky man. If I hadn't been there, he would have had a very nasty fall.'

The Feldwebel lowered his head and stared at the floor, watching the droplets of bright-red blood that leaked from his nose. He wasn't happy. He'd only shouted '*Heil* Hitler' to impress his senior officer. Well bugger him, bugger all officers and bugger the German military, and as this was only a thought he added, and bugger Hitler too.

As soon as the Italians were settled comfortably the door was closed and Rudy started the engines – only he wasn't Rudy the German pilot. He now wore Gratwick's identity discs round his neck and in his battledress pocket he had Gratwick's paybook. The uniform was almost tight enough to be ludicrous but then not many of these uniforms were made to fit.

'Where the hell is that woman?' shouted Sparks leaning out the door. 'Yasmin,' he yelled at the top of his voice.

But she couldn't hear him. She was in the hotel

seeking Carlo. Her eyes quickly scanned the room, and she found him sitting at a corner table hunched over a glass of red wine. Quickly she hurried over and sat down opposite. He lifted his bleary eyes, then sat bolt upright in alarm.

'Is something wrong?' he asked.

'No, no, Carlo. It's just something I'd like to know.' She looked round quickly to make sure there was no one to overhear. 'Tell me, Carlo,' she said, 'when you originally moved in here, did you have girls?'

'Girls?' he said, not understanding.

'Yes, girls. This was meant to be a place for senior Italian officers to relax, yes?'

He nodded, then the lira dropped. 'Ah, girls. What a difference they would have made.' He smiled dreamily. 'Oh yes, they were promised – beautiful girls of all nations. They were promised but they never came. Every day I say "Where are the girls?". "They are coming," I'm told. But, no, and the war goes badly for us.' He shrugged expressively. 'So we never got the girls.'

'Thanks, Carlo,' she said, and patting his hand she hurried out, leaving Carlo with a dreamy smile on his face, remembering what might have been.

Suddenly he stiffened and slapped his forehead. '*Mama mia,*' he ejaculated. 'I did not wish them good luck.' And his chair toppled backward in his haste to get out.

Yasmin settled into the seat next to Rudy, who buckled her into the straps. Behind them Sparks and Miller sat on the floor behind each seat. There was an air of apprehension as Rudy revved up the engines. As they reached maximum revs, he released the brakes and the plane rolled forward, bumping at first, then picking up speed, and as he eased back on the stick the motion became smooth and they were airborne. The Italians broke into spontaneous applause.

As the plane disappeared into the blackness, Carlo arrived breathless to meet Gratwick at the end of the runway, a heavy blanket round his thin shoulders, and they waved until the sound of the engines died away. Together they made their way to the hotel. Perhaps a bottle of brandy would ease the pain.

Squatting on the floor of the vibrating aircraft, Sergeant Sparks blew into his cold hands. Why the bloody hell did he let Miller talk him into these messes? He stuffed his hands under his armpits for warmth and tried to sleep. It was a black night and a new moon was obscured from time to time by clouds casting a veil over the stars.

But there was a good pyrotechnical display several miles off the port side, and to the north flashes lit the horizon. After the first half-hour the happy murmurs of the Italians interspersed with snatches of arias gradually died away and the only sound was the monotonous drone of the three engines.

It's bloody freezing, thought Miller. If I'd known it was going to be this cold I'd have walked. If things didn't warm up soon, they'd have to be lifted out of the plane like carcasses at Smithfield.

Yasmin drowsed in the navigator's seat and suddenly was aware that something was different. The plane was banking gently towards the rising sun. She put her hand up to shield her eyes from the glare and when she felt a tap on her arm she turned to Rudy, who handed her a pair of earphones. She clamped them over her head and Rudy spoke into his mouthpiece.

'We should be there in an hour or so.'

Yasmin looked at her watch incredulously.

'Surely we're not that far from Alexandria?' she asked. But he had to reach out and flick her speak button. She repeated her question.

'No,' he replied, 'we're not going to Alexandria. It's too dangerous. We've got away with it so far but now it is light . . . I don't fancy my chances with the English fighters.' She stared at him blankly. He shrugged. 'It was Sergeant Miller's suggestion and I'm inclined to agree with him.'

Yasmin groaned inwardly. Did not the poor fool realise the only reason they'd had a peaceful passage was that they were expected? Outwardly calm, she asked, 'If we're not going to Alexandria, what is our new destination?'

'It is a little place about sixty miles away called Alam Farâfa, and I know a little airstrip there. It is not a very large . . .' But the rest of his words were drowned by a loud roar and a plane flashed over the perspex of the cockpit and dwindled into the distance ahead.

Sparks and Miller clawed themselves to their feet.

'What the bloody 'ell was that?' shouted Miller over the pilot's shoulder but Rudy was struggling with the controls as the Junkers wallowed in the backwash.

Rudy leant his head back. 'A Spitfire,' he yelled.

'Oh, no,' groaned Miller. 'I knew it wouldn't last.' He ducked instinctively as they were buzzed again by another Spitfire. Rudy tried to keep the plane straight and level. There was no evasive action he could take short of diving into the ground.

In the back of the plane the prisoners were on the verge of panic and the smell of fear was almost tangible – or it might have been something more basic.

Miller grabbed Sparks's arm. 'Why don't they get it over with?' he yelled, and without waiting for a reply he shook Rudy's shoulder. But Rudy waved him away. He was busy twiddling a knob on his radio, listening intently.

A voice came through his headphones. 'This is Red Leader to Bandit. Are you receiving me now? Over.'

Rudy's adjustment to a new frequency was spot-on. 'Loud and clear. Over,' he replied.

'Red Leader to Bandit. You are veering off course.

Reset your heading to one six eight. We will escort you on to the airfield. Out.'

Rudy eased off his headphones. 'They're not hostile,' he said. 'We have an escort into Alex.' And with that he banked the plane gently round on to its original setting.

Yasmin breathed a sigh of relief. At least the wireless message had got through.

Thirty minutes later as they approached the airstrip the Spitfires peeled away with a final 'Good Luck' and, as Rudy lowered the flaps, he couldn't help feeling they were going to need all the good fortune they could handle, and more.

Miller's nose was crushed against the perspex of the side window as he gazed down on the welcoming committee. The whole place was seething with Military Police. Redcaps were everywhere. It was like landing in a poppy field. Miller's stomach churned. But what had he been expecting – a band playing 'Rule Britannia'?

Rudy was about to put the plane down gently, like a butterfly with burnt feet, when he suddenly remembered just in time that he wasn't der Fliegerhauptmann von Bosch: he was Driver Gratwick, a rusty prewar pilot taking holidaymakers on trips round the Island of Jersey. He slammed the plane down on to the runway and bounced several times before it came to rest skewwhiff at the end of the runway. It must have been a bad landing, even had Albie been a pilot and not just a cover story . . .

As the Junkers came to a halt Miller opened the door and pushed out the steps, but before he could alight a Squadron Leader shoved him back, pulled up the steps and slammed the door.

'Squadron Leader Dankworth,' he said by way of introduction. Then he leant over Rudy, giving him instructions to follow the truck that had pulled in front of them. Rudy released the brakes and they were guided to a remote part of the airfield into a heavily guarded hanger. From there the Italians and the German aircrew disembarked and were helped into three-ton Bedfords and taken away with an escort of Military Police motorcycles.

Der Oberst der Luftwaffe, being of importance, was ushered into a staff car with cool formality and whisked off to a safe house for interrogation. Sparks and Miller and the ersatz Gratwick were kept under close guard aboard the aircraft. They watched curiously as Yasmin was allowed to leave the plane in order to speak quietly to Squadron Leader Dankworth, who saluted and escorted her out into the bright sunlight.

Miller looked at Sparks. 'What did she say to him?'

Sparks shrugged. 'How the hell should I know?' he snarled, angry at his weakness in the feeling of jealousy that swept through him.

Miller turned away dejected. This was hardly the conquering heroes' welcome he'd envisaged – cheering crowds, a military band, flashbulbs, a short speech, tea with the Air Marshal's wife, a ride round the city in an open car and dinner at Government House. 'Bugger this for a game of skittles,' he said out loud and ducked through the doorway. But immediately he was facing a large Military Police Captain.

'I'm sorry, Sergeant,' he said officially. 'No one else is to leave the plane.' Then with a surreptitious glance over his shoulder he took his pay book from his tunic pocket and unclipped a pen. Thrusting these towards Miller he whispered, 'Could you sign this "To Len. With Best Wishes"?'

Colonel Brunswick sat at his desk wondering what fairy story they'd concocted this time. Sergeants Sparks and Miller were under heavy guard at the airfield and would stay there until he sent for them, and this might not be until the war was over. If General Montgomery insisted on meeting them during the next six months he'd know exactly where to find them. They'd be in that hanger at the end of the airfield. He pulled himself together; there were more important things to see to. He took a batch of intelligence reports from a drawer and began to peruse them.

There was a discreet knock on the door and his Adjutant entered.

'Not now, Jimmy,' he growled. 'I'm busy.'

'There's an Estelle Chambertin to see you, sir.'

Colonel Brunswick stared at him. 'A woman?' he asked stupidly.

The Adjutant was unmoved. 'Yes, sir.'

Brunswick exploded. 'What's the matter with you, Captain?' he yelled. 'Here I am, saddled with probably the greatest crisis of my military career and you come in here, trying to organise my sex life.'

'No, sir,' replied the Adjutant. 'Her code name is Yasmin.'

'Yasmin!' breathed the Colonel. Then he rose, all businesslike. He donned his tunic and smoothed his hair back. 'Send her in immediately, Jimmy. If anybody can pick the bones out of all this, she can.'

A few minutes later the girl was ushered in. She was still clad in the black chador of the desert.

'Yasmin, I presume,' said the Colonel with out-stretched hand.

She ignored it. When she bared her head and face he was staggered by her beauty.

'I understood you were dead,' he spluttered, off his guard.

'Then you have been misinformed,' she replied, and looked over pointedly at the Adjutant.

'Ah yes,' said Colonel Brunswick. 'This is my Adjutant, Captain Shelley.'

There was an awkward pause, then, after a moment,

the Colonel got the message. He coughed. 'Perhaps, Jimmy, it would be better if you left us alone for a while.

Without a word the Adjutant left quietly.

When he'd gone Colonel Brunswick said, 'Will you have a seat?' And when they were settled he became businesslike again. 'And to what do we owe the pleasure of this visit?'

Yasmin didn't waste any time. Quickly she explained the history and present activities of the Italian camp at the El Waddim Oasis; the twice-weekly visits of the German supply plane and the lack of morale leading up to the flight of the Junkers. It was precise and detailed as one would expect from a highly trained operative.

Brunswick nodded. He had the picture and was wondering what was coming next.

'As we are both aware,' she went on, 'the Germans are not a benevolent society. They do not send a supply plane in twice a week out of the goodness of their hearts just to feed their Italian allies.'

Colonel Brunswick stared at her fixedly, still waiting for the punchline. This wasn't the big picture – it was only the trailer. 'Please go on, mam'selle,' he said.

She leant forward. 'I think the supplies the Germans fly in is merely a smokescreen. It is what they take back with them that's important.'

After a moment Colonel Brunswick asked, 'And what would that be?'

She shrugged. 'What indeed? It is my intention to find out but I know in my bones that with the tight secrecy that surrounds it, it could be something extremely important.'

The Colonel swivelled his chair and looked out of the window. He wished to God he hadn't dismissed his Adjutant. His usual 'What do you think, Jimmy?' had seen him out of many tight corners in the past. After a time he swung round to face her.

'If this information is as important as you say, how do we acquire it?'

She seemed puzzled by the question. 'By returning to El Waddim Oasis, of course.'

'And how do you propose to return?'

'By the Junkers, naturally.'

Brunswick pondered her answer. This was not as simple as it sounded. He could authorise many things but to send her back in the Junkers was beyond even his capacity. He would have to go through all the official rigmarole again with the Air Force for fighter protection and with the Artillery to alert their batteries along the route.

'And Sergeants Sparks and Miller?' he asked, more for something to say than anything else.

Yasmin raised her eyebrows. 'Well naturally they will return with me. Everything must appear to be normal. If we did not return the Italians would be suspicious and the whole operation would be a nonstarter.'

Colonel Brunswick sighed and began to write hurriedly on his pad. And when he had jabbed the paper with a full stop he threw down his pencil. 'You realise, of course, that what you are proposing is beyond my authority and I will have to get clearance from higher up.'

She nodded quickly. 'I understand,' she said, 'but it is imperative that we return tonight.'

Colonel Brunswick sat bolt upright. 'Tonight?' he spluttered . . . he iffed and butted and supposed and finally snatched up the telephone. 'I want you in here, Jimmy, a.s.a.p.' He slammed the phone down.

All the intricate planning and arrangements would have to be done in any case by his Adjutant. It didn't appear to be too difficult and, with this highly trained intelligence agent, the pickings might be enormous.

'Come in,' he said in response to the familiar knock. And when the Adjutant was seated, pencil and pad in hand, Brunswick explained briefly what had to be done.

It didn't take long, and when the Adjutant rose to set the wheels in motion, Yasmin said, 'There is something more I would ask.'

The Colonel and his Adjutant froze, and she went on.

'I have explained to you, Colonel Brunswick, the purpose of the El Waddim Oasis and the original intention as to the activities that would be carried out there.'

The Colonel nodded. 'Yes, I understand it was to be a holiday camp for top-ranking Italian officers – in other words a high-class brothel.'

She nodded. 'And if it was restored it would attract many high-ranking officers, only this time they would be German.'

The Adjutant caught on at once. 'It's an idea, sir,' he said.

But it was well beyond Brunswick's comprehension. 'Are you suggesting,' he said, outraged, 'that we set up a brothel for German officers?'

Yasmin was unabashed. 'That is exactly what I am suggesting, Colonel. The oasis could be one of the most important centres of intelligence gathering in the Middle East. Take it from me, Colonel, when I was working on the German transmitter case at Abdul's, his girls were my best sources of information. Be assured, Colonel, brains are useless when the cock does the thinking.'

Brunswick harrumphed at this crudity, but he let it pass.

'Are there girls there already?' asked the Adjutant.

'No,' replied Yasmin coolly. 'But since you closed Abdul's place I know where to recruit some. I know where they live and three of them speak German fluently. And believe me, Colonel, they could use the work.'

Colonel Brunswick was almost at panic stations. He was out of his depth – more than that, he was in

226

mid-Atlantic with a hole in his waterwings. He could imagine the faces of the men in Whitehall when he put forward the proposal to airlift eight girls to a remote part of the desert to set up a brothel. He would certainly be sent for a medical and, even if the transportation of the girls was successful, the Germans would certainly be extremely suspicious of eight beauties suddenly appearing from nowhere. On the plus side, if they did take the bait, he recognised the importance of the intelligence that could be passed on.

He looked hopefully at his Adjutant, who turned away and looked out of the window. There was no help from that quarter.

As if reading his mind, Yasmin went on. 'I fully understand your worries regarding the eight girls but I have considered this very carefully and with a proper cover story it should not be too difficult.'

They listened intently while she outlined her plan and when she'd finished it not only seemed logical, but, better than that, it looked like a brilliant idea. Even Colonel Brunswick was impressed, so much so that he couldn't wait to expound the theory to his superiors as his own idea.

Yasmin rose and said, 'If that is all, Colonel, I'll get back to the airfield to await your decision.'

And before Colonel Brunswick could say 'Well goodbye, then', she was gone.

'Well, Jimmy,' said the Colonel briskly, 'you know what the situation is.'

'Yes, sir, we haven't much time.' And he hurried down the corridor to his own office in order to set the wheels in motion for an emergency high-level meeting. It was urgent, top-priority, most immediate, and within half an hour dispatch riders roared madly from one office block to another, telephone operators had no time for tea breaks, and the teleprinter machines clacked frantically and incessantly between Whitehall

227

and Alexandria. There was no time for long discussion – it was either yes or no and it was the reputation of Sergeants Sparks and Miller that won the day.

Even as the Junkers rose into the dark African night on its way back to El Waddim Oasis, there were still final arrangements to be made and okayed.

The Germans, alerted by all this increased activity, dispatched half a dozen more agents into Alexandria to find out what was going on – they didn't have long to wait.

The following day all the British newspapers flooded the streets with glaring headlines such as

EIGHT DANCING GIRLS LOST IN DESERT
ENSA ANGRY AT DANCING TROOP
THEY WENT WITHOUT PERMISSION,
SAYS UNION OFFICIAL
WHERE ARE THEY?

The stories were similar: 'The girls, called "The Tip Top Eight", had gone into the desert to entertain the troops, the last reported sightings being twelve miles out from Alexandria.' To all intents and purposes they'd disappeared into the blue, but the German Intelligence were not impressed. The story of the eight girls was obviously a fabrication to divert the minds of the British people from the ultimate loss of Africa. The Tip Top Eight were a fantasy dreamt up by the Propaganda Ministry. They didn't even exist. Even so, along with British patrols, the Germans had also sent out search parties for the missing girls.

On 19 August the nonexistent girls were enjoying a hearty breakfast at the El Waddim Oasis. On the plane over they had been in trepidation and even scared of what they'd let themselves in for. By the airstrip about sixty Italians had cheered as the plane had come in to

228

land and when it finally came to a stop they all surged forward. But when the cabin door opened the Italians were cut off in mid-cheer and stared in astonishment as a beautiful girl appeared. Then after a moment's stunned silence pandemonium broke out, wolf whistles, whoops and applause. Then, incredibly, another girl appeared, followed by another.

Eyes on stalks the Italians tried to take it all in. Perhaps there would be one for each of them. But when Miller was next to show his face, they realised the parade was over. The girls felt like film stars; they'd never had so much attention in the whole of their lives and all their past fears on the journey were a distant memory.

Miller, still framed in the doorway, watched happily. He'd already picked his girl. Then Sparks nudged him in the back with a suitcase and he became all business again.

'Oi,' he shouted after the Italians, 'what about giving us a hand with this luggage?'

There was still much to do – the plane had to be towed off the runway to a spot some distance into the desert, then blanketed with several tons of sand until it became just another dune. The wheel tracks had to be obliterated and Junkers 498 cease to exist until the next trip.

Carlo was overjoyed when the girls trooped in. He couldn't believe it. With tears streaming down his face, he embraced them all in turn and afterwards looked round for Yasmin. This time it was an embrace and a kiss on both cheeks. 'You are my Mother Christmas,' he said embracing her again.

And while her cheek was next to his she spoke into his ear, 'Carlo, we have to talk.'

'Later,' he said happily. 'Now we drink champagne.'

'We have to talk now, Carlo. It's important.'

Carlo looked at her and his face went serious. 'Come with me,' he said and led her into a side room.

Yasmin quickly filled him in with the girls' cover story. It didn't take long and Carlo got it in one.

'I understand,' he said quietly.

'This cover story must be drilled into every member of your staff. There must be no slip-ups when the German investigation team arrive.'

Carlo's eyes panicked for a second.

'Oh yes, they'll come,' insisted Yasmin. 'They're not going to let a plane disappear without a thorough investigation.'

'Yes, I was forgetting them.' His face fell. 'The Germans are not fools – I think the story of the lost dancing girls will not convince them.'

Yasmin smiled. 'It will, Carlo, it will; I can promise you that. By now it will be in all the English papers.'

A howl of laughter came through from the dining room and Carlo straightened his tunic. 'The sooner they all know of the situation the better.' He opened the door and strode into the happy crowd clapping his hands for attention. He stood on a chair and addressed the assembly. 'You must treat these girls with care and courtesy.' They cheered and whooped but he silenced them as he continued gravely. 'These poor girls, the Tip Top Eight, came into the desert to entertain the troops when, *zump*, the bus on which they travel breaks down and they are stranded.'

Murmurs of condolence went round the room.

'Three days,' went on Carlo, 'they wander through the vast unforgiving desert and with only a half-litre of water between them, they found this camp.'

He bowed as if he'd just recited 'To be or not to be', and dutifully they applauded. When the clapping had died down one of the Italians raised his hand and said, 'Capitano Abruzzi, this cannot be true. Did we not help them down from the plane ten minutes ago?'

There was a stunned silence and they looked towards Carlo to see how he would get out of this. They need not have worried, he was equal to the occasion.

'My friend,' he said laughing, 'you must remember in future to put your hat on when you go out into the sun. What plane did you help them down from? I have seen no plane.' He looked innocently round at all the faces. 'Did anyone here see a plane arrive ten minutes ago? And if a plane landed, where is it now?'

This was the trigger and someone started to laugh and say 'Yes, where is it now?'. Others joined in the laughter and Carlo went on. 'And when the Germans come to ask you about their missing supply plane, what do we say?' The reply came with a unanimous roar. '*What supply plane?*' they yelled and the moment was saved.

Carlo gazed down. His wireless operator was tugging at his trouser leg and holding out a sheet of paper. He took the message and read it carefully. The happy sound of laughter and ribaldry tailed off as they watched their *Commandante* anxiously. He cleared his throat.

'My friends,' he said, 'I have just received a wireless message.' He paused to let this sink in and then went on. 'Tomorrow night a German plane will arrive carrying members of the Military Police, and a man from the Gestapo. They are here from die Luftwaffepolizei to investigate the loss of Junkers 498.'

That killed the celebrations like a bucket of cold spaghetti. The Germans weren't wasting much time.

The investigating officers from die Luftwaffepolizei arrived by plane the following night and Carlo was there to greet them as they disembarked. He led them towards the hotel with a torch, talking ten to the dozen – commiserations for the missing flight crew, assuring them over and over that no one was more surprised when it didn't arrive. And just before they entered the hotel he halted and turned towards them.

'And, gentlemen,' he said in a conspiratorial voice, 'I

231

have a very pleasant surprise for you. Eight little angels who dropped in out of heaven a few days ago! You like surprises, yes?' he asked.

The man in civilian clothes growled, 'Anything is better than standing out here in the freezing cold.'

'*Si, si*,' said Carlo, and ushered them into the light and warmth of the hotel.

As they stepped inside they screwed up their eyes to adjust to the bright lights. All sound died away leaving only the click-click of the gramophone as the record reached its end. With a sudden screech someone lifted the needle.

At a bar in the corner eight girls and their attendants stared at the newcomers. Carlo wished desperately they hadn't removed the fountain – the trickle of water might have soothed the moment. Suddenly the stalemate was broken when one of the Germans yelped excitedly and pointed to the girls.

'Tip Top Eight!' He whirled to his comrades. 'Haven't you heard? These are the eight dancing girls that were missing in the desert.'

The girls had been well briefed. They looked at one another. They were good actresses. Being on the game, they had to be. One of them slid from her stool and took a pace towards the men.

'Yes,' she said in a small voice, 'we are the Tip Top Girls.'

There was a moment's silence. Then the German who had spoken said, 'I knew it.' He laughed. 'Everyone in North Africa is searching for you, even from our base. Planes have been sent out to reconnoitre.' He laughed again. 'And here you are.'

The girls still pretended to look frightened and it did not take much effort.

The man chuckled. 'As we have found you, do not we deserve a prize?' He shrugged out of his greatcoat and rubbing his hands walked confidently to the bar. 'At least we can have a drink together.' His comrade, now following his example, joined him.

Carlo was in his element – he clapped his hands. 'What will you have to drink, gentlemen? My men will serve you whatever you like.'

The girls began to smile tentatively. 'Come now, girls,' said Carlo heartily. 'They will not bite you – make them welcome.'

And the ice was broken – almost.

Carlo noticed that the man in a leather top coat, the standard Gestapo uniform, had taken a bottle and a glass to a side table; he was sitting there alone. Capitano Abruzzi, once more the head waiter, wandered over genially.

'Why not join the party?' He gestured towards the bar.

The man stared up at him coldly and in a quiet voice replied, 'They look in remarkably good condition.'

Carlo's smile froze but he recovered quickly and laughed, 'Ah yes, they look very well, but,' he said, leaning forward confidentially, 'when they arrived four days ago, oh what a mess.' He shrugged. 'But they are young and what different girls they are now after sleep, good food, wine.' He laughed again.

'They didn't walk from Alexandria,' said the man.

Carlo feigned surprise but had his answer ready. Yasmin had rehearsed him. 'No, no, no, it is impossible – they came in a bus.' And remembered in time, 'A yellow one.'

The man poured himself another glass and drank. Carlo watched him uneasily; he knew what the next question would be.

'And where is the yellow bus now?'

As per script, thought Carlo smugly, and replied, face darkening, 'The girls leave it just over the hill.' He pointed. 'Not two hundred metres from here and – ecco! – in the morning it is gone, disappeared. I know

233

where it will be.' He pointed in another direction. 'Down there in that stinking Arab village are thieves, villains, criminals.' He leant over the table. 'While you are here, I implore you and your comrades to search that encampment and should you come across eight Dovunque 35 trucks they are mine. But you must take care when entering: they will have your boots while you're walking.' He laughed at his little joke and was about to return to the bar when the man spoke again.

'And what happened to the driver?'

'The driver?' asked Carlo, his composure gone. Yasmin hadn't mentioned a driver at the briefing. Then inspiration hit him. 'Ah, the driver,' he repeated, 'he was an Arab.' And in order to hammer this one down tight he nodded. 'That place down there –' he pointed in the direction of the Arab camp '– is very likely his village. They're all related – husbands, brothers, wives. Even camels.'

'Do you have schnapps?' interrupted the man.

Carlo bowed with a sigh of relief. The act was over and he was secretly pleased with his performance. He hadn't had a standing ovation but on the other hand no one had asked for his money back.

When he returned from the bar with the schnapps he was also escorting a buxom blonde. 'Sir,' said Carlo, 'a little surprise.'

He ushered the girl forward. 'This is Inga.'

The German did not rise. He looked up at the girl. 'You are German?' he asked.

'*Ja*,' she said with a quick curtsey. 'I am from Flensburg.'

'Won't you sit down?'

'Thank you,' she said demurely, and with a shy smile took the seat opposite him.

Carlo bowed to both of them and moved away. She wouldn't be a problem. She had been well rehearsed with her cover story. He heard her begin the tale of her life but winced when he heard her say they'd emigrated to England in 1938 when she was just fifteen. Silly cow. She was thirty-five if she was a day.

Looking back at the Gestapo man over his shoulder, Carlo relaxed. The Gestapo man wasn't listening too hard. He was gazing at the two large breasts resting docilely on the table. It was going to be a long night.

Carlo joined the group at the bar, smiling happily. The party was already up and running. One of die Luftwaffepolizei with head tilted back was balancing a glass of beer on his forehead.

The investigators stayed for three days but there was very little investigation. In fact, they didn't really question the Italians at all. The Germans believed that the supply plane had crashed or been shot down somewhere on the way. After all, if it had landed yesterday the girls would have noticed. Little did the Germans realise that in giving the Italians a clean bill of health, they had saved their own lives. Had their suspicions been aroused they would never have survived the flight back. Carlo had one or two men on his staff who knew how to tinker with aero engines.

Two hours after the German plane had taken off, the first intelligence report from El Waddim Oasis was on Colonel Brunswick's desk – alongside a memo from his nephew requesting immediate dispatch of three dozen pairs of Indian clubs.

Captain Jampton looked forward to his PT sessions. Although he directed them wearing singlet and shorts, he never joined in – he wouldn't have lasted a day.

'Hup two three! Down two three! Hup two three!'

The lads were doing press-ups but in that heat it would have been frowned upon in the toughest glasshouse.

'Hup two three! Hup two three and stop!' As a body they collapsed on the sand but on a sharp, peremptory

235

blast of the whistle they sprang to their feet, or to be more exact they got up; some of them couldn't and just lay there, gathering their strength. Jampton blew his whistle again and clapped his hands as well.

Sergeant Major Puller winced as the men struggled upright. One man, however, remained flat on his face. Sergeant Major Puller's fists clenched. He recognised Jim Butterworth, who was nearly fifty, for God's sake, and he wasn't even military. Settling in Tobruk after World War One, he was the owner of the antique shop. But he wasn't there when one of the first bombs from the Stukas had flattened it. Unfortunately his wife and two children were still in bed when it happened. This was how he'd come to join Sergeant Major Puller's convoy into the blue.

'That man there,' squeaked Jampton, 'on your feet!'

The man lay prone, gasping for breath. He got slowly on to his hands and knees.

The Sergeant Major tensed. As the man was still in a kneeling position, his hand closed over a large stone. He rose slowly and took a step towards the CO.

'Butterworth!'

Puller's voice could be heard half a mile away. Butterworth stopped but his eyes never left Jampton.

'Drop it, lad,' said the Sergeant Major quietly.

Butterworth didn't move, then with a quick motion he flung down the stone and staggered off the parade ground.

Jampton was paralysed but quickly recovered himself enough to shout, 'Sergeant Major! Take that man's name!'

Puller stared back at him, white-faced with anger. You could have cut the tension with a butter knife. The whole scene was a still photograph – everyone frozen in a grand tableau. Even Prince, the flea-bitten mongrel, stood motionless by the side of the Sergeant Major with the hairs on his back stiffly upright. God knows what might have happened next.

But suddenly the spell was broken. Approaching the

camp in a large cloud of dust were two heavily armed 30-cwt Chevrolet trucks. Sergeant Major Puller recognised them as a long-range desert group patrol.

Jampton hadn't a clue who they were. They could have been collecting the dustbins for all he knew. However, he swelled with pride as the guard in tin helmet and heavily blancoed webbing ran out of the guard tent. From the distance his tinny voice rang out, 'Halt, who goes there?'

Jampton swelled with outrage as the two vehicles ignored the challenge, swept slowly past the guard and ground to a halt by the mess tent. Jampton clucked his tongue in annoyance. This wouldn't have happened had the red-striped pole been in place.

Sergeant Major Puller, all his black thoughts of the past few moments gone, chuckled softly. He, too, was thinking of the large red-and-white guard pole which had mysteriously disappeared one night. There had been one helluva flap over that, and Jampton had been beside himself with rage. In truth it was too juvenile to describe his behaviour as angry. It was more of a childish tantrum, akin to refusing to eat his prunes at teatime.

The whole of the Special Ordnance Group had been paraded while he began a tent search, although how in God's name anyone could hide a fifteen-foot pole in a two-man tent was beyond comprehension. The Sergeant Major smiled at the recollection as he made his way over to meet the visitors.

They were bone weary, alighting from their battle wagons like old men. He was only twenty yards away when the guard rushed past him breathing hard. He levelled his rifle. 'Halt! Who goes there?' he croaked.

Again he was ignored. The Sergeant Major patted him on the shoulder and said soothingly, 'You did your best, lad.' Mollified, the guard returned to his post.

The SM followed the visitors into the mess tent but

Captain Jampton was there before him. He wasn't an impressive sight: his shorts and singlet had been a goodbye present from the last batch of deserters. The man had been taller and three stone heavier than Jampton, which didn't make for a perfect fit, and for the first time Sergeant Major Puller felt embarrassed in the company of these hard-fighting men.

'Who's in charge here?' piped up Jampton.

One of them stepped forward, still sipping a mug of hot sweet tea.

'What's the problem, mate?' he said in a nasal Australian accent.

Jampton squared his shoulders. 'I am Captain Jampton, Commanding Officer.'

The man blowing on his steaming brew eyed him over the rim of his mug, then his face broke into a tired smile. 'Where the hell did you get those rompers from?' he said.

The others now turned to join the fun. Jampton drew himself up to his full five foot eight inches and eyed the man coldly. 'If it's not too much trouble,' he asked sarcastically, 'would you mind telling me who you are?'

The man didn't hesitate. 'Captain White, Long Range Desert Group.'

Immediately Jampton's manner changed. He knew of the LRDG. Stories of them and their exploits were a big part of his boyhood dreams. He put out his hand. 'Make yourself at home,' he said and shouted across to the sweating cook, 'Look after them.' Whirling round so quickly that his baggy shorts had difficulty keeping up and facing the Sergeant Major, he snapped, 'See to it.' After which he completed a full circle to face the Australian again. 'Come over to my tent when you're rested.' And he added manfully, 'We can have a tot and a yarn.' With that he marched out of the tent, back straight, a military man to his fingertips, he thought, although his large flapping shorts rather let him down.

* * *

Some hours later Captain Jampton sat at the table in his tent. He was looking forward to meeting Captain White. Before him was spread out the inevitable map. It was his way of appearing to be busy. When his guest arrived he'd fling down his dividers and mutter something like 'What a stinking mess', or, better still, 'Roll on peace'.

There was a knock on the tent pole. 'Come in,' he said and without looking up muttered, 'I'll take a patrol out tonight,' and flung his pencil down. As he looked up he frowned. It wasn't the Australian Captain: it was Jackson, his batman.

'Yes, what is it?' snapped Jampton, wishing he hadn't muttered that bit about the patrol. It would be all over the camp in less than five minutes and the MOs tent would be heaving with mystery ailments.

'Captain White's compliments, sir, and he'll be right over.'

Jampton perked up. 'Thank you, Jackson,' he said. 'Lay out a bottle of whisky and two glasses.'

Jackson stared at the little prat, dumbfounded. 'Sir?' he croaked.

'You heard me, Jackson. Surely you know what whisky is.'

'Yes, sir,' and he hurried from the tent to spread the tale of his CO's conversion to the hard stuff. He was back in five minutes with a bottle and two glasses. 'Got the whisky from the MO, sir. Said he might join you later – and he'll bring his own glass.'

Jampton shuddered. The last thing he wanted was the company of Captain Witherspoon. When Jackson had gone he examined the bottle and, taking the cork out gingerly, he sniffed at its contents, staggering back as if somebody had hit him. It was awful! He pushed the cork back in and was wiping his eyes when, without ceremony, Captain White entered, looking rested and younger.

239

'This is mighty nice of you,' he said, 'but I can't stay long. We're off in half an hour.'

'Time for a quick one, then,' said Jampton manfully. He sloshed half a tumblerful and handed it over, then attended to his own, pouring barely enough to cover the bottom of the glass.

'This is better than Horlicks,' he said and put the glass to his lips although he didn't open his mouth. The Australian didn't seem to notice as he took a large gulp from his own.

'Jesus,' he breathed, 'a drop of good stuff you've got here, mate.' And he sat in the chair facing the table.

Jampton sat himself down opposite, eager to get this man talking. What a letter to Aunt Dorothy! He kicked off with: 'Was it rough last night?'

The Captain took another drink. 'Average,' he said laconically, then: 'You know, I have a confession to make.' He looked down at his glass. Jampton was all ears. 'We didn't drop in on you accidentally, like.' Jampton's eyebrows went up. 'We were on our way back to base and we made a detour of ten miles for this.'

Jampton was beside himself with pride and joy. He knocked back his teaspoon of whisky to hide his pleasure. And when he managed to control his coughing he noticed that his glass had been replenished. He waved a casual hand. 'Yes I suppose word gets around.' Then added modestly, 'Like you, we're just doing our job.'

The Captain eyed him curiously. 'This is the Special Ordnance Group, isn't it?'

Even that small sip of whisky was beginning to affect Jampton. 'Right on the button,' he said, laughing, and took a large drink. This seemed to go down much easier.

There was a long pause. The Captain was puzzled. From the stories he'd heard Captain Jampton was the guiding light behind the exploits of Sergeants Sparks

240

and Miller. He didn't look like a hero, more like a trainee bus conductor. But then this could only be a façade, a front behind which lurked a brain cool, determined and razor sharp. He decided to give Jampton the benefit of the doubt. After all, Lawrence of Arabia was no great shakes in a civvy suit. And noticing his host's glass was empty he took the bottle and said, 'Let me top you up, sir.'

'Why not?' said Jampton grandly, contentment seeping through him. 'No need to call me "sir",' he said expansively. 'My name is Wilfred.'

Captain White raised his glass. 'Well thank you, Wilf,' he said.

Jampton winced. He wasn't all that drunk but recovering himself with gay abandon he gulped down a mouthful and almost fell over the back of his chair. This time it took him a little longer to recover but he was game. 'First today,' he gasped, smiling through his tears.

The Australian nodded sympathetically. It was obvious the lad wasn't used to it. This was probably the first ever. What must he have been through in his short military career? He coughed, embarrassed. 'Besides yourself, the two drongos the lads would really like to meet are your two Sergeants.'

Jampton eyed the two waving images in the chair opposite.

'You know, Sparks and Miller.' White's voice was getting quieter.

Jampton pulled himself together with a monumental effort. 'Ah,' he said, 'Sergeants Sparks and Miller.' He struggled to control his diction. 'I'm sorry to disappoint you, Captain,' he said slowly, 'but you can't. They've disappeared.' He waved his now empty glass into the air and crooned: 'Gone . . . over the hills and far away.' Then the glass fell from his hand and he slumped face down on to the map of Africa – Abyssinia to be exact.

Captain White rose and looked down at one of his heroes. 'Sod the bloody war. This poor bastard's coming apart at the seams.' And he dragged Jampton over to his bed and laid him out gently.'

As he ducked out of the tent he almost ran into Sergeant Major Puller. The man made a drinking gesture with his hand and shrugged. 'Poor sod.'

The Sergeant Major's eyebrows went up in amazement and, gazing towards the CO's tent, he whistled softly. The little man was human after all.

'Well,' he said, 'your lads are ready and waiting.'

'Thanks.' The Captain nodded. 'Oh, and by the way, I'm sorry to hear about Sergeants Sparks and Miller.'

'What?' said Puller.

'I gather they've bought it.'

Puller jerked his thumb over his shoulder. 'Is that what he's been telling you?'

The Captain replied, 'Well that's what I gathered from his conversation.'

'Take my word, sir, I'll bet my last pay parade they're living it up somewhere, maybe Alex for all I know.'

The Captain was intrigued as Puller filled him in briefly about the night of the great sandstorm, and when he had finished the Australian thought for a moment. Then: 'Southwest?' he said.

Puller nodded. And after a time the Captain rubbed his chin. 'There's nothing down there for most of three hundred kilometres – well there is. There's an oasis, about fifteen miles in that direction – El something or other . . . never been there meself. It's a little off the beaten track. Well,' he finished, 'we'll be off. Thank him for all his hospitality when he wakes up.' And with a flip of his hand he hurried over to his own mob.

Puller waved them off into the blue, then he gazed over to the southwest. It's worth a try, he mused. Yes, just the place that might appeal to those two bastards. And with mind made up he strode into the CO's tent.

242

But when he stuck his head through the flap he almost gagged. Not only had Jampton been sick all over himself, but also the bed and a large part of the floor as well. The Sergeant Major didn't envy Jackson having to clean this lot up. The uniform was only fit for burning, but that wasn't an option. It was all Jampton had to stand up in until his suitcase turned up. There'd be no chance of putting forward his idea today, probably not for three days at least.

He moved over to the table and lifted the bottle of whisky and shook his head. Then, taking the cork out, he helped himself to a fair swig. He belched pleasurably and put the bottle back on the table and left the tent.

The first intelligence report from the El Waddim Oasis was dynamite. Colonel Brunswick could hardly believe his luck when he read through it. It was brief and to the point as one would expect from a highly trained intelligence agent, albeit French. The girls had passed on pillow talk, everything they could remember, to Yasmin but the Colonel was spared banalities such as 'After the war I am going to marry you' and 'You are more beautiful than the moon over Wilhelmstrasse'.

Even so it was a long report, but after half an hour Brunswick felt he had struck the Mother Lode. 'I'll take you back to Alexandria.' 'When?' 'It won't be long – only a few more days.' And, more importantly, 'The Tommies will not be searching for you on Friday – they will have other things to worry about.'

From these and other drunken boasts, a pattern began to emerge – Rommel was up to something, something big in the next few days – and it could only be Alexandria. And in order to gain this objective the British defence line would have to be breached at Alam el Halfa Ridge.

Colonel Brunswick, eyes gleaming with excitement, reached for the telephone. It was the vital information that General Montgomery's headquarters had been waiting for and the action taken was immediate. The weak gaps in the defence line were strengthened by New Zealand and Indian divisions. Tanks moved into position, antitank guns were dug in and, most important of all, the minefields on the approach to Alam el Halfa were heavily reinforced. General Montgomery was facing the bowling and this was his first ball but now he knew which side of the wicket it would break.

On 31 August the Germans rolled into the attack but it was against an infinitely superior force to what their intelligence had led them to believe. From the beginning of the battle when their panzer tanks foundered in a bigger minefield than they had expected, holding up their advances, it was a series of disasters for the vaunted Afrika Korps. After five days Rommel, battered, bruised and bewildered, was forced to retreat. It was General Montgomery's first victory. It wasn't the match, but it was at least a boundary. Perhaps he was the right man even if he was a teetotaller, didn't smoke and wore two cap badges.

From this victory tiny seeds of optimism began to grow. Plans were now being discussed, not for the defence of Alexandria, but for an all-out offensive. To the troops of the Eighth Army, General Montgomery, or Monty as he was popularly known, was welcomed wherever he went. He was here, there and everywhere seemingly in several different locations at the same time. It was rumoured that the General had four lookalikes.

On the other hand, the newly promoted Field Marshal Rommel, frustrated and angry, could only wait, hamstrung by his lack of fuel. If supplies didn't get through the British sea blockade, his panzer tanks would have to go into battle pushed by the infantry.

Colonel Brunswick was revitalised and his meetings

with General Montgomery became more frequent. It wasn't exactly 'Charles' and 'Monty' yet but they were shaking hands now. On their last meeting in Monty's caravan, much to his astonishment the General asked him if he would like a glass of whisky and Brunswick astonished himself even more by turning it down; they discussed further stratagems over two glasses of lemonade.

September stepped back in order to give October a chance. During the last few weeks there hadn't been much intelligence from El Waddim Oasis but what little snippets arrived at British Military Intelligence were encouraging.

The girls reported to Yasmin that their high-ranking German clients were becoming a bit heavy and not much fun. Their bombast and arrogance were now replaced by gloom and probably apprehension and their visits were less frequent. In fact, the cup presented to the girl pulling the highest-ranking officer had lost its flavour. All this information gathered together in a bundle was invaluable to the British, direct proof of the low morale pervading the enemy forces.

The Tip Top Eight, however, were glad to see the backs of the master race. What the hell – the Italians were better lovers anyway, and some of the girls quite enjoyed the change; not only that, it was a great improvement on Abdul's lousy setup. Here they were coining it and, more important, engaged in vital war work. They just lay back and thought of England, Germany, Poland and Lithuania, and the other three with no homeland thought of their old-age pension.

This turn of events didn't suit Miller at all. No one was volunteering for the next flight to Alexandria. They were having too much of a good time with the girls and you didn't get that in a prisoner-of-war camp. Miller fretted; if he didn't get back to Alexandria his biscuit tin full of valuables was useless.

Colonel Brunswick waited eagerly for Yasmin's report regarding the German supply plane. It could be of low priority, or it could be of vital importance. Whichever way the ball bounced, Charles Brunswick was a born-again Colonel in British Military Intelligence. Oh yes, there had been those foolish enough to snigger behind his back when he'd mooted his idea to plant eight girls in the oasis, but those unbelievers were now hailing it as a stroke of genius. He rang down to the canteen and asked for a cup of tea to be sent up. His sun was shining and there wasn't a cloud in the sky.

Little did he know that, somewhere out in the desert, the lid was off a tin of ointment and a small fly was already buzzing around.

Captain Jampton stumbled through the soft sand. The night was black and any sound was too far away to cause concern. It was Jampton's third night patrol, or Exercise Spiller 3, a clever composition of the names of his missing Sergeants with the number 3 denoting his number of previous missions. Sergeant Major Puller, next in line behind his Commanding Officer, eyed Jampton's crouching, weaving shape. He shook his head; the little pillock was also holding his pistol. He hoped to God it wasn't loaded.

Suddnely he froze and cocked his head to one side. It was the sound of an approaching aircraft and, from the uneven throb of its engines, it certainly wasn't British. The sound of the engines got louder as if it was above them. It was certainly close, and then to their right the sky was lit by a faint gleam of light. With a final crescendo the plane's engines cut abruptly, and the lights were extinguished, leaving the night blacker and more fearful.

Jampton's mouth was dry. 'Sar'nt Major,' he hissed.

But the Sergeant Major wasn't there. Louder this time he repeated it, then anxiety began to crawl up his legs. Where the dickens was the patrol? It was a simple explanation. When the column halted on hearing the plane, Jampton hadn't. He'd been wrapped in his own fantasy world and it had been the gleam of the flare path that had brought him back to earth. He was well ahead of the patrol, that was all. But then rationality had never been one of Jampton's strong points. He turned full circle in an attempt to pierce the night, and then something sprang into his mind, something he'd read in a book by Baden-Powell – 'When separated from your comrades on a dark night, drop instantly to a prone position. The sky with stars is lighter than the ground and against this backcloth silhouettes may be discerned.' Jampton got down on his belly and was searching fiercely in the darkness when somebody tripped over him.

'Ouch!' he yelped as the man stumbled.

'Bloody 'ell,' said Private Summerskill, 'who's that?'

'It's me, Captain Jampton,' muttered the CO, brushing sand from himself as he rose to his feet.

'Sorry, sir,' mumbled Summerskill. 'I hope I didn't wake you.'

The Sergeant Major, guided by the prattle of their exchange, joined them. 'Keep your voices down,' he hissed. 'Sound travels a long way in the desert.'

Jampton was about to reply sternly to this usurping of his command but the Sergeant Major was already addressing the man. 'Go on, lad,' he whispered.

Summerskill had been scouting well ahead of the column when the plane approached. In fact he had actually been in the oasis when the kerosene lamps of the flare path were lit and as shapes had hurried towards the plane when it had finally braked to a stop. As he made his report he became more excited.

'You're not going to believe this,' he said, 'but I swear I could hear dance music coming from one of the buildings and women laughing.'

'Guards?' snapped Jampton regaining his superiority. 'I didn't see anybody – nobody challenged me.'

'Did you see the plane?' asked Puller.

'Yes, sir. It was German all right. Bloody great swastikas on it.'

Eagerly Jampton chipped in. 'Then if Sergeants Sparks and Miller are here, they are being held prisoner.'

Jampton swung round, staring in the direction of the oasis. His heart was beating faster as heroic thoughts sprang to mind. According to Summerskill it was very sloppily defended, if at all. And what a feather in his cap if he were to lead his patrol in and free the two Sergeants. He whirled towards Puller and Summerskill but now there were more dark shapes. The patrol wanted to know what was in the wind.

'We're going in,' he hissed. He wished it was light so he could see their faces as he uttered these momentous words. Luckily for him, though, it was dark and he couldn't see them edging surreptitiously away.

'Right Sar'nt Major,' he said. 'Take six men and deploy round that side of the camp.' His pointing finger was invisible in the darkness.

The Sergeant Major interrupted the half-baked diatribe. 'Sir,' he said patiently, 'with due respect, from Summerskill's report this could be a German camp and I wouldn't give much for our chances – twenty rifles against God knows what.'

'Under cover of darkness?' said Jampton. 'And with the element of surprise?'

'It may be dark now, sir, but it won't be for long.'

'We need only reconnoitre,' pleaded Jampton, modifying his plan somewhat.

'Believe me, sir, it's not our bag. This is a job for three companies of light infantry.'

In any case the discussion was academic; the patrol were well on their way back to the vehicles.

* * *

At first light Alexandria began to wake up. Traffic became heavier, noises increased and somewhere a cock crowed. Colonel Brunswick lay in bed listening to Bing Crosby on his shortwave wireless. He harmonised a little, softly so as not to blot out the Master's voice. He was a happy man.

The phone rang and, switching off the set, he lifted the receiver and rapped in a brisk voice, 'Brunswick.' He'd learnt his lesson – he'd once picked up the phone and yelled 'What the hell d'you want now, Agnes!'. It was a mistake – it turned out to be the Minister of War.

'Message from the oasis, sir.' It was his Adjutant.

'Well,' snapped Brunswick, 'what's it say?'

'I'd rather not over the telephone, sir, but I think you'll like it.'

The Colonel sat up. 'Quite right, Jimmy. I was out of order there. Have my car here in ten minutes – coffee and toast.' He slammed down the receiver and jumped out of bed. He was intrigued and a feeling of happiness swept over him – this was going to be a good day. He switched on the wireless to continue hearing the voice of Bing while he dressed, but a slow, ponderous voice assured him that carrots are good to eat and the nutritional val–

'Bollocks,' he said and switched it off. He padded into his bathroom and stood under the shower – but not for the first time there was no water. However, his mind was elsewhere. He stepped out of the nonexistent shower and from force of habit towelled himself briskly.

Captain Shelley was his usual urbane, unflappable self when his superior strode in, flung his cap on the desk and lifted his coffee cup, which was still tolerably warm. First he sniffed at it, then swallowed a large mouthful, sighing with satisfaction. His Adjutant didn't forget a thing. It had been laced with Dimple Haig; pity about the coffee. Then he sat in his chair and looked up expectantly.

'Well, come on, Jimmy, let's have it,' he said.

'Well, sir,' he began. 'It would appear that Yasmin has struck oil – literally.'

Colonel Brunswick frowned as the report was placed before him. He put on his glasses and began to read. He read for only a short time, then he looked up. 'I don't understand,' he said. 'Supply plane arrives with rations, they load it up with oil for the trip back.'

His Adjutant pointed to the report. 'That's only the first paragraph, sir.'

'I'm aware of that, but the amount of oil taken away is hardly enough to service Rommel's car, let alone ultimate victory.'

'It's a little more than that, sir,' said the Adjutant, twisting his body to look over the desk at the message. 'According to this a Junkers 52 carries a payload of –' he tilted his head further '– approximately three thousand nine hundred kilos and with two trips a week that makes seven thousand eight hundred kilos, and that's enough to keep a flight of Focke Wolf 190s in the air.'

Brunswick stared at him. 'Then why isn't the oil going to Rommel? It's the only thing that's holding him back.'

'The only explanation I can think of,' replied the Adjutant, 'is that Rommel isn't aware of what's going on. After all, there's no love lost between the Luftwaffe and the Afrika Korps. The Wermacht being the star of the show, the flying men are not too happy as the supporting cast.'

Brunswick nodded and went on with his reading – it was a long, detailed report. Captain Shelley watched him patiently. It wasn't long in coming.

Brunswick's face broke into a smile. 'Ah,' he said and jabbed his finger down on the paper. 'That's more like it,' he said. 'By God, Jimmy, that girl Yasmin is worth a squadron of tanks.'

He'd every reason to be pleased. According to the report, the oil taken away by the Junkers was only the tip of the iceberg. Yasmin had discovered several more camouflage dunes under which lay a vastly greater amount of oil and most likely ammunition as well. Naturally this was only a calculated guess but the enormity of the dump was not in question – it was more than enough to take Rommel's troops into Alexandria and beyond.

Colonel Brunswick rubbed his hands together with a feeling of excitement and chuckled. News of the oil would certainly send his stock soaring in the War Cabinet. He might even get a pat on the head from Winston himself. Yes sir, the war was looking up!

The intelligence report arrived in Whitehall like warm sunshine in the middle of December. Its impact was electrifying. It couldn't have had more of an effect if Hitler had applied for political asylum. It was obvious that the Luftwaffe had no knowledge of the immense reserves of fuel at their disposal, otherwise they would have passed on the information to Field Marshal Rommel and more than likely Rommel and his headquarters staff would be whooping it up in Cairo by now. It was imperative that the British take possession without delay. Whichever side had use of this gigantic oil supply would be two goals up at half-time.

The stratagem concocted by the brass hats in Whitehall was put at the top of the priority list.

Object: oil from El Waddim Oasis to be transferred to Alexandria, British War Effort, for the use of. This was passed down to the planners, the outcome being that twelve Dakotas carrying paratroops would make their way to El Waddim Oasis, the airborne soldiers would be dropped and, after securing their objective, a Dakota would land to be loaded with oil for Alexandria followed by a second Dakota to repeat this action, and subsequently until all twelve had completed the operation.

Further trips to El Waddim Oasis would depend on the quantity of oil. This was then passed down the ladder for the more mundane operating details to be worked out. The stumbling block that took up most of the time was the selection of a code name for the operation. It was finally decided to call it Operation Jupiter. Having accomplished this it was rushed back to the top of the heap and Winston Churchill, peering through his cigar smoke, grunted and wrote across the bottom of the message 'Action This Day'.

Every contingency had been gone over thoroughly. It wasn't a difficult operation and nothing had been overlooked. However, there was a snag that not even the sharpest brains in Whitehall could have foreseen. It was another assault on El Waddim Oasis but this one was code named Exercise Spiller 4.

NINE

The Special Ordnance Group led by the indomitable Captain Jampton were back among the dunes surrounding the oasis. But this time it was midday and a full turnout, nearly sixty men, carried rifles and some of the more experienced of the old 41st Infantry were equipped with light machine guns.

They were on the brink of exhaustion when they reached the start point. It had been a torturous trek through the soft sand in a temperature over a hundred degrees. The high-noon strategy had been Jampton's idea – hit them when they were at their most vulnerable during their siesta, sleeping and dozing in the midday heat. It had never occurred to him that his own troops would also be suffering and certainly no match for an enemy refreshed by sleep under some shade or other.

Now Captain Jampton, face red as a turkey cock and shirt black with sweat, was reluctantly coming to the conclusion that his idea wasn't a good one after all. He ordered a halt and assembled his men in a long line on either side of him and passed the order for a ten-minute break. They were now only six or seven hundred yards from their objective.

Sergeant Major Puller struggled wearily through the treacherous sand towards him. Thinking back, he decided that the horrendous convoy through the sandstorm was infinitely better than today. How the hell were they supposed to take this camp was beyond him. By the time they reached the oasis the lads wouldn't have the strength to lift their arms in surrender and he was damn certain it wasn't worth all this effort just to free Sergeants Sparks and Miller. As far as he was concerned he was glad to be shot of them.

He watched as Jampton sat on the sand, immediately springing back on to his feet as if he'd bounced off a trampoline and patting his backside.

Sergeant Major Puller was too far gone to smile. The little pillock hadn't even got the sense to realise the sand would be like a hotplate. He slithered over to where his CO was still patting his backside.

'It's no good, sir,' he said, 'the lads are knackered. In their condition they couldn't beat a junior girls' netball team.'

There was a silence between them then Jampton said in a dry voice, 'What are you trying to say, Sar'nt Major?'

The Sergeant Major said it and Jampton was off the hook.

'All right,' he sighed. 'At the end of the break, pass the word along to make tracks for the vehicles.'

When the order was passed on that they were returning to camp it was a shot in the arm. Several of them rose to their feet, brushing sand from their uniforms. They didn't want a break: they wanted to be off. They were rejuvenated like school boys at the end of term. The whitewashed stones and the replacement red-and-white pole of the Special Ordnance Group had never been more appreciated.

But, sadly, many of them would never see the camp again. That break of ten minutes was to be the last they would ever enjoy. For those who survived, it would haunt them for the rest of their lives.

It all began at the far end of the extended skirmishing line. Nobby Clark stared around him through a pair of binoculars, twiddling the focusing wheel. 'Where'd you get these from?' he asked his mate, who winked and patted them. 'Zeiss,' he said, and made to take them back.

'Hang on,' said Nobby, jerking his arm away. He started to slither and stagger to the top of a high dune. When he reached the summit he couldn't get his breath and had to take the cigarette out of his mouth in order to cough. This done he replaced the cigarette and raised the binoculars to his eyes and stared into the distance. Then he swivelled to the right and as he did so he had a feeling that something was wrong. He looked down at his feet and then moved to one side, and looked again. It wasn't sand – it looked like canvas or tarpaulin. He took the cigarette from his lips and shouted, 'Hey Jacko, there's something funny about this lot . . .' He never finished his sentence. There was a ripping noise and with a yelp Nobby disappeared from view.

Jacko looked up, perplexed. It was the last thing he ever saw. A burning cigarette and high-octane fuel are a lethal mix – the explosion was horrendous.

The dune was ripped apart by a second, louder, explosion as burning fuel shot hundreds of feet into the air. The sun was blotted out by the oily black smoke. All the men unfortunate enough to be in the vicinity were never seen again. Others were screaming and writhing in the sand in a vain attempt to put out the flames engulfing them.

Jampton stared in horrified fascination. Some of the soldiers ran for protection behind the next dune but it was a mistake. Burning fuel from the first silo was already eating through the thin covering of sand, and with another shattering explosion the second dune erupted taking all the men with it.

The Sergeant Major, face blackened with smoke, realised the situation at once. They were trapped in a blazing oil dump. From another dune a further explosion, and this was accompanied by flying tracer bullets. 'God Almighty!' he breathed. 'That's ammo.' He grabbed Jampton's arm. They had to get out of the valley. Every dune was suspect. God only knew how much stuff was hidden away here and with the domino effect as other dunes went up, death was creeping towards them.

He tried to drag Jampton away but the little man had found some strength from somewhere. He wouldn't budge and was staring at the carnage, eyes like headlamps. Puller grabbed his arm again. The heat was now unbearable and Puller's eyebrows were singed and his hair was beginning to crackle. He dragged Jampton a yard or two but the little bastard shook himself free and began to run towards the inferno.

Another explosion ripped the air, slamming him back, and something rolled towards him. He didn't move as it came to rest at his feet but when he saw what it was he began screaming like a young girl on the big dipper. Puller looked down. It was a man's head, blackened out of recognition.

Jampton was still screaming at the top of his voice and when the Sergeant Major grabbed his arm again he fought himself free and, still screaming, he scrabbled for his pistol. But the Sergeant Major had had enough. He smashed his fist into Jampton's face, caught the sagging body and humped it over his shoulder, staggering off to God knew where, any place to get out of this blistering deathtrap. 'You stupid bastard,' he yelled at the top of his voice. 'You wanted to see action,' he screamed, tears rolling down his face. 'I hope you're satisfied, you useless pillock.'

Jampton, lolling over the Sergeant Major's shoulder, didn't mind. He was out to the wide.

The shock of the first explosion jerked the Italians in the oasis out of sleep. Sparks and Miller, who had been dozing at the table in the shade of the palm, sprang instantly to their feet as the blast shredded all the leaves from the tops of the trees, exposing them both to bright sunlight.

Italians in various stages of undress ran from their billets in a mad stampede. There was another, louder, explosion and immediately the whole mass of them veered in a different direction.

Sparks and Miller ran round the corner of the hotel as another explosion hurled Sparks against the wall. Miller hauled him to his feet, scanning the sky for the bombers. In complete disorientation they ran to a corner of the building and immediately stopped dead in their tracks, frozen with horror – the whole desert was ablaze and creeping towards them was a burning river of oil. They were transfixed, too paralysed with the enormity of the scene to move, when out of the smoke staggered someone carrying what looked like a sack of potatoes over his shoulders. He almost collapsed in front of them and Miller grabbed his burden. It was a man, and, laying him gently on the ground, he wiped some of the grime from the man's face and then stopped and jerked back.

'What's up?' said Sparks.

Miller didn't look around. 'Take a look for yourself. You're not going to believe this. It's Hugh.' And on hearing his voice Captain Jampton sat up and wiped his eyes.

'I thought it might be,' said Sparks. 'This one's the Sergeant Major.'

'Can you walk, sir?' asked Miller.

Jampton turned towards him with vacant eyes and a beatific smile on his face but he didn't say anything. Miller didn't like the look of him at all. He held up his hand in front of Jampton's face. 'How many fingers have I got up?' he said. But Jampton stared at him with eyes that didn't look as if they could see. A rivulet of burning oil crept round the corner. It was enough. Miller picked up his CO and slung him over his shoulder and the three of them began to run towards the comparative safety of the lake.

At 2300 hours the first Dakota took off from Aboukir and when all twelve planes were airborne, they set course for El Waddim Oasis under an umbrella of night fighters equipped with extra fuel tanks. Operation Jupiter was well into Phase One. The two companies of paratroops occupied the first four Dakotas. They had been well briefed. It should be a soft landing and opposition was likely to be nonexistent. Some of them, those who'd seen action in the past, weren't convinced – they'd heard it all before.

Apart from a hairy five minutes from a hostile anti-aircraft battery, probably British, the flight was uneventful. The Squadron Leader at the controls in the leading Dakota with thirty-five minutes to his ETA was puzzled. What had seemed to be a red glare ahead in the far distance was confirmed. The glare was getting brighter and, whatever it was, it was something immense. After a few more minutes' flying his worst fear became a certainty. It could only be El Waddim Oasis – what the hell was going on?

The Paratroop Captain was leaning over his shoulder. Bloody hell, he thought. It's a bit too big for a barbecue. In another fifteen minutes they were right over the target; at 2,000 feet they circled the conflagration. The pilot was thinking hard – his orders had been clear. The only word to be transmitted would be 'Bingo' and only then on completion of a successful mission. The wireless operator came forward and looked down – even at this height his horror-stricken face was lit by the flames.

The skipper decided to break radio silence and instructed his operator to inform base of the situation.

Target in flames – landing impossible – await further orders.

On the ground it could only be assumed that the last of the deadly silos had been detonated. There had not been an explosion for some time. Most of the survivors were on the other side of the lake in comparative safety. Shocked, blackened and dishevelled, they stood apathetically amidst the groans and screams of the badly burnt survivors. Several men and some of the girls did their utmost to comfort them but with few supplies of medicine and certainly no morphine they could do little to alleviate the suffering. They didn't even bother to look up as the Dakotas thundered overhead.

At first light the paratroopers jumped out of the Dakotas, parachutes blossoming as they floated down some miles to the north of the oasis, the Dakotas peeling away to make their way to Alexandria, one Dakota remaining to circle the oasis in order to maintain wireless contact with the paratroopers when they hit the ground.

Colonel Brunswick was apprised of the situation as he was rushed to Aboukir and inside ten minutes he was airborne in a Lysander. At the oasis the paratroopers had taken command of the situation and were doing all they could for the survivors, but it was a hopeless task. Although they had two medical orderlies and supplies of morphine, there was little they could do. Even so, their presence was a comfort.

At ten o'clock the light plane was circling the oasis and Colonel Brunswick stared down, white-faced. The whole area was decimated. Fires still blazing here and there, it was like looking down into the gaping mouth of an active volcano. The pilot tapped him on the shoulder. 'It's OK to land, sir. They've cleared the strip.'

Ten minutes later Colonel Brunswick took in the scene from ground level. He was appalled as he walked slowly through the blanket-covered bodies arranged in neat rows by the lake. The carnage about him was indescribable.

'Sir.' He whirled round. Staring into the blackened, exhausted face of Sergeant Major Puller, he wasn't even surprised to see him there. In some strange way he'd known all along. He couldn't bring himself to speak. He waved his arms ineffectually at the carnage around him and shook his head.

'How did it happen?' he asked finally in a low voice.

Briefly Puller explained about Exercise Spiller, how Captain Jampton had passed on orders to abort the operation when the first dune went up. He couldn't explain why or how.

The Colonel sighed heavily and looked round at the devastation. At least, he thought, it'll deny Rommel the use of it. Then, turning to the Sergeant Major, he asked, 'And how is my nephew?'

'Captain Jampton, sir . . .' Puller was uncomfortable. 'I'm afraid they'll send him home, sir.'

Brunswick looked at him sharply.

'Oh he's not wounded, sir. Not physically that is, but, er, mentally I'm afraid he's . . .'

Again the Colonel said nothing.

'I'm sorry, sir,' added the Sergeant Major. 'I think he felt responsible and it was all too much for him.' His voice tailed off.

'Thank you, Sar'nt Major. I understand.'

He understood all too well. It had been his brilliant idea to form the Special Ordnance Group, and an even brighter one to place it under the command of his nephew. The blame rested squarely on his own shoulders. The responsibility for this tragedy was his alone and he knew the guilt would trouble him for the rest of his life.

The Colonel glanced down at the blackened and burned hands and arms, then up into the Sergeant Major's tired face.

'I think it's time you got yourself some medical attention,' he said gruffly.

'Yes, sir,' snapped Puller. 'Just as soon as some more medical supplies come in.' He saluted wearily and made his way towards the huts. The Colonel watched him go then turned to survey the long rows of blanket-covered bodies. God what a mess. The roar of a landing Dakota caused him to look towards the air strip and at the pathetic line of stretcher cases and walking wounded, some assisted by the girls, patiently waiting to board the planes. When this plane was loaded, another would take its place, and then another, until the evacuation was complete.

Colonel Brunswick lit a cigarette. It wasn't easy. He hoped no one noticed his trembling hand. As a Director of British Intelligence he know that in the next few days there would be many more deaths. The war in North Africa was about to explode and every war threw up its casualties – but then, did there really have to be wars? He shook his head sadly. He thought of his wife, Lady Dorothy, and her high-born relations, and the power they wielded behind the scene – unelected, unaccountable and yet influencing the tide of history with aristocratic disdain for all those beneath them. No one had asked the Gallant Six Hundred if they wanted to ride into the cannons of the Turks, or the 60,000 casualties on the Somme as they marched with their rifles at high port across no man's land to be cut down row upon row by the German machine guns. These mass suicides had been approved and in many cases instigated over vintage claret in cut-crystal glasses. Whoever carried the can, the aristocracy always survived.

Yet again, was the alternative any better? The French revolution had been a disaster. In Russia, Stalin was infinitely more dangerous than the Tzar and his relations. Hitler wasn't far behind him, either. The

Colonel winced as the cigarette burned his fingers. It had burned right down without him even taking a drag. The Dakota lumbered into the air and another was already in the circuit waiting to land. This broke his train of thought. He took out his handkerchief and blew his nose, then shrugged. Politics and philosophising weren't his pigeon. He had a war to run ... and where the hell were Sparks and Miller?

Sparks and Miller went to find Carlo. He was in the hotel, or what was left of it. There was just enough roof left to provide the shade under which Carlo sat at a table staring morosely into a glass of wine. They stood awkwardly in front of him. He looked up.

'My dear friends, you have come to say goodbye.' He shook his head. 'I see you have still got your biscuit tin.'

Miller, embarrassed, shuffled uneasily. 'Yes, sir, er, and I'm sorry about, er, what's happened and that.'

'Ach,' said Carlo. 'Is not your fault. And since you two arrive we have fun, yes? And excitement and what about the girls? The last few weeks have been happy. At last the El Waddim Oasis became what it was originally designed to be.' A tired smile crossed his face. 'What did you call it once? The best little knocking shop in Africa?'

The Sergeant Major walked in and broke up the party, saluting Carlo smartly.

'Colonel Brunswick's compliments, sir. And would you get your lads assembled, taking only what they can carry. It's an hour or two's march to the truck line.'

Carlo thanked him, and came round the table to embrace Sparks and Miller. 'If you are ever in Roma,' he said, 'ask for Carlo and I will give you the best table.'

Two hours later, the long line of three-ton Bedfords, packed with Italians, rolled out along the flat stony surface towards Alexandria. Then the Sergeant Major turned back to his own convoy for the survivors of Special Ordnance – just two trucks, and these half empty. Forty-seven dead and injured was a helluva price to pay. Sparks and Miller were about to clamber aboard when Puller stopped them.

'Not you lads. They've laid on a special treat for you.'

The two Sergeants looked at each other.

'Like what, sir?' asked Miller, but the Sergeant Major didn't reply. He shaded his eyes at a small speck in the distance, creating a very impressive dust trail. As it got nearer they could see it was an open touring car. When it drew up in a cloud of dust, Miller whistled softly.

'Blimey,' he said. 'Where're we off to?'

The Sergeant Major thrust an envelope at Miller. 'There's your marching orders,' he said. He turned towards his own truck, then stopped and turned back again. 'By the way,' he asked in a curious voice, 'what have you got in the biscuit tin?'

Miller didn't look up. 'Ginger nuts,' he said, struggling to open the envelope.

Sparks took it from him and proceeded to read: '. . . to make all speed to General Montgomery's caravan, reference 607982. As from 22nd you are promoted to the rank of Warrant Officer and will be attached to General Montgomery's personal staff.'

Sergeant Major Puller looked away disgustedly. 'If you two fell head first down a Whitechapel sewer, you'd come up smelling of roses.'

He watched as they made themselves comfortable in the back seats. Miller leant forward and tapped the driver on the shoulder. 'Who's this General Montgomery?' he said.

Before the driver could reply, the Sergeant Major strolled over and leant on the door. 'General Montgomery?' he asked. 'Oh yes, you don't know him yet, do you? He came over when you were on your holidays.'

Miller leant forward to the driver and said, 'Do you know where this reference place is?'

'Yes, sir,' replied the driver.

'Well then, let's go,' said Miller and waved grandly at the Sergeant Major as he passed him in a cloud of dust. 'This is the life,' said Miller, beaming all over his face.

Sparks didn't reply.

'Warrant Officers, eh?' went on Miller proudly. 'Next thing you know we'll be Brigadier Generals.'

They'd been travelling for half an hour when Sparks leant forward and, tapping the driver on his shoulder, said, 'Stop here, mate.'

The driver pulled up and Sparks got out. Miller looked at him curiously. 'You should have gone before we set out,' he said, but he didn't like the way his oppo was smiling at him.

'What's up?' he asked.

Sparks sighed. 'This is as far as I go, Dusty. It's been nice knowing you.'

Miller stared at him uncomprehendingly. 'What the bloody hell are you on about?'

Sparks looked at him for a minute. 'I don't want to join General Montgomery's staff. I don't want to be a Warrant Officer, and I've got enough medals.'

Miller looked at him and then noticed a movement on top of a ridge behind his mate. He squinted – it was an Arab woman in the black robes of the desert. 'Yasmin?' he asked softly.

Sparks shrugged.

Miller was worried. 'What shall I tell the General?' he asked.

'You'll think of something,' said Sparks and turning on his heel he walked away.

'Oi,' shouted Miller half-heartedly as Sparks continued.

Miller watched him join the Arab woman, who turned and waved. Miller waved back and they drove on.

The car trundled on. Miller was deep in thought. He was miserable and panic surged through him at the vision of life without Sparks.

'Ah well,' he muttered, 'I'll miss him, you know.'

The driver looked at him through the mirror. 'Yes, Sergeant,' he replied in a neutral voice.

It was going to be a long trip and he didn't want to be involved in a maudlin diatribe about comradeship and brotherly love. The car lurched up a slight rise and before them stretched a flat bit of the Sahara. This made driving easier and they increased speed. The driver squinted his eyes as in the distance he saw indistinct shapes coming slowly towards them. Miller had also spotted them and craned forward over the back of the front seat. Then as the figures became recognisable he relaxed and flopped back against the leather upholstery.

'Bloody Arab and his camel,' he said with a smile. 'He doesn't have to worry about who's winning as long as he can sell his fruit.'

The driver smiled, then Miller tapped him eagerly on his shoulder. 'Here,' he said, 'fancy a melon?' And before the driver had time to decide whether he fancied a melon there came a loud whooshing of air and a twenty-five-pound shell blew the car and its occupants to a better place.

The Arab, never deviating, continued his regular journey passing the burning wreck with hardly a glance. The date was 23 October and when darkness fell the greatest artillery barrage in military history was unleashed at a little town called Alamein, heralding the beginning of the end.

EPILOGUE

OCTOBER 1947

Five years after the decisive battle of Alamein, the North African desert, having staged this devastating extravaganza, settled itself back into its thousands of years of anonymity.

The camel and its driver plod through the desert skirting the detritus of war, rusting hulks of tanks, burnt out wagons, ugly, spent scrap metal . . .

Sir Charles Brunswick now serves as Governor of a little island in the South Seas, one of the last outposts of the Empire. Not a fitting promotion perhaps, but then anything was better than pushing his nephew's wheelchair through the leafy lanes of Shropshire . . .

At the Aeolian Hall in Bond Street, London, where the BBC records many shows, a commissionaire will open the door for you. Two rows of medal ribbons brighten the breast of his black uniform. He has only one arm, having been one of the first casualties of Sword Beach during the D-Day Landings in Normandy. Most of the employees hurry past him into the building with scarcely a nod, medal ribbons mean nothing to them and amongst themselves they refer to him as Granddad. Ex Sergeant Major Puller is not yet forty . . .

The camel perks up as it reaches the soft sand now on home territory the journey almost at an end . . .

Albert Gratwick and Rudolph Borsch run a children's

266

book shop in Amsterdam ... they were married in August 1946 ...

The camel, led by its driver, entered the El Waddim Oasis with a look of smug satisfaction on its face. It's mission was once more complete. A goat came out of the front door of the ramshackle hotel and surveyed the camel with arrogant eyes and a hen fussed around it, clucking and whinging at some imagined outrage. From one of the huts, a handful of small children ran, skipped and stumbled, joyously surrounding the man, holding on to his legs and laughing. He bent to pick up the smallest toddler, lifting him high on the camel's saddle, then, taking down the cloth that protected his mouth and nose he smiled. He turned towards the building – 'Yasmin!' he yelled. 'Where's my bloody tea?'